'I can unde

revenge,' Be

'If your purpos [...]
you would do so directly.' She took a deep
breath. 'When I met you, two nights ago, you
said I owe you a debt and you told me what
you consider payment. I will give you what you
ask if you will promise to leave Chloe alone.'

'You do understand what I want, do you not?'
Justin had moved closer to her and she resisted
the urge to back up.

'I believe you wish me to...to spend a night
with you,' she said calmly.

'A night? Not precisely. If you recall, I was to
have you for a week. But of course there is
interest, which by now is quite considerable.'

'What is it you want?' She could barely speak.

'I want you to be my mistress until the end of
the Season.'

Ann Elizabeth Cree is married and lives in Boise, Idaho, with her family. She has worked as a nutritionist and an accountant. Her favourite form of day-dreaming has always been weaving romantic stories in her head. With the encouragement of a friend, she started putting those stories on to paper. In addition to writing and caring for two lively boys, two cats and two dogs, she enjoys gardening, playing the piano, and, of course, reading.

Recent titles by the same author:

THE DUKE'S MISTRESS

Ann Elizabeth Cree

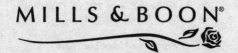

First published in Great Britain 2002
Harlequin Mills & Boon Limited,
Eton House, 18-24 Paradise Road, Richmond, Surrey TW9 1SR

© Annemarie Hasnain 2002

ISBN 0 263 83141 8

Set in Times Roman 10½ on 12 pt.
04-1002-83834

Printed and bound in Spain
by Litografía Rosés S.A., Barcelona

THE DUKE'S MISTRESS

Prologue

Sussex, July 1813

He never would have anticipated that the means for his revenge would come through his wife. But when he saw how Justin Everard, the young Marquis of Wroth, looked at Isabelle, the sudden admiration in his eye, the way his gaze frequently fell on her during the interminable dinners, he knew he had found his tool. He would destroy Wroth, and with that destruction bring about the destruction of Wroth's father, the Duke of Westmore. And then his own father's death would be avenged at last.

He had made his plans carefully. The two-week house party had proved perfect. He had thrown Isabelle in Wroth's way as frequently as possible, appealing to her disgustingly sweet nature to befriend him. With satisfaction, he had watched Wroth become more enamoured with his wife each day. But, despite Wroth's reputation, he made no move to actually seduce Isabelle, instead treating her with a protective chivalry which set his teeth on edge. For he needed an excuse to call Wroth out. To his fury, he realised his wife was succumbing to Wroth's charm. There was nothing overt in her behaviour, for after two years of marriage she was still too prudish, too rigidly moral to ever display an illicit passion. If anything, she was undoubtedly horrified at her lapse.

He did not love Isabelle. He had married her because, as Baron Allingham's only child, she had brought to the marriage a generous portion. And in two years, on her twenty-fourth birthday, she would inherit a sizeable fortune from her grandmother.

He had married her as well because he desperately wanted an heir but, despite her lovely body with its supple curves and his persistent efforts, she had failed him. Her barrenness only made him despise her more. But she belonged to him and he could not let her go unpunished.

So the plan he had devised would destroy not only Wroth, but humiliate and chastise Isabelle as well.

The knock on the door startled Belle. She had crept upstairs early as she had every night since arriving at Greystone nearly a fortnight ago. The other female guests of Sir Farley Greystone were too busy with their cards and gossip and lovers to notice or care if she left.

She rose from the edge of the bed, her heart thudding. She unlocked the door and opened it. Eliza Pomeroy, her husband's current mistress, stood on the other side. 'Your husband wants you below,' Eliza said without preamble.

Belle stared at her, her stomach taking a sickening turn. 'But why? Is he still not at play?' She could not imagine what he could possibly want.

Eliza looked at her, and her expression was not unkind. 'Yes, and he wants you there. I think you had best go straight away. He is not in a pleasant mood.'

But then Lucien rarely was, except when it served a purpose. And since she had served her purpose when he married her, she rarely saw the charm he could turn on at will. She followed Eliza down the hallway and down the winding staircase to the floor below. To her bewilderment, Eliza led her to the small saloon where there always seemed to be a card game in progress. She stepped inside the dimly lit room, its stale, rancid scent of smoke, sweat and alcohol assailing her senses. Confused, she saw several men still sitting around one of the small tables. She looked away, embarrassed to be there.

Lucien rose in a fluid motion that was rarely impaired by drink. He had removed his coat and his elegant waistcoat was rumpled. He came to her side, smelling of brandy. 'Ah, my lovely wife.' His eyes glittered down at her with an odd sort of excitement.

She suppressed the shiver that darted through her and forced herself to look at him and speak calmly. 'Mrs Pomeroy said that you wished to see me.'

'Yes. I do.' His mouth curved in a cruel smile. He caught her wrist in a hard grip and pulled her around so she was forced to face the others. 'My wife, gentlemen. And my next stake.'

She froze. She heard Sir Farley say, 'Damn it, Milborne. It's one thing to wager your doxy, but your wife. Not at all the thing.'

Lucien's grip tightened on her wrist. He laughed. 'Why not? I've nothing else left. She is my possession, even more so than any man's doxy. So, who will cover?'

'You are mad.' Lord Wroth spoke. Belle's head jerked up. She had not known he was there. For an instant his eyes met hers, but there was none of the warmth and laughter that had lurked there since she had arrived at this hellish house party.

She looked away, humiliated and ashamed beyond belief. 'Lucien, please do not do this,' she said softly.

He didn't glance at her, his fingers only dug into her arm more, his gaze fixed on Wroth. 'So, what do you wish to wager for a week with my wife?'

'What do you want?' Wroth asked.

Her stomach turned even more sickeningly. He couldn't possibly be considering Lucien's offer.

'Five hundred pounds,' Lucien said.

'One thousand,' Lord Banbury said. His gaze went to her face and fear shot through her. He was thin and had a pallor that seemed unnatural and the whispers she had heard of his sexual proclivities had sickened her.

'Two thousand,' Wroth said. His voice was so cold she hardly recognised it.

'Very well. Two thousand.' Lucien laughed again. He released her so abruptly, she nearly stumbled. With a numb horror she watched him take his seat.

Her eyes never wavered from the game but she hardly knew what took place. Her mind and body no longer seemed connected and when the last of the cards were played, it hardly registered. Not until Lucien stood. 'She is yours, Wroth.'

Shock coursed through her. 'No,' she whispered.

Wroth rose and came towards her. 'Come with me, Belle.'

She backed away. 'No. I cannot.'

'You must come with me. You cannot stay here.'

She stared at him. 'I will not do this.'

Lucien was at her side. 'You have no choice, Belle.' He glanced at Wroth. 'Leave us for a moment.' He took her arm and dragged her from the room to the hallway.

His eyes glinted. 'Do not worry, my dear. It will not be a permanent arrangement. Just a week.' He cupped her chin, his fingers hard against her flesh. She kept perfectly still. 'Although I've no idea why you find the idea so repugnant. I have seen how he looks at you, and how you look at him. I only trust you will show more willingness in his bed than you do in mine, or I doubt he will feel you are worth two thousand pounds. On the other hand, he may enjoy tutoring you. I will own, I've not much patience for blushing virgins. I had thought at your age you might prove a more adept student, but I was wrong. At least you've no fear of his getting you with child.'

His cruelty still managed to pierce her like a sword. She resisted the urge to beg for she knew it would only inflame him more.

He dropped his hand away. 'Go upstairs and pack.'

She watched him walk away, then forced herself up the stairs and to her room. Once inside she shut the door and sat down on the bed, a cold numbness seeping through her. How could Justin betray her in such a way? She had thought that, of all the people at this nightmarish house party, he had been the one person she could call a friend. Older than her by a mere four months, at two and twenty, he possessed a boyish charm with his slightly rakish smile. She had been wary when she found him frequently at her side and thought he had chosen her for a flirtation.

Gradually it dawned upon her that he was at her side because he meant to protect her from the others. She was shocked when one of the other women told her he had mowed down Lord Amberly for insulting her. And although she suspected he had developed a *tendre* for her, the advances she was certain he would make had not come. Instead he had teased her and talked to her, and told her of his own family: his strict but just father, and the generous, warm woman who was his mother and who was not very well. She had envied him, for her own parents had died of diphtheria when she was twelve. As loving as her grandmother, Lady Townsend, had been, she still missed her parents and the family life they had shared.

And for the first time since entering the prison that was her marriage, she had started to feel a little of her own self again.

She had thought they were friends. But he was no different from her husband. In fact, he was worse. She had trusted him. She had never trusted Lucien.

She forced herself to rise and found the portmanteau. She started to pack, hardly caring what she put into it. She hesitated over the jewels Lucien had given her. She hated most of them. They were heavy and ornate and reminded her she was nothing more than a prisoner. She picked up one of the necklaces, a circlet of rubies and diamonds that felt like a collar around her neck. She stuffed it into her reticule. She could sell it if she needed money. With more than a little surprise she realised she did not intend to return to Lucien.

Nor would she allow Justin to touch her. She would die first.

She left the rest of her jewellery except for the pearls her grandmother had given her for her first Season. Her fingers brushed over the smooth strand and she fought back the tears that sprang to her eyes. 'Oh, Grandmama,' she whispered. 'You were right about him.' Lady Townsend had considered Lucien cold and calculating. But after Lady Townsend's death, when Belle was just nineteen, he had been so charming and solicitous to Belle that she thought Grandmama had been wrong.

She sat back down and put on her stockings and a pair of half-boots. The knock on the door startled her. She looked up, expecting to see Lucien, which made no sense because he never knocked. But it was Justin. Stunned, she could only stare at him.

He stepped into the room and shut the door behind him. 'Are you ready?' There was no boyish smile on his face. Instead, his dark eyes were hard and cold, his expression impossible to read. He looked almost a stranger to her.

'Yes,' she said coolly. She stood and draped her travelling cloak over one arm and then picked up her portmanteau.

He looked at her. For a moment she sensed he did not know quite what to do, but the impression quickly vanished. He stepped towards her. 'I will take that. We are leaving now.'

'I can carry it myself.' She started to walk by him.

He blocked her way. His brow crashed down. 'Give it to me, Belle.'

'I prefer to carry it.' She forced herself to meet his gaze.

'This is not the time to argue. You can do that as much as you please in my coach.'

'Can I? You did not buy my tongue as well as my body?'

He flinched. 'The portmanteau.' His hand closed around her wrist and he easily removed it from her grasp. His touch sent a shiver through her.

Justin took her hand, his fingers strong and warm around hers. She realised she had not put on gloves, and for the first time her bare flesh contacted his. She had a sudden vision of those hands on her and she felt almost shaky.

He did not seem to notice her reaction as he led her down the dimly lit hall. To her astonishment, he did not head for the main but the back staircase.

'Why are we going down here?'

'Do you want the rest of the company to see you are leaving with me?' He did not look down at her.

'If you must know, it really does not matter.'

His mouth tightened but he said nothing. He kept her hand tightly in his as he led her down the staircase to the small hall below. He paused and glanced at her.

'Damn it, Belle, don't look like that. I will not hurt you,' he said roughly. He touched her face, his hand gentle.

She flinched. She thought then that she hated him. 'You already have.'

He looked as if she had slapped him. His hand dropped from her face, his eyes cold and hooded. 'My carriage is outside.'

She went with him, careful not to touch him. The cold night air whipped around her and she drew her cloak tighter around her. She would rather die than let him touch her. And she would die a thousand deaths before she returned to Lucien.

He helped her into the carriage. 'I will ride,' he said. His voice was expressionless before he turned away and then the door was shut.

As the coach started to move, the thought crossed her mind she should jump. But where would she go? She could not return to Greystone and Lucien. But surely they would need to stop somewhere and then she could escape.

But if she did manage to escape, what would she do

next? Lord Ralston was her only relation, but he was Lucien's stepfather and what explanation could she possibly give them? And Maria adored her only son and could never see any fault in him. She had never been happier than on the day Belle had wed Lucien. She had clasped Belle to her breast with tears in her eyes. 'Now you are truly my daughter!'

Belle had pushed away her doubts. She had gone to live with Lucien's stepfather, the Earl of Ralston, who had been a distant cousin of Lady Townsend's as well as her closest neighbour. Lucien's mother, Maria, had done everything she could to encourage a match and, after a while, Belle had started to believe herself in love with Lucien. Maria had been so kind to Belle, treating her as a second daughter, and their own daughter, Chloe, six years younger than Belle, had been the sister Belle had always wanted. When Lucien had offered her marriage a year after Lady Townsend's death, it seemed ungrateful to refuse. So she had married him, despite the fact he sometimes scared her with his temper and that he frequently seemed to drink to excess. But then, she knew so little of fashionable gentlemen that perhaps being frequently in one's cups was normal. And his temper had never been turned directly on her. That is, until after they were wed, and she failed to produce an heir.

By the time the carriage halted, she was no closer to a solution. She saw they were in an inn yard and that faint fingers of light were creeping across the sky. The coach doors opened and Justin waited for her. He helped her down and then released her. 'We will stop here and rest.' He made no move to touch her as they walked across the silent yard and into the inn. The proprietor came out and Justin bespoke two rooms. If the proprietor doubted that they were brother and sister, he did not reveal it. He showed them to a private parlour where they were to wait until their rooms were ready. He shut the door behind him.

'What are you going to do with me?' she asked. She was beginning to feel an odd calmness.

'I have a lodge in Scotland. You will be safe there.' He looked down at her.

'Will I?' she said bitterly.

'Yes.' He took a step towards hers. 'I love you, Belle,' he said hoarsely.

'And so you buy me for two thousand pounds. I fear, my lord, that is not enough to induce me to share your bed. I will never let you touch me.' She was angry and scared and confused. Her eyes searched his face. Lucien had said those words to her when he was courting her, but she soon learned they meant nothing. But he had never looked at her with the sort of despairing longing she saw on Justin's face.

'Is that why you think I wagered for you? So I might force you to my bed? I love you,' he said again.

Something painful and raw twisted inside of her at his words. 'No, do not say that to me! I do not want your love. I cannot bear it!' The door opened and she turned, a terrible shock coursing through her. Lucien stood there, a pistol in his hand. His gaze went from her face to Justin's. 'Very touching, but alas, I fear I must put an end to your impassioned declaration.' He motioned with his pistol. 'Come here, Belle. I must applaud you on your performance, but it is time for the farce to end.'

She stared at him. 'What are you talking about?'

Lucien smiled, a cold cruel smile that sent a sliver of fear through her. 'You are coming home with me, just as we planned.' He looked at Justin. 'As for you, I fear

I must call you out for abducting my wife. She is a splendid actress, do you not think? She played the role of innocent, betrayed wife to perfection and, as we had planned, you walked neatly into her trap.'

Justin's face turned to stone but not before she caught a flash of anguish that tore at her being. 'Is this true, Belle?' His cold gaze bore into hers.

'No!'

Lucien caught her arm and pulled her to him. 'My love, there is no need to continue the act.' His mouth crashed down on hers in a hard, possessive kiss that reminded her of exactly who was master. He lifted his head a little. 'If you continue to deny this, I will shoot Wroth on the spot. Do you understand?' he said against her mouth.

She nodded, sick with fear. He released her. 'Tell him the truth, Belle.'

She forced herself to look at Justin. 'Very well. It…it was a trap.'

His eyes remained on her face, the coldness in them chilling her soul. 'Why?' he asked.

'I…' With sickening clarity she knew what Lucien meant to do. How could she have been so blind, so stupid to not suspect his motives for telling her to pay attention to Justin? When Lucien was only ten, his father had lost most of his fortune to Justin's father, the Duke of Westmore, in a London gaming hell. That night he had shut himself up in his study and put a bullet through his head. Lucien made no attempt to hide the fact he considered Justin's father a murderer.

Lucien's grip tightened on her arm. 'Can you not guess? I am going to avenge my father's death.'

Justin's gaze did not waver. 'My father was not responsible for your father's death.'

Lucien laughed. 'Oh, but he was. Westmore took everything from him without mercy. Your father did everything but put the gun to his head. And so I plan to take everything from your father. Without mercy.'

'So you will murder me. Then you will hang. I fail to see how that will give you satisfaction.'

'But I do not plan to murder you. There will be a duel. And alas, you will be the loser.'

There must be a way to stop him. Lucien was a deadly shot; he spent hours practising—it had of late become an obsession and now she knew why. No matter why Justin had wagered for her—she could not let him be killed.

'Because I abducted your wife? I won your wife, if you recall. There were witnesses.' Justin had folded his arms. His voice was deadly calm, almost conversational as if he were merely curious about what Lucien planned.

'There were witnesses to the fact you cheated.' Lucien smiled gently. He pulled two sheets of paper from his pocket. 'After you left, we discovered some of the cards were marked. I have signed statements from both Farley and Banbury, who by the way, was not pleased you stole the prize. So it will be an affair of honour. You may examine them if you wish.'

Justin ignored his offer. 'I assume there will be the usual witnesses to this affair of honour.' His voice held more than a trace of a sneer.

'Banbury will be my second and...' Lucien paused deliberately '...your cousin will be yours.'

'My cousin! Damn you!' He started to move forward, then checked himself. 'Why the hell did you involve Brandt?'

'So there would be no questions about the fairness of the duel.' He glanced towards the window. 'It is nearly dawn. It is time to proceed. There is a field across the road which will serve our purpose.' He looked down at Belle. 'You will come as well.' He motioned with his pistol. 'Go, Wroth. I trust you will not attempt to escape or I will shoot Isabelle.'

Justin finally looked at her, his eyes so full of contempt, she nearly quailed. 'That is a matter of supreme indifference to me.'

But he made no move to run and merely went with them across the inn yard, now coming to life. With the sensation of a nightmare she saw Eliza Pomeroy was there as well as Lord Banbury and Justin's cousin, Lord Salcombe. Banbury's expression was indifferent but Salcombe's was grim. He was a year older than Justin, and tall and broad-shouldered, with the same handsome dark looks.

Still in a dream, she crossed the road to the field with the others. She watched as a short balding man arrived. From his manner, and the bag he carried, she presumed he was the local surgeon. Lucien had released her and seemed to have forgotten her presence. She closed her eyes for a brief moment. If only she could stop this. But Lucien was beyond reason.

Justin stood with his cousin. He had removed his coat and stood in breeches, waistcoat and linen shirt. Belle started towards him. He looked up, his eyes boring into her. 'What do you want?'

'You must not do this! He never misses and he means to kill you.' Justin merely looked at her. She turned to Salcombe. 'Can you not stop this?'

Salcombe met her eyes, his own hard. 'It is too late for an attack of conscience, Lady Milborne. It is a pity it did not happen two weeks ago before you ensnared my cousin.' He turned to Justin. 'It is time.'

She felt as if she had been slapped. Salcombe walked towards Banbury, who held the pistol case. Justin started after him and then paused. He turned and looked down at Belle, his dark eyes remote. 'Why did you do this?'

'I had no idea...I did not know what Lucien meant to do.' She looked at him, willing him to understand.

A cold smile touched his mouth. 'There is no need to continue the act. We are not on stage.' He stepped towards her and she made herself remain still. 'By the way, I was acting as well. I intended to bed you using any means possible. But for now, I will have to be content with this.' Before she could protest he had pulled her against his hard unyielding chest. He tilted her chin and then his lips found hers. His kiss was bruising and punishing, and when he released her she stumbled. But he was already striding across the field.

She watched as they took their pistols and paced off. It all happened in such slow motion. The handkerchief dropping and the shots and then Justin falling to the ground. She started to run forward and then in a sort of shock realised Salcombe had helped Justin to a sitting position. She heard shouts and saw the surgeon was at Lucien's side. Eliza caught her arm. 'You must go to your husband. Salcombe will see to Justin.' Confused, she allowed Eliza to lead her across the grass. Lucien lay there, a dark red stain spreading across his shirt. The surgeon had pressed a pad to his shoulder. Belle fell to her knees on the other side of him. As if sensing her presence he opened his eyes and his eyes glittered. 'I will still win. Even if I die, Wroth will hang for my death. And you, Isabelle, will learn that allowing your affections to stray is fatal.' Then his eyes closed.

* * *

Justin kept his gaze on his father. 'So when do I leave England?'

'You will leave for Dover with Giles tonight,' the Duke said coolly.

A sob escaped the Duchess's throat. Justin was consumed with guilt and anger that he had brought her such anguish. He forced his own voice to remain expressionless. 'And if Milborne lives, when can I return?'

'When the affair has died down. Unfortunately duelling is illegal and despite the fact you had no choice, you could be tried for his murder.' His father's expression was grim. The Duke's immense position and power had not been enough to quell the rumours that Justin had cheated at cards and when Milborne had called him out, Justin had callously shot him. At least there had been no mention of Belle. For some reason Milborne had not seen fit to spread that tale. 'You may be in even more trouble if he lives. He will do everything in his power to harm me through you. You will have some measure of protection away from England.'

'I would rather take my chances in England.' He could not bear to leave when his mother was so ill.

'No, my dearest, you must go.' The Duchess rose from the sofa and came to his side. 'You will be safe with Lord Haversham, and I will not worry that Milborne will seek to have you arrested.' She caught his hands. 'How I wish you were not going so far away, but I cannot see what else is to be done!'

The tears in her eyes tore at his heart. She was so thin and fragile and her hand so delicate in his that he felt he held a small bird in his palm. 'I will return as soon as possible. I promise you that,' he said roughly.

'I will not let you forget.' She reached up and brushed her lips over his cheek. She smelled softly of roses, a

scent he always associated with her. He brought her hand
to his lips and then released it, fighting down the pre-
monition that he would not see her again.

If it were possible to damn Belle Milborne to hell at
that moment, he would have. He cursed himself for his
gullibility. From the first moment he saw her on Milborne's arm, her face as lovely and pure as a Madonna's,
her expression apprehensive as she surveyed the company, he had wanted to protect her. Milborne's evident
neglect and her unhappiness had aroused chivalrous instincts he'd never suspected he possessed and within a
week he had tumbled head over heels in love for the first
time. He could talk to her and she listened as if she truly
cared about him, rather than the fact he was heir to a
dukedom.

But it had all been the performance of a consummate
actress. She must have laughed when he made his impassioned declaration of love. Laughed to think he was
so infatuated with her that he paid two thousand pounds
to save her from her husband's schemes. He shoved
aside the image of her anguished face when she pleaded
with him not to accept Milborne's challenge. He had no
idea whether she had actually felt a twinge of guilt or
whether she was merely acting. It made no difference.
He hated her more than he had hated anyone in his life.

Three years later, he stood at the rail of the ship that
carried him towards England. He had not seen his
mother again. Or his father. He had spent the last three
years in the army under Lord Haversham. When his
mother had finally succumbed to the wasting illness,
three months after he left England, he had been on the
Peninsula. His father had died a year and a half later
from pneumonia, but by then Justin was in Brussels. The

news of his father's death had been delayed so by the time it reached him his father had been laid to rest in the cool marble tomb next to the woman he had loved since childhood.

He watched the seabirds circle and dive as the cliffs of Dover slowly appeared on the horizon. He was returning home. Home to England. And to Isabelle Milborne. The hot, passionate anger he had felt over her treachery had cooled to a cold desire for revenge.

Milborne was dead; he had finally died months after the duel from a lingering infection. He despised Milborne, but in some sense he could understand the man's obsession for revenge. But Belle's complicity was beyond his comprehension. That she had participated in a plot that was to result in his death was despicable enough, but that she had hastened his mother's death was unforgivable. He had no doubt his mother's distress had only served to weaken her already fragile health. And because of Belle Milborne, his father had died without the comfort of wife or son at his side.

So, Belle Milborne would pay in hell for her treachery. Even if he went there with her.

Chapter One

London, 1816

Belle took one last glance at herself in the looking glass. Her soft grey silk ball gown was elegant but severe. As was the rest of her appearance. Which was exactly what she wanted. She knew certain males of the *ton* considered her cold and had unkindly dubbed her 'the unassailable' but she had no desire to be viewed as anything but unapproachable.

She picked up her gloves and tried to quell the nervous flutter in her stomach. She had been in London ten days and had accompanied her mother-in-law, Lady Ralston, and her sister-in-law, Chloe, to half a dozen affairs already, including a ball, without such apprehension. But tonight was different. The Duke of Westmore was in London.

She very much dreaded he would be at the Hartford ball. She had not seen Justin since he returned to England nine months ago. Lord Ralston had died six months before that and they had still been in mourning and had not gone out into society until now. But she had heard enough about him. About how, despite a broken arm, he had returned to the battlefield at Waterloo and braved the enemy lines to rescue his wounded superior, Lord Haversham, from certain death. He had left England in disgrace but had returned to it a hero. And a duke, for his father had died on the eve of the battle.

The thought of possibly meeting him nearly threw her into a panic. Only last night at a rout, she had heard two women discussing him. Usually, she did not eavesdrop but the mention of his name had drawn her attention like a magnet. By the time the women had moved away, she had learned he had just arrived in town and that his aunt, the Dowager Countess of Knowles intended to find him a wife and every mama in London was nearly in a swoon over the idea.

Perhaps he would be so preoccupied with swooning mamas and daughters he would hardly notice her. Belle was not hopeful. Lucien had not destroyed him physically, but had managed to ruin his life in every way possible. She doubted he had forgotten that.

Or that Belle had confessed to taking part in Lucien's plan.

If it weren't for her mother-in-law and Chloe, she would be tempted to flee London. But Maria, who suffered from a nervous constitution, insisted she badly needed Belle's support during the ordeal of a London Season. And Belle loved Chloe as dearly as if she was her own sister, and had wanted to be in London with her.

The scratch on her door jerked her from her thoughts and reminded her she had a ball to attend. Her housekeeper, Mrs Bates, entered. 'Lord Ralston is below. Impatient as usual.' She sniffed. 'I don't know why since you are always prompt.'

'Tell him I will be with him shortly.'

She sighed. Arthur was another ordeal. He was the reason she had insisted on staying in the comfortable townhouse in Gower Street her grandmother had left her. Maria and Chloe were staying with Arthur, now the Earl of Ralston. Arthur was also Chloe's guardian, and although Belle tried to like him, she could not like someone who so thoroughly disapproved of her. The idea of living under the same roof as Arthur had been unthinkable and so, over Maria's protests that Belle could not possibly manage on her own, she had opened the house for the Season. Once a year, from the time she had been thirteen until Lady Townsend had become ill, they had come to London. Maria had not been able to understand that Belle wanted to surround herself with something of her family and had exclaimed that she and Chloe were her family. Belle had not even bothered to explain that she looked forward to the silence as well. A place where she could be left to her own thoughts and do as she wished.

She left her bedchamber and went to the drawing room. Arthur was standing in front of the mantelpiece, hands clasped behind his back. He turned when he saw her and moved towards her. He was dressed as usual in black, a colour that only served to make his bony features even more severe. Only four years older than her five and twenty, he seemed a decade older than that. 'Good evening, Belle,' he said, without smiling. He ran his eyes over her dress and frowned. 'Must you persist in dressing as if you were a governess or a poor relation? It will hardly help Chloe's chances at making a good match if her sister-in-law is considered an eccentric.'

'We will hope that any man who truly cares for her would be willing to overlook her eccentric relations.'

His thin lips tightened. 'And if you truly cared for her you would see to it that you do nothing to call attention to yourself.'

What did he think she would do? Run about in her shift in the middle of a ballroom? She bit back a sharp retort. 'I intend to behave with the utmost decorum.' As she always did.

Maria and Chloe waited for them in Arthur's carriage. Belle seated herself next to the younger woman. Chloe leaned towards her. 'Did he lecture you very much?' she whispered to Belle.

'I fear I dress like a poor relation,' she whispered back.

Chloe made a face. At nineteen she was very pretty with a pair of sparkling brown eyes and a smile that often held a hint of mischief. She tended to laugh off much of Arthur's admonitions although she always gave the air of listening intently. And then she did as she pleased.

Nearly three-quarters of an hour later they finally stepped into the Hartfords' small ballroom. The room was already crowded with fashionable members of society—the women in silks and muslin and jewels, the men in elegantly cut evening clothes. Chloe was soon engaged for the first dance and, after giving his approval, Arthur wandered off towards the card room. Maria and Belle started towards the wall where the chaperons congregated.

They were just about to join two of Maria's friends, when Maria gave a sharp gasp. She stared towards the double doors that led from the ballroom to the hall, her face white.

'Maria, what is it?' Belle said, alarmed.

'Oh, dear God! He is here! Whatever shall we do?'

Belle looked towards the doors. A dark-haired man was just bowing over Lady Hartford's hand. Then he straightened and her heart nearly stopped. Even after three years, she could not fail to recognise him. Her worst fear had just come true. The Duke of Westmore had arrived.

'I do not think we must do anything.' She put a re-assuring hand on Maria's arm. 'The best thing would be for you to pretend as if nothing is amiss.'

'But what if he should approach us? I daresay he blames Lucien for exiling him to the continent although it was completely his fault.'

'I doubt if he will even notice us.'

But a half-hour later, despite her best efforts to remain hidden behind a potted plant, Belle knew she was wrong. She glanced across the room and found herself staring into his dark cool face. She yanked her gaze away, but not before she saw the slight inclination of his head. He had not forgotten her and she had no doubt he had not forgotten the past at all.

Justin finally managed to extricate himself from his aunt's side. Since his arrival in London, Lady Georgina had been determined that he meet every young lady she considered eligible for the next Duchess of Westmore. He had already met half a dozen girls under the age of twenty who either stammered and blushed or coyly dropped their gazes upon his being presented to him. However, none of them interested him in the least. The only woman who did had just left the ballroom.

And he did not intend to allow her to leave the ball without confronting her.

He stalked to the hall. At first he did not see her

among the guests who had also decided to escape the hot, crowded ballroom. Then he spotted her. She stood near a long window, partially hidden by a statue, her back to him. She was alone. Despite his desire to remain detached, his pulse quickened as he approached her.

She seemed to be staring out the window and did not turn until he was right behind her. She spun around, almost running into him, then she took a step back and paled, her eyes widened with shock.

'Hello, Belle,' he said softly.

'I…' She stared at him as if he were a ghost.

He allowed his gaze to wander over her face. 'I had heard you were in London, and had hoped I might see you this evening. And here you are, nearly throwing yourself into my arms. Dare I hope that means you are pleased to see me?'

She might have flinched, but he could not be certain. Her eyes were fixed on his face. 'I cannot imagine why you would want to see me.'

'Can't you? You are still the most beautiful woman I know. And you owe me a debt.'

She flushed, something that surprised him, but then she was a consummate actress. This time he insolently ran his eyes over her, allowing his gaze to linger on the creamy flesh above her modest bodice. Desire, hard and swift, shot through him. Hell. After all this time, he should feel nothing for her but contempt.

Worse, he did not lie. Despite the unbecoming grey gown she wore, she was even more beautiful at five and twenty than she had been at two and twenty. Her oval face with its slightly patrician nose, and her rosebud mouth and expressive hazel eyes had only improved with maturity. She still reminded him of a Madonna, a lovely, untouchable virgin, but now he knew what lay beneath that lovely façade.

'A debt? Do you mean the two thousand pounds?' The flush on her face made her look vulnerable. 'I want to repay it but I cannot do so all at once.'

He shrugged. 'Two thousand pounds is mere pin money to me. No, I want something else.'

'What is it? I have only the money my grandmother left me. And her townhouse, which is not very grand. That is all I can give you.'

'Not quite all.' He kept his gaze on her face. 'If you recall, I bought your company for two thousand pounds. That is what you owe me.'

She paled so much he thought she was about to swoon. She backed away as if she feared he planned to ravish her on the spot. 'But I thought… You cannot possibly want my company! I would give you anything but that.'

'I do not want anything else.'

She stared at him, a flash of anger in her eyes. 'I would rather die than consider such a thing! I did not make that wager, my husband did. I went with you because I had no alternative.'

'Didn't you? If I recall, your choice was to deliberately participate in a scheme to bring about my demise. Do you deny that you told me that it was a trap?'

'No, but Lucien left me no choice. He would have shot you on the spot if I did not,' she said quietly.

For an insane moment, he almost believed her. But then he recalled how she had repulsed him when he said he loved her. Nor had she once, in the aftermath of the duel, made any attempt to deny the lies her husband had spread about his cheating at the card game. All the bitterness and anger rose up again.

He smiled coldly. 'Very convenient of you to cast the blame on your husband, particularly since he is dead. The debts may have been his, but they now are yours. I want to collect what you owe me. I would prefer to continue this conversation in private, however.'

'And I do not want to continue the conversation at all.' She lifted her chin. 'I will not deny we…I did you a great wrong. You do not know how many times I wished it had all been different. But I will not do this!'

'No? I have no doubt I can change your mind.'

'You never will.' She started to move past him. 'If you will please allow me to pass. I must return to the ballroom. I have been gone far too long. They will notice.'

'Perhaps you will honour me with a dance.'

'I never dance with anyone. There would be talk.'

'That matters little to me. I have no doubt I would survive a dance with you.'

She bit her lip. 'But I will not. My sister-in-law is here. This is her first Season and I cannot do anything that will ruin her chances. She is an innocent child and does not deserve to be caught up in this. None of this is her doing.'

'No? It is a pity you did not think of these things three years ago.' He stepped aside. 'But I will have my payment.' He did not give her a chance to reply but turned and walked away. But not before he saw the stricken look on her face. He shoved down the twinge of conscience that smote him and cursed himself for still wanting to think her innocent. He had no intention of allowing anything to get in the way of his revenge.

Belle returned to the ballroom, and paused inside the double doors, her breathing hard almost as if she had been running. Which she had been for all purposes.

She forced herself to take a breath. She could not let anyone see how agitated she was. It would not be at all in keeping with the cool, remote persona she had cultivated since Lucien's death.

But one encounter had managed to strip that coolness away and she had felt as exposed as she had that horrible night. Why ever had she left the ballroom? She should have suspected he would follow her. Despite her best efforts to remain invisible, he had spotted her within a half-hour of his arrival. More than once she had found his cold gaze on her and she knew that a confrontation was inevitable. Perhaps by leaving the ballroom she had hoped it would force his hand and she would know what he wanted.

And now she did.

He wanted her.

She felt almost sick at the thought. He had a ruthlessness about him that had not been there before and she knew he would grant her no mercy. There had been nothing of the charming young man she had known in his hard, handsome face. But then she had watched that young man disappear three years ago. If he had ever existed.

Belle realised the music had stopped and the dancers were dispersing. She looked around and saw Chloe, standing near the side of the ballroom with her friend, Serena, and Serena's mother, Mrs Hurst. She looked so normal that Belle thought that perhaps the whole scene had merely been a bad dream. She made her way to Chloe's side and the young girl looked over, her lovely oval face lit with a smile. 'Where were you? Arthur was looking for you. He seemed quite out of sorts that you had left the ballroom.' She lowered her voice. 'I suggested that perhaps you had an assignation and he looked quite apoplectic. Mama was looking for you also. She also seemed somewhat distressed.' Chloe peered more closely at Belle. 'Are you well? You look rather peculiar.'

'It is the heat.' She managed a smile. 'I merely left the ballroom for a few moments in hopes it would be cooler in the hall.'

'If that is all,' Chloe said. Her attention was caught by Serena who wanted to point out a particularly amazing headdress worn by one of the dowagers.

Mrs Hurst moved to Belle's side and began to talk about the shocking expense of living in London. Belle half-listened to her light chatter, but she felt distracted, waiting for Westmore to appear. Had he entered the ballroom or was he still in the hall or perhaps the card room? But surely there was nothing he could do in the middle of a ball.

Serena's hand was solicited for the next dance and Mrs Hurst moved off. Maria bustled up to them a few minutes later. 'Here you are my love, thank goodness.' Her voice was quite agitated. 'I saw you leave and then he left just after you and I feared he had followed you. Oh, how can he be here, so haughty and proud, as if he had never done such a despicable thing! And everyone thinks he is a hero!'

Guilt shot through Belle as it always did when Maria spoke of Justin in such terms. No matter what she felt about Justin, Lucien had cruelly used him.

'But he did save his superior officer's life at Waterloo and if the tales are to be believed, in a most heroic fashion,' she said lightly. 'Would you like a lemonade? I would be happy to fetch one for you.'

As Belle had hoped, Maria was distracted. 'How kind you are. A lemonade would be just the thing but I do hope it is not too strong. Perhaps you could add a little water if it appears to be so.'

'Of course.' She started to move away and then she saw Lady Hartford coming towards them. To her horror, she saw Justin was with her.

She froze. At the same time she heard Maria gasp. Dear lord. Surely he could not be planning to speak to them!

But he was. Lady Hartford stopped in front of them, the smile on her face a trifle strained. Maria's face was rigid with shock and disapproval. Belle prayed she would not do or say anything to create a scene.

Lady Hartford cleared her throat. 'Maria, his Grace wishes to be presented to you and Lady Chloe.' She cast Belle a nervous glance. 'I believe you have made his acquaintance, Lady Milborne.'

'Yes, we are acquainted,' Belle said. 'Good evening, your Grace.' She kept her voice as even as possible despite the knot in her stomach.

'Good evening, Lady Milborne.' His voice was polite, but the sardonic gleam in his eye filled her with apprehension. She had done him a terrible wrong and she could not fault him for being angry, but why must he throw down the gauntlet so publicly?

For he would have to be supremely insensitive not to realise they were the centre of attention as Lady Hartford performed the introductions. Maria barely held out her hand, her lips set in tight lines as he bowed over it. She snatched it away as soon as he released her as if she had just touched something nasty. Chloe greeted him properly, her expression hard to read.

At least no one had said anything amiss. If only Westmore would go away. But he still held Chloe's hand. 'Will you do me the honour of standing up with me for the next dance, Lady Chloe?'

Chloe stared at him. Belle felt almost light-headed and even Lady Hartford appeared stunned. Maria gasped. 'Most certainly n—'

Chloe recovered first. 'I would like to, Mama.' She gave Belle an imploring look.

'I am certain it would be a great honour.' Belle hardly knew what she said. She had never expected him to ask Chloe for a dance, but to refuse him would only cause gossip, something Chloe seemed to recognise. She attempted a reassuring smile. 'Shall I fetch the lemonade you wanted, Maria?'

'I...' Maria's face had taken on a most alarming colour and, for a moment, Belle feared she was about to swoon. She caught Maria's arm. 'Perhaps you should sit.'

'An excellent notion,' Lady Hartford said. Her colour was almost as high as Maria's.

Belle glared at Justin, angry he was causing so much distress. He met her eyes, an expression crossing his face she could not fathom and then he yanked his gaze back to Chloe. 'Lady Chloe, should we join the next set?' He held out his arm.

'If you please.' Chloe laid her gloved hand on his arm, her face still worried, but she went with him.

Belle watched them for a moment, Chloe looking young and vulnerable next to his dark, forceful figure. If only she could march up to him and demand he release Chloe instantly, but that would only cause the sort of scene she wanted to avoid. Maria's soft moan forced her attention back to her mother-in-law.

She and Lady Hartford helped Maria to a place near

the wall and a footman quickly procured a chair before
he was sent off for a glass of watery lemonade. Belle
pulled out the smelling salts Maria kept in her reticule
but Maria waved them away. Her normal colour was
starting to return and she sat more stiffly upright. Several
of her friends had by this time gathered to offer their
assistance and she managed a weak smile. 'I am quite
recovered. It was only the shock of... My love—' she
looked at Belle '—you will see to Chloe, if you please.'

'Yes.' Belle hastened away, glad to leave the circle
of chattering women.

Arthur joined Belle just as she reached the side of the
ballroom. 'Is it true Westmore has asked Chloe to stand
up with him?' he demanded.

'Yes, unfortunately.'

'Unfortunately? Not at all, my dear, not at all.' His
eyes gleamed. 'Having Westmore's attentions will only
serve to secure her place in society. It is quite fortunate.'

'He has distressed Maria no end by doing so. She
nearly swooned and I could clearly see Chloe was
equally distressed. I cannot imagine how you consider it
a good thing!'

He looked down his thin nose at her. 'I had hoped
that, after all this time, you would have forgotten the
affair. Apparently Westmore has. And may I remind
you, he is a duke and very powerful, so I trust you will
do nothing to provoke him.'

It was all she could do to hold her tongue. She turned
towards the dancers and looked for Chloe and Justin.
They were not hard to find. Justin could not be considered exceptionally tall, but his dark head and arrogant
grace stood out. She watched as he and Chloe came
together. He said something to Chloe and she shook her
head, a slight smile on her face. At least he was not

doing anything to distress her, thank goodness, but even that did not provide much reassurance. She had no idea why he had sought out her sister-in-law and none of the suspicions whirling in her head gave her the least comfort. Had he meant to punish her for refusing him by approaching Chloe? A shiver darted through her. She knew without a doubt he was not about to let things rest.

She felt overwhelming relief when the music finally stopped. She waited while Justin tucked Chloe's hand beneath his and brought her to their side. Arthur pasted a smile to his face. 'Good evening, Westmore. We are most honoured by the compliment you paid my ward by asking her to stand up with you.'

Justin released Chloe's hand and glanced at Belle. 'And is Lady Milborne honoured as well?'

Arthur looked at her, his expression daring her to disagree. 'Most certainly Lady Milborne is honoured. Quite honoured, in fact.'

'Is she?' A slight smile touched Justin's mouth. 'I am delighted to know that.' He turned back to Chloe. The smile at his lips was full of charm. 'Good evening, Lady Chloe. I hope you will stand up with me again.' He inclined his head towards Arthur and Belle. 'Ralston, Lady Milborne.' He walked off.

Belle was too furious to speak. Chloe's face was anxious. 'Is Mama well?'

'I think so. When I left her, she was drinking lemonade. She refused her smelling salts.'

Chloe sighed. 'Then it wasn't so bad.'

'You should be grateful Westmore stood up with you. As should Maria,' Arthur said. 'I will talk to her and make certain she understands that.' He stalked off before she could say a thing and Belle hoped he was not planning to accost Maria just now.

She linked her arm through Chloe's. 'I must bring you back to your mama. She will want to know you are unharmed. He did not say anything untoward to you, did he?'

'Oh, not! He was really quite…quite nice,' she said awkwardly. 'Oh, Belle I did not mean to overset her but I feared if I did not stand up with him, it would result in a horrid scene. I pray you will not think too badly of me.'

She looked at Chloe's sweet face and felt the surge of love she always did for her. 'I would never think badly of you for anything you did. You were quite right to avoid a scene. It is exactly what I would have advised.'

'I hope so.' Chloe's smile was relieved.

Belle returned her smile, not wanting Chloe to sense her distress.

But later that night, in the quiet of her bedchamber, she could not suppress the growing fear that Justin meant to use any means possible to extract payment from her. Including Chloe. Because of Lucien and because of her, he had been banished from England. And from his family. He may have acted despicably in wagering for her, but she had no doubt he had cared deeply for his family.

She sat down on her bed. Tonight's encounter had brought up memories she had thought buried. The warmth she had found in his presence. The way his eyes lit with laughter when he had teased her. Sitting with him in the secluded garden at Greystone and watching his face as he described the house that his father had just granted him for his twenty-second birthday. It was perched on a cliff in Devon, overlooking the sea, and at various times in its history had been used by smugglers.

She couldn't think of anything more romantic and for a moment, as he told her of his plans for the house, she had allowed herself to imagine being there with him.

How naïve she had been. Perhaps he had believed himself in love with her. Or confused the emotion with lust. She had almost believed his declaration of love before Lucien had burst in.

Lucien had entertained no doubts Justin had a *tendre* for her. During the time between the duel and his death he had taunted her with it often. 'How foolish of Wroth to fall in love with you. I would not have thought him capable of such weakness. But then it provided me with the perfect weapon to use against him. He would have gone to any lengths to save you.'

She set down the basin she carried on the table next to his bed. She had come to change the dressings on his arm. The wound in his shoulder had never properly healed and the physician had been forced to drain it more than once. Despite his increasing weakness, Lucien was not so ill he was unable to torment her. He insisted that only she should nurse him and refused to allow anyone else to attend him, including Maria. 'He was not in love with me,' she said.

Lucien laughed softly. 'Certainly not when he realised the woman he adored had planned to kill him. I've no doubt he quite hates you.'

She kept her gaze on the wash basin, not wanting him to see how his words hurt her. Had Justin cared for her at all, or had it merely been an act, as he had claimed? A means to bed her in any way he could? Or had her betrayal prompted his cruel words?

She forced her thoughts back to the present. It did not matter now whether he had ever cared for her, for after tonight she had no doubt he detested her. She could not imagine that he could possibly want her, but she had not mistaken the blatant desire in his eyes.

What if he decided to use Chloe as a weapon against her? She had never thought him capable of such an act. But then, the dark, cold man she saw tonight was a stranger to her, and she had no idea what he was capable of. Marriage to Lucien had taught her the capacity for anger and revenge was bottomless.

And she very much feared that, this time, Justin truly intended to use any weapon at hand to get what he wanted.

Chapter Two

When Belle called in at Grosvenor Square the next morning, she was stunned to find Maria in hysterics. Chloe knelt by her side, the relief on her face apparent when Belle was shown in. 'Thank goodness you are here!' Chloe exclaimed, rising. 'I did not want her to see the card, but she insisted.'

'What card?' Belle asked. She sat down next to Maria and took her soft, plump hand.

Maria sat up, sniffed loudly and gripped Belle's hand. 'The card on the flowers. He…he sent my innocent child flowers!'

Belle's stomach churned. 'Westmore?'

'Yes!' A militant light appeared in Maria's eye. 'I have already disposed of them. I wish I might tell him exactly what I feel to his face! If he thinks to work his wicked wiles on Chloe, he will be very sorry.'

Belle glanced up at Chloe. 'Was there something in the note to give offence?' she asked.

Chloe shook her head. 'He merely thanked me for the dance and signed his name.'

'That does not sound so dreadful.'

Maria glared at her. 'It is dreadful enough that he even

noticed her. I have no doubt that he means to cause mischief. I have no idea why when he was at fault for the whole affair. If only I could tell the entire world what really happened! Then we would see how welcome he would be!'

Oh, dear! The last thing they needed was for Maria to decide to stir up the old rumours. 'You must not say anything. Westmore was not completely at fault. Lucien wished to provoke him,' Belle said quietly.

'How can you possibly defend him?' Maria's mouth tightened. 'He cheated and then, when Lucien challenged him, instead of behaving like a gentleman and allowing himself to be shot, he killed my son. Sometimes I think you did not care for Lucien at all!'

Belle looked at her helplessly and knew she should have said nothing. She had no doubt Lucien had induced Banbury and Farley to sign the statements. Her instincts told her that Justin would not cheat. He did not need to, for one thing. She had watched him play enough during that fortnight to know his skills far exceeded those of any of the others at the house party. But trying to tell Maria that was hopeless. She would not hear anything against her beloved first-born. Any of Belle's efforts to suggest that Justin was not completely at fault was met with recriminations and palpitations.

'Of course I cared for Lucien,' she told Maria. The lie fell easily from her tongue, adding one more sin to her long list. She had cared for Lucien at first, had wanted to love the handsome man with his fair hair and charming smiles, but his charm faded almost as soon as the vows had been said. Under his continuous mockery and derision, her fragile love had withered away. She had not let on to Maria, however, not wanting to hurt the woman who had been so kind to her, almost a second mother. After her parents had died and Belle had gone to live with her grandmother, Maria had often invited Belle to her home on the rambling estate that bordered her grandmother's more modest property. Maria had welcomed Belle as a second daughter and mothered her in her rather fussy, warm way. Lord Ralston, although more reserved, had been kind as well. And after Lady Townsend had died, and Belle had nowhere else to go, Maria had insisted she must live with them.

Maria was finally calmed. By the time they had set out for Bond Street, she had been distracted by thoughts of ribbons, gloves and stockings and a visit to Gunther's for ices. She chatted happily about the soirée they were to attend the following night and the small dinner at the Sherwoods' that night. The Duke of Westmore was not mentioned at all.

Belle only wished it were possible for her to be so easily distracted. She could think of nothing but Westmore and it took all of her willpower to concentrate on the matching of ribbons to a new gown and later, to force a few bites of lemon ice down her throat.

For she very much feared that for once Maria was right, he meant mischief. He meant to force her to do his bidding.

And if he intended to use Chloe to achieve his ends, Belle would have no choice but to do what he wanted.

Justin rose from behind his desk as his aunt was shown into his study. From the bright colour in her plump cheeks he surmised she was in high dudgeon over something. She sailed towards his desk and stopped in front of it. 'What do you mean by standing up with Lady

Chloe Daventry last night?' she demanded. 'Have you gone mad?'

His brow rose. 'Not at all. Why would you think that?'

'Why?' She fixed him with her sharp blue eyes. 'Because she is Isabelle Milborne's sister-in-law, not to mention the sister of the man who nearly ruined you.'

'Perhaps so, but Lady Chloe is also very lovely. And very eligible.'

She gasped. 'You do not mean...really, Westmore, you could not possibly consider her!'

'Why not? She is the daughter of an earl and has a significant portion. Her family is old and respectable. I see no reason why she should not be considered in the running.'

'You would have Lady Milborne as your sister-in-law! I could never countenance that!'

'Indeed.' He smiled a little. 'However, your worries are premature, for I've not made up my mind at all.'

She did not look particularly mollified but, after spending a few more minutes attempting to dissuade him from the notion, finally gave up. She left shortly after that and said she hoped he would come to his senses.

He watched her go and then sat back down. He did not intend to marry Lady Chloe, but he was not above using her for his own purposes. That Belle was fond of her sister-in-law, he had no doubt. He wondered how far she would be willing to go to stop him if she thought he did intend to wed her.

He had very little else to use. None of his discreet inquiries had revealed the slightest hint of scandal attached to her. After her husband's death, she had gone to live with her in-laws. This Season was her first venture into society since then. Milborne's stepfather had died a year after Milborne and she, Lady Ralston and

Lady Chloe had remained in mourning until a few months ago. She had inherited a sizeable sum from her grandmother as well as a townhouse, but continued to live in a modest fashion. Since coming to London she never stood up with anyone and had made it clear she was not interested in either an affair or marriage. She had been nicknamed 'the unassailable'.

He could understand why. She had a remoteness about her that had not been there three years ago. The plain clothing she now wore gave her the appearance of a nun and only added to her air of aloofness.

He intended to change all of that.

Belle forced her attention to remain on the voluptuous soprano who stood in front of the assembled guests in Mrs Beaufort's drawing room. Her voice was lovely, pure and sweet, and quite in tune, but Belle had scarcely heard the performance. Her thoughts were preoccupied—this time by Justin's latest move.

Thank goodness he was not here tonight or Maria would probably have hysterics on the spot. Belle had no idea whether she wanted to kill Justin for his despicable behaviour or Arthur for gleefully telling Maria every detail, sending her into hysterics and distressing Chloe. Chloe had been driving with Serena and her brother, Roland, in the park. And as Arthur told them, Justin rode by their carriage for a full five minutes.

Belle was about to depart for her house so she might have a light dinner and then prepare for tonight's musical, when Arthur had arrived.

'He has made it quite clear he has an interest in Chloe.' He clasped his hands behind his back and smiled in a superior fashion at the women seated in the drawing room. 'What would you say to having your daughter a duchess?' he asked Maria.

'I would rather see her in a convent than marry him! Have you no conscience, no sensibility! He murdered my son!'

'Hardly, madam. If you recall, Lucien did not die for months after the duel. A healthy man would have recovered instead of developing such a putrid infection, which was no doubt due to his excessive fondness for drink.'

'His infection was due to the fatal wound he sustained from the duel! The only reason that…that creature is not hanging from the gallows is because he is a duke!'

'You are ridiculous,' Arthur snapped.

'And you are unfeeling and callous and disrespectful! My daughter will never marry him!'

All this time Chloe had sat on the sofa, her expression increasingly stricken with each word. Belle had finally got up. 'This entire conversation is ridiculous. Arthur, I pray you will restrain yourself from speculating on Westmore's intentions. I doubt very much he wishes to marry Chloe.'

As she had hoped, her words managed to turn Arthur's attention away from Maria. 'And how would you know Westmore's intentions? Are you in his confidence?'

'Of course not. But one dance and a brief meeting in the park hardly constitutes a proposal of marriage. I've no doubt he has paid such attentions to dozens of young ladies. Besides, you are distressing both Chloe and Maria. Until there is an actual proposal, I would suggest you not say a word on this topic again.'

His lips tightened. 'May I remind you that none of this is your concern? I could forbid you to see Chloe, if I wish.'

Maria promptly burst into noisy tears and Arthur, who could not tolerate one of her outbursts, finally took his leave. It took nearly three-quarters of an hour for Belle and Chloe, with the assistance of Maria's maid, to calm her. After that she had to be coaxed to eat a few bites of a light repast. Belle barely had time to return home and change her muslin for a silk lavender gown that was more suitable for a musical soirée before she turned around again and headed back to Grosvenor Square.

By the time they had arrived at Mrs Beaufort's elegant townhouse, vexation was her overriding emotion and she thought if she saw Justin, she could cheerfully strangle him.

But there was no sign of his dark-haired figure when they first arrived. His paternal aunt, Lady Georgina, was there. As they took their places in the second row of chairs, she turned and fixed Chloe with a pair of sharp blue eyes. She was an intimidating figure: thin and upright, her features patrician and she held herself with regal bearing.

There was nothing in the look she bestowed upon Chloe to indicate approval. Chloe, thank goodness, was not aware of her perusal, but Belle was. She stared at Lady Georgina until the lady allowed her gaze to fall on her. Her stare was so icy Belle nearly quailed, but she would not let her gaze drop. Lady Georgina finally looked away, but not before Belle knew she had made an enemy.

Oh, dear. She turned and sighed. Why could she not let things alone? Now she would worry Lady Georgina would take her wrath out on Chloe. Arthur might welcome a match between Justin and Chloe, but it was more than apparent Lady Georgina would not. From what little she knew of Lady Georgina, she was not a woman to cross.

Belle had met her once, over a decade ago, when she had come to London with her grandmother for her first and only Season. Belle and Lady Townsend had been about to leave a rout when they came face to face with Lady Georgina. Grandmama had greeted Lady Georgina politely, but Belle had never forgotten the hostile stare Lady Georgina had bestowed upon the other woman before saying, 'Good evening, Sarah.' She had turned equally cold eyes upon Belle. 'I suppose this is your granddaughter. She resembles you.' Belle had known her words were not a compliment. She had been glad to escape the cold, aristocratic Countess who so intently disliked her grandmother. Grandmama had said nothing about Lady Georgina and had instead gone on to talk about the people they had met at the rout.

Belle's hand tightened around her fan. She could not allow him or his family to hurt Chloe, which made it even more imperative for her to deal with Justin.

The soprano had just begun her last aria when someone entered the room. There was a slight stir among the guests. Belle glanced towards the door almost without thinking. Her heart pounded and her hand trembled around her fan when he strode through the double door. He glanced around. She dropped her gaze and hoped he would not see her. If only she could crawl under the chair, but it would not do.

She forced herself to look towards the door again. He stood near the wall, arms folded. He looked every bit as male and elegant as he had two nights ago. And every bit as dangerous.

She yanked her gaze away. How could she ever confront him? But she must before he caused any more trouble. She would do it for Chloe's sake. And for Maria's.

She belatedly realised the soprano had finished and she had forgotten to applaud altogether. Chloe was already standing, as were many of the other guests. The first half of the performance had ended and the guests were milling towards a smaller room next to the drawing room where refreshments had been laid out. Belle forced herself to not look in Justin's direction. She smiled at Maria. 'I think we should find some refreshment. Shall I escort you there?' If only she could move Maria from the room before she spotted Justin.

'I do not know.' Maria looked around. Belle moved in front of her, hoping she could block Maria's view. 'Perhaps a small cake and some punch. I believe I would prefer to stay here, however. I am feeling rather fatigued as I always do after such a disagreeable scene. Thank goodness, Arthur cannot abide music. But you and Chloe must go and if you wish you may bring me back a little refreshment.'

'Would you like me to stay with you?' Chloe asked.

'Oh, no.' She smiled wanly.

Belle glanced around. To her horror, she saw Justin stood a few feet away with a tall, dark-haired man she recognised as his cousin, Lord Salcombe. Justin suddenly glanced up and met her eyes. The mocking look that crossed his expression did not bode well. She turned away and touched Chloe's arm. 'Shall we get refreshment, then? I see Serena near the door.' She moved down the short row of chairs away from Justin. Chloe, who appeared rather bewildered, followed.

They were just about to leave the refreshment room when she saw that Westmore and Salcombe now stood directly near the doors between the rooms. Unless she and Chloe were to turn around, making it quite obvious they wanted to avoid the men, they had no choice but to pass them.

'Good evening, Lady Milborne, Lady Chloe,' Justin said. His gaze lingered on Chloe in a way that made Belle want to hit him.

'Good evening, your Grace,' she said coolly. 'Lord Salcombe.'

Salcombe inclined his head but his expression was icy. Chloe looked confused. Belle would have just walked past them, but Justin spoke. 'I hope you enjoyed your drive in the park, Lady Chloe.'

'Very much,' Chloe said politely. Slight colour stained her cheek.

A slight smile touched his mouth. A smile Belle considered predatory. 'I am glad,' he said. 'Perhaps you will do me the honour of driving with me some time.'

Chloe raised startled eyes to his face. 'I—'

'No, she most certainly will not,' Belle snapped. She had the satisfaction of seeing Justin start.

Then his brow rose. 'No? But you are not her guardian, are you?' His smile was lazy. And dangerous.

'No. But I am her friend.' She turned to Chloe. 'Can you manage the refreshments? I will join you in a moment, but I have something I wish to say to the Duke.'

Chloe's eyes widened. 'Belle, I do not think—'

'I will be fine. Just tell your mama that I was feeling rather warm and I wished to sit in the hall for a moment where it is cooler.'

Chloe nodded. After casting a worried look at Justin, she left. Belle looked at him. 'I would like a word with you, your Grace. In private.'

By now many of the guests had taken their places. He

glanced around. 'I am your servant, of course. However, this does not seem the place for a tête-à-tête.'

'We can step into the hall, then.'

Salcombe spoke. 'Anything you wish to say to my cousin, you may say in front of me.' He looked down at her, his dislike for her evident.

'This does not concern you, my lord.' She turned back to Justin. His expression was unreadable but she sensed he was enjoying her discomfort. Well, she could not stand here and argue with him in full view of the rest of the guests. She could see Lady Georgina staring at her and feared any moment she would come forward to forbid her to talk to him. And if Maria should happen to notice...she did not want to think of that. 'I am going to the hall. I would like to talk to you.' She turned and walked away.

By the time she reached the hallway, her knees were shaking. What had she done? It was just that Justin had made her so angry that she felt if she did not say something she would explode. She doubted that he would follow her. He probably enjoyed tormenting her too much.

An even worse thought occurred. What if he really did intend to pursue Chloe? That he wasn't merely trying to bend her to his will but actually had an interest in Chloe? The idea was too awful to contemplate.

'I believe you wished to talk to me.'

She whirled around and gasped and his brow rose at her expression. 'Or was I mistaken?'

'I...I did not think you would come.'

'After such a forceful demand, I had no choice. Come into Beaufort's study. We can be more private there.'

She nodded. She did not want anyone to know what she said. She stepped past him into the small room and he shut the door. He leaned against it and fixed his gaze on her. 'What is it you wish to say to me?'

For some reason the cool indifference in his voice steadied her. 'I have no doubt you know very well. But rather than play games with you, I will tell you. I want you to cease your pursuit of Lady Chloe.'

'Am I pursuing her?'

'I pray you will not fence with me. You are, and I cannot think what you hope to accomplish by doing so. I can understand your desire for revenge, but I pray you will not use Chloe to accomplish it.'

'And how do you know my purpose is for revenge? She is a lovely girl and I am in need of a wife. There is no reason why she would not make a suitable duchess.'

Her blood ran cold. 'No. You cannot possibly consider such a thing. You would make her miserable. If your purpose is to punish me then I wish you would do so directly.'

She took a deep breath. 'When I met you, two nights ago, you said I owed you a debt and you told me what you considered payment. I will give you what you ask if you will promise to leave Chloe alone.'

'You do understand what I want, do you not?' He had moved closer to her and she resisted the urge to back up.

'I believe you wish me to...to spend a night with you,' she said calmly.

'A night? Not precisely. If you recall, I was to have you for a week. But of course, there is interest which by now is quite considerable.'

'What is it you want?' She could barely speak.

'I want you to be my mistress until the end of the Season.'

The world seemed to spin for a moment. She felt as

unfocused as if she had sustained a blow. Her vision cleared. 'Until the end of the Season? I…I cannot do that.'

'Then I will continue my pursuit of your sister-in-law. You might consider that although you object, Lord Ralston does not. And he is her guardian, not you.'

Dear God. She could perhaps bear one night, but how could she stand to come to him night after night? But if she did not, Chloe would pay for her debts, just as Lucien had made Justin pay for the wrong done his father. Another innocent would suffer. And that she could not bear at all.

She looked into his cool, haughty face and took a breath. 'Very well, your Grace. I will be your mistress until the end of the Season. But I want a contract outlining the terms.'

He frowned. 'A contract? Do you want my solicitor to draw it up?'

'No! I…I don't want any one to know about this. I will prepare the papers myself.'

'Will you? If no one knows, then how do you know I won't cheat you? Once you come to me, the advantage will all be on my side.'

'I will trust that you won't.' Her gaze did not waver from his face.

'Will you?' An odd expression appeared in his eyes. 'I will call on you tomorrow. We will discuss the terms then. And you must hope I will prove to be more trustworthy than you.'

She bit her lip. 'I must return to the drawing room before my in-laws worry.'

'Yes.' He looked at her, his eyes darkening and her breath caught. For a moment, she thought he was about to kiss her and then he pulled away. 'You are right, you had best go.' His voice was cold.

She left him without looking back.

Belle stared at the paper in front of her. She usually spent Tuesday mornings in her study, answering her correspondence and going over her accounts. She supposed she was over-cautious but Lucien had never paid attention to such things. He had left behind a mound of debts after his death. The dowry she had brought to her marriage was gone; spent on gaming and horses and jewels. Even after she had sold everything she could, there had been more bills. If the former Lord Ralston had not stepped in, she had no doubt she would have ended up in debtors' prison, for until she turned four and twenty, she had had no money of her own.

But today she had not even glanced at the business that awaited her. She had spent the morning on something else entirely. Even after wasting several sheets of paper, she still was not certain she was pleased with the results. She rubbed her neck and then nearly jumped when the footman appeared in the door of the small room. She looked up. 'Yes?'

She did not even need to look at the calling card he carried to know who it was. 'The Duke of Westmore is below.'

She stared at him, her heart starting to pound, and then realised he still waited expectantly. 'Please, show him up.'

She shoved the paper aside she had been working on since she had risen far too early and, after a moment of hesitation, placed a dictionary on top of it. The last thing she wanted was to have him catch a glimpse of the contract before she presented it to him. She rose, feeling as if she waited for her executioner. Surely he didn't plan to seduce her in the middle of the morning. Not that she knew a thing about how these affairs were arranged.

His footsteps sounded outside the door and then he stood in the doorway. Her mind suddenly went blank.

He spoke. 'Good day, Belle.'

She started. 'Your Grace. Please, come in.'

He stepped into the room and she knew it was a mistake to have him here. For some reason the thought of discussing such business in the drawing room seemed inappropriate, but the study seemed to shrink with his presence.

He came towards her. He was dressed in a dark coat and buff breeches, his cravat starched and tied in an elaborate knot. She backed up against the desk, her eyes on his face. He stopped in front of her and his brow shot up. 'There is no need to look so frightened. I have no intention of ravishing you at this moment. In general, I prefer more comfortable surroundings.'

'Oh. Of course.' She felt a flush steal to her cheeks in spite of her efforts to remain composed. 'Will you not be seated? Would you care for refreshment?'

'No, refreshments are not necessary.' He remained standing and she hastily seated herself in the chair behind her desk. He moved around the side of it to the window at her back and although he appeared to be merely observing the view, he had neatly blocked her in. And he was still standing, which gave him an unfair advantage. He looked down at her. 'Have you changed your mind since last night?'

She stood again, hoping to feel less intimidated. 'No. Have you?'

'No.'

'Very well. I have drawn up the contract. If you would

care to look at it.' She reached for the dictionary and
moved it, then picked up the paper.

She held it out to him and he looked at her face for
a moment before taking it. He moved away from the
window and she folded her arms, her eyes on him as she
waited in silence for him to finish. He had changed. His
shoulders were broader and tapered to narrow hips. The
youthful handsomeness of his face had matured into an
arresting maleness. She felt a peculiar tremble go
through her. Since Lucien's death she had never thought
about lying in a man's arms again. She had wanted to
forget that part of her marriage along with the rest of it.

All last night, as she'd tossed and turned, and again
this morning when she had sat and written the contract,
she had tried to put the physical intimacy aside. But now
with Justin standing in front of her, the full implication
of what she had agreed to hit her.

She tore her gaze away. Oh, lord. Could she really do
this? But what choice did she have? None if she wished
to protect Chloe. Just as Lucien had wanted payment for
the wrong done his father, Justin wanted payment for
the wrong done to him. She was the one to pay.

'I must compliment you.' His voice broke into her
thoughts. 'This would put my solicitor's contracts to
shame. However, there are one or two points I would
like to discuss.'

She eyed him with more than a little apprehension.
'What are those?'

'You stated you would spend no more than three occasions a week in my company. I want to increase that.'

Her cheeks coloured. 'I would think that would be
enough time to…to conduct our business. I cannot spend
all of my time doing that and I am certain you have
other things to do as well.'

For the first time, a hint of amusement crossed his face. 'But none as pleasurable.'

'Perhaps for you!' Her cheeks must be on fire.

He stared at her and a rather wicked smile touched his mouth. 'I intend to see our meetings are pleasurable for you as well.'

'I...' She swallowed and wished she had held her tongue. She did not want him to flirt with her. She wanted him to be cool and controlled. And passionless. Just as she intended to be. 'Three times a week is enough for me,' she managed to say.

'But I will want your company for other things.'

'What other things?'

He shrugged. 'To attend the opera or the theatre. Perhaps Vauxhall. Or to drive with me.'

'But why? I cannot imagine why you would wish to spend any more time with me than you must.' She had not expected this. She had thought they would meet clandestinely and then pretend they hardly knew one another in public.

His expression cooled. 'I wish to make it very clear you are mine.'

'I see.' She moved away from him. 'You wish to publicly shame me. But I fear you will hurt my mother-in-law and my sister-in-law as well. And perhaps your own family. Surely they will not be pleased that I am in your company.'

'No, but it will tell society that you do not hold me responsible for your husband's death.'

'Will it? And will I have paid my debt—Lucien's debt—at the end of the Season? Because I do not want to pay forever. Nor do I want my sister-in-law or any one other person to pay as well.'

'It will be paid.'

She took a deep breath. 'Very well. How often do you want my company?'

'Three nights a week and for other occasions as I demand.'

'I will not be at your beck and call, your Grace.' She lifted her chin and met his eyes squarely. 'If I am available I will consider your request, but I certainly have no intention of ordering my life around your convenience.'

His eyes never left hers. 'Then three nights a week and two other occasions at my request. Any more than that will be at your convenience.' His voice held a note of mockery.

She had not realised she was holding her breath. 'That will be acceptable. Do you wish to add the amendments or should I? Then I suggest we sign the contract. I have made two copies.'

He gave a short surprised laugh. 'I had no idea your mind ran along such damnably methodical lines. How many of these contracts have you drawn up?'

She gave him a cold look. 'None. But I have read enough contracts to know what they should contain. If it were possible, I have often thought I would like to study law.'

'I've no doubt you would do admirably. I have always thought you were one of the most intelligent women of my acquaintance.'

The words seemed to surprise him as much as they did her. For a moment, they stared at one another and then she looked away, oddly unsettled. He took a pace towards the mantelpiece before looking at her. 'You may add the amendments. We will sign them tonight when you come to dine with me.'

She faltered. 'Dine with you? Tonight?'

'Yes. I see no reason to delay.'

'But…' Her stomach had started to knot again. 'I have promised Chloe and my mother-in-law that I would accompany them to Lady Fairfield's rout and then there is some other affair after that.'

'Lady Montgomery's soirée. I assure you both affairs will be dead bores. You will be much better off dining with me.'

A little smile had touched his mouth and for a moment she was swept back into the time before he had come to hate her. Regret and a bittersweet longing shot through her. 'Will I?'

His smile faded. 'Yes. Can you cry off? The sooner you fulfil your terms the sooner I will fulfil mine.'

She understood his meaning perfectly. She took a deep breath. 'Very well. I will dine with you tonight.'

'I will send a carriage for you at eight.'

She frowned. 'I can take my own.'

'It will be less obvious if I send one of mine.'

She raised her brow. 'I hardly think a carriage with a ducal crest would be less obvious.'

He scowled. 'I have a plain, unmarked carriage.'

'The one you always use for your mistresses?'

'No.' His voice had lost all trace of warmth and he moved towards her. 'I will see you tonight, Belle.' His gaze went to her face and then strayed to her lips. For a moment, just as she had last night, she thought he would kiss her. Instead, he backed away. 'Goodbye.'

She watched him leave the room and heard his footsteps echoing down the hall. She had no idea what to think. None of it made sense at all.

Chapter Three

Belle followed the housekeeper into the drawing room. The lamps had been lit and cast a warm glow around the elegant room. The housekeeper, a stocky woman with greying hair and a brisk manner, regarded her with a not unkind expression. 'His Grace will be with you soon. Please be seated, my lady.'

Belle managed a thank-you and took the nearest chair. She pulled her cloak more tightly around her and watched the stout woman bustle away. She took a deep breath and tried to force herself to be calm, but her heart was beating as fast and loudly as the clock on the mantelpiece.

She had told Chloe and Maria that she feared she was developing the headache...which was not exactly untrue, for an acute attack of nerves was doing just that. A particular spot at the back of her neck had started to ache, a sure sign of an impending headache. She had not even considered using that as an excuse to avoid Justin tonight for she doubted he would believe her and for the most part her headaches were infrequent and usually not very bad. So, promptly at eight, she had climbed into the comfortable coach and after an all-too-brief ride through the streets of London, had arrived at his townhouse.

She rubbed her neck and closed her eyes for a moment. What was she doing here? No, she knew exactly what she was doing. She was paying off the enormous wrong Lucien had done Justin. And she was protecting Chloe. She had tried to tell herself that surely she could endure his touch. She could endure anything after marriage to Lucien where she had learned to shut her mind far away from what happened to her body. She opened her eyes. It would not do to think of such things now.

The ticking of the clock only increased her apprehension. She finally rose and went to look at the landscape over the mantelpiece.

'Good evening.'

Her heart slammed to her throat. She whirled around to find Justin behind her. 'I did not hear you!'

Slight amusement showed in his face. 'You seemed to be engrossed in the painting.'

Her mouth suddenly went dry. 'It is fascinating. Is it of the Yorkshire moors?'

He looked a little surprised. 'Yes. Have you been there?'

'Once. With my parents when I was twelve. They wanted to tour some of the more remote parts of the kingdom and so we went to Yorkshire and even to Northumberland. I especially remember the moors. They looked so wild and I instantly thought of *Udolpho*.' It was the last trip she had taken with her parents before they died and she went to live with her grandmother.

'You were allowed to read such a work then?'

'Well, no. Mama was very strict about such things. A young lady on the neighbouring estate loaned me her copy and I read it in great secrecy whenever I could manage. As well as several other romances.'

His mouth curved in a smile. 'I had no idea you were a secret romantic.'

'I was. Once.' The smile made her catch her breath. Oh, lord. The last thing she wanted was to feel some sort of attraction towards him.

'But no longer.'

'No.'

The smile faded. 'We can dine in my apartments.' His voice was impersonal. She nodded. The coolness had returned to his face, thank goodness. He made no move to touch her as they left the drawing room and passed through the hallway. They went up the tall winding staircase to the floor above. The house was quiet and their footsteps were a soft pad on the rugs. He pushed open a door to a room and allowed her to precede him. She stepped in and saw it was a large sitting room. In one corner was a long table covered with papers. A sofa flanked one side of the fireplace.

She stood in the room, having no idea what to do. He came up behind her and his hands were on her shoulders. Belle jumped and then froze.

'I am only intending to take your cloak,' he said. 'Don't run.'

She stood perfectly still as he removed the garment from her shoulders. His fingers brushed her nape and she shivered. But she had no idea whether it was from fear or something else.

He draped her cloak over a chair. Despite the modest cut of her gown she felt exposed. But his expression was still polite when he looked at her.

'Would you like something to drink?' he asked. 'Wine?'

She almost refused and then decided that perhaps it was exactly what she needed. She watched as he strode across the room to the wine, which sat on a table. He poured two glasses then came back and gave one to her. Her hand was not quite steady as she took it.

'I wasn't certain if you would come tonight,' he said.

'Why? I told you I would be here.'

'You must be very fond of Lady Chloe.'

'She is like a sister to me. I would not see her hurt for the world.' She looked at him. 'Or Lady Ralston.'

He was silent for a moment and then his gaze moved to the papers she still held in one hand. His brow rose slightly. 'The contract?'

'Yes. I would like you to sign it before we…we…'

'Dine?'

'Yes.' Colour tinged her cheeks.

'Come and sit down, then.' He held out one chair at the table. She sat down and he took the chair across from her. She gave him the paper then took a nervous sip from her wine, watching him as he perused the document. He finally looked up. 'It seems to be in order.'

'Should we sign the contracts, your Grace?' She attempted to keep her voice detached as if the papers merely contained the terms for the sale of a piece of property.

'Yes. Although I am beginning to think we need to clarify that you are to call me by my given name. Under the circumstances, ''your Grace'' does not seem appropriate.'

'We are entering into a business arrangement. It does not mean we must be on…on intimate terms with each other.'

A sardonic light leapt to his eye. 'You don't think coming to my bed constitutes intimate terms?'

'No, not necessarily. I think true intimacy can only be based on mutual affection and trust. Since we do not have those between us then we cannot truly be on intimate terms. I do not think a mere physical relationship can be defined as an intimate one.'

'So you consider our relationship to be a form of prostitution?' His eyes narrowed.

She flinched but forced herself to meet his eyes. 'Yes, of course.'

'You are remarkably matter of fact about this affair. I would almost suspect you have entered into such a relationship before.' His words were deliberate and cruel.

Anger shot through her. 'Perhaps I have. Although I was young and naïve and thought physical intimacy was equivalent to love. I know better now.'

She was unprepared for the blaze of fury in his eyes. 'Who was he?'

'That is not your concern.' She had undoubtedly had too much wine or she would not have provoked him in such a way.

He stared at her for a moment longer. 'We will sign the documents and then eat.' His voice was indifferent again.

He crossed to the small desk to find an inkpot and pen.

His shoulders were broad beneath his coat and his thick hair, slightly longer than the fashion, brushed against his collar. A peculiar pit began to form in her stomach. She should not have made him so angry but his words had pierced her. And why should he be so angry? In another man she would have thought he was jealous, but of course that could not be it. She picked up her wine again and took another sip and realised she had just finished the entire glass.

She watched him with the pen in his strong, lean fingers. He signed both copies and then pushed them towards her. 'Your signature.' He gave her the pen, his fingers brushing hers. A dart of awareness shot through her and she took it with a shaky hand. She had no idea whether it was from the wine or his touch.

She wrote her name beneath his bold, impatient signature and then gave him one copy. He took it and put it on the desk behind him.

She nearly jumped when the door opened. She turned and saw two footmen enter, carrying trays. She moved away from the table and watched while they deftly laid the covers then they departed as quietly as they had come. 'Sit down, Belle,' Justin said.

She took the chair he held out for her and sat. He again took his place across from her. Her appetite had fled, but at least if she made some pretence of eating she could put off the inevitable.

She glanced across the table at him. The candle flickered over his strong features and she could tell herself and him that there was no intimacy between them, but the setting itself conspired against her. Her gaze fell to his lips and she swallowed. She took another sip of wine. The smell of the food drifted up and to her surprise she felt a pang of hunger. At least eating would be something to do besides staring at him and anticipating what was certain to come after dinner so she picked up her fork.

The food was good. She had eaten several mouthfuls before she looked up to find Justin had stopped eating and was watching her instead. 'Must you stare at me?'

His eyes drifted over her face. 'You are very beautiful.'

Her face heated. 'I wish you would not pay me compliments.'

'I am merely stating a fact.' His eyes remained on her.

She put her fork down, feeling self-conscious. 'I would prefer it if you would not make such personal remarks.'

'Ah, yes. The business relationship we are embarking on. Very well, then talk to me.'

'Talk to you?' She started. Her hand hit the empty wine glass and it fell to the floor and rolled under the table. Mortified, she pushed her chair back with some idea of retrieving it. And then froze when his hand closed around her wrist. Her eyes flew to his face. His mouth twitched and he released her hand. 'Sit down. There's no need to panic yet. I was merely suggesting conversation.'

'Oh.' She took her seat, feeling foolish.

'More wine?' he asked.

She glanced swiftly at him. 'Yes, if you please.' She rarely drank wine, but perhaps if she had a bit more she would not be so…so nervous. It seemed to have dulled her emotions and thankfully her headache as well.

He poured her another glass and brought it to her. She sipped it and watched him take his place across from her. She was suddenly aware of the broadness of his shoulders and the lock of hair that had fallen across his forehead. With a sort of detached fascination she stared as he picked up his own wine glass and brought it to his lips. Lips that would soon be on hers. As would those strong lean hands that were now wrapped around the stem of his glass.

Heat coursed through her and she felt almost dizzy.
She set her glass down and nearly set it on her plate.
She stared down and realised she was having a difficult
time focusing. Oh, lord. She was not just relaxed but on
her way to becoming inebriated. Only once before had
it happened, when she was only eighteen, and it had not
been an unpleasant experience. Except for the dull headache and horrid taste in her mouth the next day.

Perhaps becoming foxed was not a bad idea. When he
started to…to…seduce her she might not mind so much.
Or maybe she would not mind at all.

'You are not hungry?' he asked.

His voice jerked her from her contemplation of the
plate. 'No, not very.' She glanced at him and forced
herself to focus. 'Are you?'

'No.' His eyes met hers. Despite the amount of wine
she'd drunk, she could not mistake the desire in his eyes.
He pushed back his chair and stood. 'Come here, Belle,'
he said roughly.

Her heart leapt to her throat. She started to rise and
knocked her chair over.

Her cheeks burned as she stared at the downed chair.
'You must think I intend to destroy your house.'

He came around the table and set the chair upright
then he turned to look at her. 'Not at all. I do think,
however, you have had too much wine.'

'Do you? I am not certain I've had enough,' she
blurted out.

'It won't be that bad,' he said almost gently.

'Won't it?' Her eyes searched his face and what she
saw there made her tremble. She stepped back and stumbled into the chair.

He caught her against his chest. 'You are foxed.' He
sounded bemused.

'No, I am not. Perhaps if I sat down.' His chest felt hard and strong and warm. He smelled nice, she thought with vague surprise. Unlike Lucien, whose odour had been harsh and unpleasant.

'I think that is a good idea,' he said.

He took her arm and led her to the sofa. To her dismay, her gait was unsteady and it took all her willpower to keep from swaying. She sank down on the sofa and closed her eyes. Everything spun for a brief moment. Then he was beside her, his thigh pressed against hers. The sensation was not unpleasant. She opened her eyes. 'I never drink wine,' she told him.

'I thought not.' His eyes were on her face. 'As soon as you have er…sobered a bit, I will take you home. First you need some tea.' He started to rise.

'No!' She grabbed his coat sleeve. 'I…I think we should start the contract.'

He sat down and stared at her. 'As tempting as the offer is, I think it best if we wait until we are both sober.'

'No. I really prefer we start now.' She must be mad or perhaps he was. 'Otherwise I…I will be afraid.' She undoubtedly made no sense at all.

'Of me?'

'Of…of any man.'

Something flickered in his eyes. 'Then come here.' He held out his arm.

She scooted next to him and he pulled her to his side. He bent his head towards her, and she felt a bolt of panic as she always had with Lucien. He stilled for a moment. 'You can kiss me first,' he said.

She stared at his mouth, firm and sensuous, with a hint of dark beard around the edges. His eyes were dark and still and waiting. She closed her eyes and forced herself to lean towards him.

Her mouth found his. His lips were warm and firm. He made no move to possess her and merely waited. She tentatively nibbled at him and then kissed him more firmly. Her hands caught his arms so she might brace herself and she realised with a sense of wonder she had never explored a man's mouth before. She lightly ran her tongue over his lips, tasting him. A low sound escaped from his throat, almost a groan, and his muscles tensed under her hands.

She lifted her head and opened her eyes. 'Is something wrong?' she whispered. 'I have not done this before.'

'No.' His eyes shot open.

She touched his face. His cheek was rough under her palm. 'Should I kiss you again?'

'No!' He looked as if she'd offered to shoot him. 'That is…' He ran a hand through his hair. 'If you continue kissing me like that you will end up in my bed.'

Perhaps she was more drunk than she thought. She blinked, trying to clear her vision. And her hearing. 'Isn't that what you wanted?'

'No. At least not tonight. Hell.' He stood. 'I thought—' He stopped and turned to look at her. 'I'd best take you home.'

'Why?' She seemed to be rapidly sobering. 'Why not tonight?'

'Because I have no intention of taking advantage of you. I would prefer that you are sober and fully conscious of what you are doing.'

'I see.' She rose, feeling a little dizzy. She supposed she should be relieved, but she only felt confused. To make matters worse, her headache was returning in full force and she rubbed the back of her neck.

'What is wrong?'

''Tis nothing. I have had a slight headache most of the day.' She was beginning to feel a little sick as well.

His brow shot up. 'And you drank three glasses of wine? My dear, you will have the devil of a head to-morrow.'

'Was it three? I thought it was only two.' She sat back down as another wave of light-headedness overcame her. Why must this happen now?

'Most definitely three.' He looked down at her for a moment. 'I will take you home,' he said abruptly.

Although he draped the cloak over her shoulders and helped her into his carriage, his touch was as impersonal as her maid's. Once in the carriage, he sat in the corner opposite her, his legs stretched in front of him and said nothing. Belle tried to look anywhere but at him as they made the short journey to Gower Street.

Once they arrived, he stepped down and then held out his hand to assist her. Despite his hand, she stumbled. His arms closed around her. 'Please 'lease me,' she said as coolly as she could but, to her chagrin, her words were slightly slurred.

'You cannot go in by yourself.'

'Yes, I c…can.' She swayed again.

'No.' Before she could protest, he had swung her up in his arms. She hardly registered the bewilderment on the face of James, her footman, before Justin was carrying her up the stairs. They met Mrs Bates at the top.

'My lady?' Mrs Bates said, her face alarmed.

'Your mistress has the headache,' Justin said. 'If you show me her bedchamber, I will take her there.'

'It is this way.'

He did not put her down until Mrs Bates had pulled back the covers and then he gently laid her on the bed. Belle thought she would die of humiliation. She closed her eyes and hoped it was all a bad dream brought about by too much wine.

'Belle.'

She was not dreaming. She opened her eyes to find Justin bent over her. 'Will you be all right?'

No, she was dreaming after all. He sounded almost concerned, which was impossible. 'Yes, of course.'

He straightened. 'Then I will leave you. Goodnight, Belle.'

'Goodnight,' she whispered. But he had already left the room. To her chagrin, she felt tears prick her lids. Why did he have to behave in such a gentlemanly fashion? She wanted to think him cold and callous. Otherwise, she could never keep her emotions uninvolved.

Justin asked himself the same question the next day. He threw a punch that nearly sent Brandt reeling. Brandt held up his hand. 'Wait! What are you trying to do, bloody my nose? Might I remind you we are relations? Damn, Westmore, what's the occasion?'

Justin scowled at his cousin, still breathing hard. 'None,' he finally said. They were at Gentleman Jackson's. He'd hoped a good sparring match would at least temporarily distract his thoughts from Belle. However, it seemed to have the opposite effect and he could think of nothing but when he would see her again.

What the hell was wrong with him? He had had her exactly where he wanted her last night, in his arms and kissing him, her body soft and pliant against his. The contract aside, taking her would have been easy—he had only to scoop her into his arms and carry her to his bed.

Except she had been three sheets to the wind and her pliability had little to do with wanting him. And she had said she was afraid. Perhaps he had been a fool to believe her, but something in her voice told him she did not lie. Had it been the lover she claimed had hurt her? Or her wretch of a husband?

'Let me guess. Isabelle Milborne.'

Justin yanked his thoughts back to his cousin. 'What?'

'Lady Milborne. She was not seen at all last night although her relations were. Nor were you.' He picked up a cloth and threw it to Justin.

'So?'

'Completely unremarkable except you were seen calling on her yesterday morning.'

'Who the devil saw that?' He wiped the sweat from his brow and frowned at Brandt.

'Percy Ormund. He was calling on an acquaintance in Gower Street.' He cocked a brow at Justin. 'Taken together with your absences, I would almost suspect you were with her last night.'

It was on the tip of his tongue to deny it, but why, since he wanted it known he had an interest in her? 'You would not be incorrect.'

Brandt stared. 'I've no desire of interfering in your business, but what the devil are you about?'

Justin shrugged. 'Payment for my two thousand pounds. With interest.'

Brandt choked. 'The hell you are!' He stared at Justin, a peculiar light coming into his eye. 'And what role does Lady Chloe play in this?'

'Lady Chloe is my trump card.'

Brandt's eyes narrowed. 'She may be the late Lord Milborne's half-sister but she's an innocent. I would hope you have the decency to leave her out of this business.'

'Precisely Belle Milborne's sentiments. Which is why she is willing to co-operate with me.'

Brandt continued to stare at him. 'Are you certain it is payment you want? Or is it revenge? Because as much as I appreciate your desire for the latter, I fear you will pay part of the price yourself.'

Justin thought of how pale and vulnerable she had looked in her bed last night then shoved the thought aside and gave a short laugh. 'That is something I do not intend to let happen.'

Chapter Four

Belle pulled on her glove and picked up her fan. She was in no mood to go to another ball but after crying off last night, she could hardly do so again. So she would go despite a heavy head and a dry mouth. Reminders of last night—a night she would have preferred to forget. Not only had she disgraced herself by drinking too much wine, she had thrown herself at Justin in a way that made her blanch just thinking about it.

Worse, was his own behaviour. He had been nothing but a gentleman even after she made it patently obvious she was willing to do whatever he wanted. Instead of taking full advantage of her, he had taken her home.

She had no idea why. She would have thought it would have suited his purposes perfectly to have seduced her last night. But he had not attempted to at all and had only insisted she kiss him after she practically begged him. Never in her life had she behaved in such a wanton and despicable way.

And, she thought bitterly, her behaviour had no doubt confirmed she was exactly what he thought her. She would not let such a thing happen again. If she saw him tonight, she would be cool and composed and completely in control. The unassailable Lady Milborne.

Justin finally spotted Belle near the faux Grecian pillars at the far end of the ballroom. She stood with her mother-in-law and Ralston. He started across the room. It was time to make his intentions public.

She stiffened at his approach and then she quickly looked away. To his annoyance, she kept her gaze on Ralston, apparently so absorbed in what he was saying that she did not notice him until he stood directly in front of them. 'Good evening, Lady Ralston, Ralston. Good evening, Lady Milborne.'

'Good evening, your Grace.' Despite the flash of apprehension in her face, her voice was polite as was her expression, as if they were nothing but mere acquaintances. He fully intended to shake that composure.

He turned to Lady Ralston, who looked as if he had come to escort her to the gallows. 'Lady Ralston, I trust you are well.'

Her eyes widened. 'I…' She swayed a little and Belle caught her arm.

She cast Justin an angry look before turning to her mother-in-law. 'Do you need to sit down, Maria?' she asked.

'Oh, no. I will be fine,' Lady Ralston said with a wan smile.

'Then perhaps you will not object if I solicit your daughter-in-law for the next dance?' Justin said.

Lady Ralston gaped at him. 'Belle? You wish to dance with Belle?'

'I fear Lady Milborne does not dance,' Ralston said icily. The ingratiating smile on his face had disappeared.

He shifted, just barely towards Belle, but the movement signalled possession.

Unaccountably annoyed, Justin's brow rose. 'I was not aware you were Lady Milborne's guardian.'

Ralston's face reddened. 'I am not, naturally, but since she never dances she should not make herself a source of gossip by doing so now unless, of course, she dances with a relation.'

'Such as yourself?'

Ralston frowned. 'I would consider that more acceptable, yes.'

'Do you wish to stand up with Lord Ralston?' Justin asked Belle who still held Lady Ralston's arm.

'No, I do not!' she snapped. 'I do not want to stand up with anyone, if you must know!'

Lady Ralston gasped and Ralston's mouth opened and closed like a landed trout. Belle coloured fiercely when she seemed to realise how much she had shocked her family. 'That is, I do not dance, your Grace.'

A cool smile curved his mouth. 'There is the contract.' He spoke softly enough that he doubted Ralston could hear him over the music and chatter.

She frowned and then her gaze went to something over his shoulder. He half-turned and saw young Roland Hurst escorting Lady Chloe towards them. Belle looked back at him. 'Very well, your Grace, I will stand up with you.'

Lady Ralston gasped. 'You cannot!'

'Belle!' Ralston exclaimed. 'I forbid you to make a spectacle of yourself.'

Justin was rapidly developing a desire to mow Ralston down. He eyed the man with a look that made him pale. 'I assure you she will not.' He turned to Belle and held out his arm. 'Shall we, Lady Milborne?'

She nodded and, after a brief hesitation, took his arm. He led her to one of the sets that was forming and released her. 'Does Ralston always attempt to dictate to you like that?' he demanded.

'He always dictates to everyone.'

He scowled. 'But why the devil do you allow him to ride roughshod over you like that?'

'Because if I do not, he will forbid me to see Chloe.'

'The devil take him,' he said softly. She merely looked at him without speaking but she did not need to. He was using her affection for Chloe to dictate to her in an even more despicable fashion than Ralston.

He looked down at her lovely face and reminded himself that she deserved no sympathy. She had used him in a way that had nearly killed him, but even worse had destroyed his parents. Her actions were every bit as despicable as his.

The music started. It did not take him long to realise that if his intentions were to shake her composure by dancing with her, he had sadly miscalculated. She was polite but she had put up that impenetrable barrier that made him want to grit his teeth. Or kiss her until she surrendered to him.

Then he wanted to curse because he did not want her to affect him in any way. He wanted no emotion involved where she was concerned because he intended to use her as heartlessly as she had used him.

By the time the dance had finished, he was in a foul mood. He led Belle from the set and to the side of the ballroom and there he looked down at her. 'I would like your company tomorrow night. You will attend the theatre with me and after that you will come to my house.'

'Tomorrow night is not convenient for me.'

'You had best make it convenient then. May I remind

you that until you start to fulfil your terms of the contract, my side is not enforceable.'

She lifted her chin. 'If you recall, you said you would
require my company on two other occasions each week.
I would consider last night one occasion and tonight another unless you wanted last night to count towards the
other part of my terms.'

The fact she could continue to look so composed and
sound so damn reasonable annoyed him even more.
'Hardly, my dear. Since very little happened.'

'That was not my doing. I was willing but you were
not.'

He stepped towards her. 'Oh, I was very willing, but
I was not about to take advantage of you.'

'How odd since that was what I thought our entire
contract was about.' A little smile touched her mouth.

Which had the unfortunate effect of drawing his attention there. He could almost taste her lips. The urge
to take her into his arms and kiss her until she was
breathless was nearly overwhelming. He took another
step towards her and her eyes widened.

'Westmore!'

His aunt's sharp voice suddenly recalled him to his
senses. He was in the middle of a ballroom. He spun
around to find Lady Georgina behind him. With her was
her latest protégée, Lady Clarissa Blackwood, an icy
beauty of eighteen, whose conversations seemed to consist solely of monosyllables. Lady Georgina's sharp gaze
went from his face to Belle's. Without acknowledging
Belle, she turned back to him. 'I have promised Lady
Clarissa that you would stand up with her for the next
dance.'

Hell. He wanted to strangle his aunt, first for cutting
Belle and then for putting him in a position where he

was obligated to dance with the girl. He could hardly refuse with Lady Clarissa standing in front of him. ''Very well,' he said coolly.

He turned to find Belle. But she had vanished. Had his aunt's snub distressed her so much that she had left? But why should he care if it had if he wanted to punish her in any way possible?

He had no answer.

Chapter Five

Belle stared down at the note she held in her hand with a great deal of dismay. It had arrived just as she sat down for breakfast and had had the immediate effect of ruining her appetite. The note was very curt and to the point.

—As one of your contractual obligations you will do me the honour of accompanying me to the Theatre Royal tonight. We will return to my house after the performance.

Westmore.

She crumpled it and resisted the urge to tear the page into small pieces and forget she had ever made such a bargain. But that would never do. Then he would distress Chloe with his attentions and poor Maria would probably go into a severe decline. Arthur would do everything in his power to make certain Chloe became a Duchess while Lady Georgina would do everything in her power to make certain Chloe did not. She shuddered just thinking about it.

Oh, dear. She took a sip from her coffee, which was now cold, and then shoved the cup aside. Agitated, she rose and went to stand near the window. Everything was about to become very complicated. She must cry off from attending the theatre with Maria, Chloe and Arthur and then they would see her there with Justin. She could hardly keep it a secret from them.

She really had no choice but to tell Maria the truth. She was going to the theatre with Justin.

Her mother-in-law stared at her, her face incredulous. Two spots of red colour appeared in her cheeks and then she fell back against the sofa with a little shriek. 'No! It was bad enough you stood up with him last night. But to attend the theatre with him?' Her voice rose. 'How can you? Are you so unfeeling that you would consort with the man who…who killed my son? You have always been a daughter to me and now you are betraying me!'

Belle tried to take Maria's hand but the older woman snatched it away. 'Please do not touch me! I do not know why you are doing this? Is it possible you are in love with him?'

Belle flinched and a wave of anger hit her with stunning force. She spoke before she could think. 'No! How can you say such a thing? How can you even think such a thing? The only reason I am doing this is to protect Chloe. He will leave Chloe alone in exchange for my company. Otherwise he will continue to pursue her.'

Maria's mouth fell open. 'You are protecting Chloe from his attentions?' She stared at Belle, her eyes growing wider. 'Oh, how can he be so wicked as to pursue her when he must know we revile him? But if you go to the theatre with him he will stop? Why?'

Belle suddenly regretted she had spoken. She said tiredly, 'I do not know. It is what he has agreed to.'

She had no idea what Maria would say but she was hardly prepared for Maria's next words. 'Oh, my dear! I quite see how it is. You are sacrificing yourself for Chloe. How could I doubt you! You must be the best of daughters-in-law!' She enfolded Belle in a swooping embrace that smelled of cloying perfume. She released her then sat back and sniffed. 'How brave you are! I do not care what anyone will think or say when they see you with him.'

'I pray you will not say a thing to anyone about this. Particularly not to Chloe.'

'Of course I will not,' she said indignantly. A little frown creased her brow. 'So you are only going to the theatre with him?'

'No, he wishes me to spend more time in his company.'

Maria stared at her. 'More time? Does he wish you to…to become his *mistress*?'

'I…' She looked at Maria, feeling helpless. Her cheeks heated. 'No, of course not.'

Maria's eyes widened. 'I am certain he does. I see everything now! He was in love with you and wished to provoke a quarrel with Lucien so he might have you. But you refused him and now he means to have you any way he can!'

'No, it is not that at all.'

Maria paid no heed. 'Oh, my love, you must be careful. You will have no reputation and then Chloe's will be quite ruined! The Duke of Westmore's mistress! I quite see, he means to ruin all of us!' She closed her eyes and emitted a wail.

'No, he will not. I will see to it he does not.'

Maria's eyes opened. 'No, I know you will not let anything happen to us. Or to harm Chloe. Which is why

I must ask that you do not see Chloe for the rest of the Season.'

Belle stared at her. 'Not see Chloe?'

'You do understand why, do you not?' Maria asked. Her eyes were fixed on Belle. 'I perfectly understand the sacrifice you are making, but others will not and if it appears we condone your association...my dear, you must see that it will not do Chloe any good at all!'

'No, it would not,' she said slowly. She rose, her legs unsteady. 'I must go. Please give Chloe my love and tell her...tell her...' but she could not finish. She picked up her reticule and bonnet and nearly ran from the room. She heard Maria's surprised protest but she had no desire to burst into tears in front of her. She climbed into her carriage and sat down, clutching her reticule and praying she would not weep. But she could not so easily stop the wretchedness in her heart that made her feel as if she had just cut herself off from all that was good.

Justin glanced at his companion who was seated next to him in the box. She had been quiet and obviously distracted ever since he had called for her three-quarters of an hour ago. She had politely answered his questions, but she might as well be on another continent as far as he was concerned.

She suddenly stiffened, her attention caught by something. He looked over and saw Lady Ralston and Lady Chloe being escorted into a box by Lord Ralston. 'Do not worry, I have given you my promise that I will not pursue your sister-in-law,' he told her.

She turned and looked at him. Her fine eyes were full of such misery that he was taken aback. Then her expression veiled. 'I am not worried,' she said politely.

'Then what is it?'

'Nothing at all.' She folded her hands back in her lap. 'I have not been in the Theatre Royal before.'

'Your husband did not bring you here?'

'No, he did not.' She made an obvious effort to look at him. 'I have heard this is an excellent play.'

'Yes. There is no need to force yourself to make conversation,' he said drily.

'I beg your pardon. I fear I cannot think of much to say tonight.'

'Apparently not. You might, however, look as if you take some pleasure in my company.'

For the first time her eyes flashed anger. 'Why? Is that part of our contract? That I must enjoy this?'

At least she showed him something besides indifference. He folded his arms. 'I would like that, yes.'

'Very well.' She gave him a tight smile. But then her gaze went in the direction of Ralston's box. She looked quickly away. Her cheeks heated with colour. The curtain went up, but not before Justin caught a glimpse of Ralston's outraged face.

Brandt was the first person to join them at the interval. With him was Henry Aubrey. Justin stood, and Belle did as well. He glanced at her. 'You know my cousin. Have you met Aubrey?'

'Yes,' Belle said. Her smile was strained. 'Good evening, Lord Salcombe, Mr Aubrey.'

Brandt inclined his head. 'Lady Milborne.' His expression was cool. 'You are enjoying the performance?'

'Very much.' She was still polite, nothing in her expression revealing how she felt at Brandt's icy manner.

For some reason Justin wanted to box his cousin's ears.

Aubrey's face held curiosity, but his manner was more

open. 'Are you? Will own I could not understand the
actress who played Perdita or Prudence or whatever the
d…she was called.'

Belle's face relaxed a little. 'Her diction was not the
best.'

Brandt had turned to Justin. 'So you purchased Chiswick's colt today.'

His preoccupation with Belle had almost made him
forget about the animal. 'I signed the papers this morning. I'll leave for Surrey tomorrow to fetch him.'

'Chiswick's bay devil?' Aubrey said. 'Good God! His
bloodlines are impeccable, but he's a nasty temper from
what I've been told. Bit a groom. Bolted with Chiswick
and dumped him in a heap of…' he glanced at Belle
'…er mud.'

'Which is precisely what I'd do if someone as heavy-
handed as Chiswick was on my back,' Brandt said.

By this time Lord Henly had joined them. He was
stout with a face that resembled a pig's and a roving
eye. He ran his gaze over Belle in a brazen fashion that
made Justin want to hit him and then positioned himself
far too close to her. When he launched into a discussion
of the various attributes of the actresses, Justin decided
it was time to leave.

He turned to Belle, who stood quietly listening.
'Come and take a turn around the lobby with me.'

She hesitated and then followed him from the box.
'Do you not wish to stay with your friends?'

'No. Henly will undoubtedly regale us with his comments on certain parts of the female anatomy. They are
not fit for your ears.'

'I can assure you that after marriage to Lucien I am
not easily shocked. Besides, Lord Henly visited Lucien

more than once.' She spoke calmly but colour touched her cheek.

'Of course. I had nearly forgotten you were married to one of the most notorious rakes in England.' As well as that beneath her quiet façade was an adventuress, and the slight flush staining her cheeks had nothing to do with modesty.

She looked at him. 'Had you? I fear that is something I have never been allowed to forget.' She glanced over his shoulder. 'Good evening, Lady Burlington.'

He started, having nearly forgotten where they were. In the middle of a London theatre where he had intended to parade to the *ton* that she was his. Certainly he had accomplished his objective if the number of curious stares they received were any indication. Only Belle did not seem to notice. She stood a little aloof and he wanted more and more to shake her out of it. He did not want to return to their box. He wanted to be alone with her. To feel her mouth beneath his and her soft curves pressed against him. He scowled. 'We are leaving,' he said abruptly.

Surprise showed in her face. 'But the next act is about to begin.'

'The prospect of missing it hardly pains me. I came to be seen with you, not because I wished to watch the play.'

'Indeed. I do not suppose it might occur to you that I might actually want to watch the play?'

'No.' He frowned at her, wanting to tell her that it did not matter what she wished, but her expression gave him pause. 'Do you?'

She lifted her chin and looked at him. 'No, for it is really not a very good play, but I might have wanted to.'

His brow shot up. 'I fail to see the point of this conversation. I wish to leave and you wish to leave.'

'The point is that I am not your lap dog. I will not allow you to dictate to me.'

He bit back his impatience. 'I was not attempting to dictate to you. I've no idea why you decided to disagree with me when there was no need to. Shall we go since we are both in agreement?'

Belle opened her mouth as if she wished to say something else and then closed it. She turned and started towards the steps. He felt his temper rise but, before he caught up with her, she stopped.

Her mother-in-law was coming towards her with Lady Chloe and he watched as Lady Ralston drifted past Belle without the least acknowledgement that she was there. Lady Chloe sent her a brief stricken glance before continuing on. Belle lifted her head and then continued walking as if nothing had happened.

He reached her side and caught her arm. 'What the devil was that all about?'

She barely looked at him. 'I have no idea what you are talking about.'

'Lady Ralston just gave you the cut direct. As did your sister-in-law.'

'Did she?' She looked straight ahead.

He realised several people watched them. His desire to be on display had been abating rapidly and now it died. 'We will discuss this later. We are leaving now.' He took her to the entrance hall and then sent for her shawl, and his hat and gloves. He did not speak again until they were in his carriage and it had started to move through the London streets.

'Do you know why your in-laws just cut you?' he demanded.

She tore her gaze from the window. 'I rather expect it was because I was with you. I would rather not discuss it, if you please.'

She sniffed as if she were fighting back tears. If she had actually cried or raged at him or raged at her in-laws, he might have remained unmoved or perhaps been even contemptuous, but that little sound took him aback. The next thing he knew he was sitting next to her. His arms went around her and he pulled her against him. 'Don't,' he said roughly.

'Don't what?'

'Cry.' Her scent filled his nostrils. A soft blend of rose and femininity. He suddenly thought of his mother, for she too had smelled of roses. But Belle's warm frame was hardly maternal. His arms tightened.

'I am not crying.' She lifted her head and looked at him. She sniffed again.

'You are.' Her lips were too invitingly close. With a groan he covered them with his. A little gasp escaped her and her hands clutched at his coat as the carriage hit a bump. His arms tightened, pulling her closer and his mouth moved roughly over hers, demanding her response.

Her lips parted slightly and he deepened the kiss. Her taste and smell intoxicated him and it wasn't until he felt her stiffen under him and heard her little sound almost of pain that he realised he was half on her in the darkened carriage.

He lifted his head and dropped his arms. 'I beg your pardon.' He moved away from her, trying to regain his senses.

'There is no need to under the circumstances. It was just my reticule was under me. I think I sat on a pin.'

'Are you hurt?'

'No. It was the merest of pin-pricks.'

Her voice was calm, too calm, whereas he felt as if he was on fire. He moved back to his seat across from her. What the devil was wrong with him? He'd nearly lost control of himself, attacking her with the loss of restraint of a callow youth with his first love.

That was not part of his plan. He had no intention of relinquishing control. He might desire her, but he intended to keep it firmly in check with no other complicating emotions.

Justin realised the carriage had halted in front of his house. He stepped down first and then helped her out.

He kept his voice and expression as cool as hers as he escorted her up the steps of his townhouse and into the entry hall. But he did not feel nearly as cool inside when he said, 'We can go to my apartments.' His voice came out rougher than he'd intended as he held out his hand.

She nodded and that was when he saw the apprehension in her eyes. It was gone quickly, but there was no mistaking it or the tremor of her hand as his closed around it. He realised then that she was not nearly as calm as she appeared to be. In fact, just the opposite. She was frightened. Which, whether he liked it or not, would complicate everything.

Her mouth dry, Belle glanced at Justin as they climbed the winding staircase. His expression was brooding. He had said little since he had kissed her in the carriage and then apologised, which had completely confused her. His manner had been polite almost as if she was a stranger he found himself entertaining, certainly not that of a potential lover.

He pushed open a door and she found herself in a

darkened bedchamber. Only the light of the full moon provided any illumination. Her legs had quit trembling and she found she was detached, the way she had been when with Lucien. With a calm indifference she noted the bed was simple and old-fashioned with brocade hangings and there was a small table next to the bed and that the wardrobe was plain. A portrait hung over the mantelpiece. He put the candle down on the small stand and then turned to look at her. 'Do you want more light?'

'No. This will be adequate.' She moved towards him. 'What would you like me to do? Should I undress?'

'No.' His eyes swept over her face and then narrowed. 'Are you always this aloof when you are with your lovers?'

'I have never had any lovers.'

'No? Then what of the man you mentioned before? The man who taught you that physical intimacy and love are not the same?' His voice had a hardness to it.

She looked at him, surprised, and then remembered what she had said to him in her anger. 'I was referring to Lucien.'

'Lucien?'

'Yes. My husband. I have never been with anyone but him.'

'Were you in love with him?' he asked harshly.

She looked away. 'I do not wish to discuss Lucien.'

'No.' He moved away from her. 'I have changed my mind. You may undress now.'

She looked up and realised he had come to lean against the bed post. His arms were folded, but the shadows prevented her from seeing his face. But she knew one thing, he was going to watch her.

Having no clue how to proceed, she finally sat down on the bed and pulled off her gloves. She placed them on the table near the bed and then bent down to remove her slippers. Her hand trembled as she untied the laces and then slipped them off. She pulled up her skirt as far as she could without baring her entire leg and started to unroll her silk stockings. She kept her eyes on the task, her face heating with unwelcome colour. She managed to get both stockings off and then rose.

Did he expect her to unlace her own dress? She had only attempted to do so a few times in her entire life. She forced herself to look at him. 'I do not think I can undo the laces of my dress myself.' Her voice did not sound at all like her own.

'I'll do it. Come here.'

She came to stand in front of him and felt his fingers at her back, cool as they brushed her bare skin. She closed her eyes as he undid the fastenings of her dress, trying to quell the disturbing sensations his touch wrought in her. And then her silk gown was falling from her shoulders and his hands were at her hips sliding the material so that it pooled at her feet.

She heard him catch his breath. 'Turn around, Belle.' His voice was husky with desire.

She did and resisted the urge to close her eyes as he looked at her. She felt vulnerable and stripped of everything as his darkening gaze rested on the mounds of her breasts pushed high by the stays. His eyes travelled to the curve of her hips and she felt almost faint with apprehension.

'You are so damnably beautiful.' He sounded almost reluctant to admit it. 'Take the pins from your hair. I want to see it around your shoulders.'

She hesitated and then lifted her hands to her hair. Her fingers shook as she removed them and she felt her hair falling to brush her bare shoulders. She put the pins on the table with her gloves and then turned. He still watched her. 'What do you want me to do now?' she asked. At least this time her voice was more contained and normal. She would get through this. Nothing he did could be any worse than being with Lucien.

He stared at her and blinked almost as if he had awoken from a trance. 'Do next? My dear Belle, does nothing shake your composure? You are standing in front of me half-dressed and you still sound as if you are inquiring whether I would like a cup of tea. Does it not fluster you in the least that I want to take you to my bed and ravish you until dawn?'

She started. 'Until dawn? I rather thought we would be finished within an hour. Perhaps two at the most.'

His smile was dangerous. 'An hour or two? That is not nearly enough time.'

'But whatever does one do for so long?'

He stepped towards her and she found herself backed up against the bed. 'That, my sweet Belle, is what I intend to show you.'

She forced herself to remain still, her eyes on his face. He looked rather angry and his eyes had a wild glitter. Her heart was beating so quickly she felt almost dizzy and her legs trembled. Justin's hand cupped the back of her head and he brought his mouth down on hers in a hard, possessive kiss. She gasped and then stilled as his mouth moved over hers, demanding her surrender. His arms locked her to his hard chest and she fought to force the panic down, forced her mind to go elsewhere as she had done with Lucien. So when his arms fell away, she felt completely disorientated. 'Damn it, Belle,' he said harshly. 'This is not what I want.'

Her eyes opened and she stared at him. 'What is wrong?'

He took a pace away from her and ran a hand through his hair. 'This. I feel as if I'm about to commit a rape. I cannot force you to my bed.'

'But you are not. I am willing.'

He gave a short laugh. 'Are you? Then why did I have the sense you were terrified when I held you? I thought you were about to swoon in my arms.'

She looked away, mortified and ashamed. 'I do not like to be held so tightly. I feel as if I cannot breathe.' Which was not exactly a lie.

'Is that all?' he demanded.

'Yes.' She forced herself to look at him. 'So, if you wish to proceed, I am more than willing.'

'Not with you so terrified. What the hell did Milborne do to you?'

'Nothing.' She rubbed her arms where his hands had grasped her. 'I did not like the marriage bed at all. He left me in no doubt that he found me quite inadequate, although he assured me that his mistresses made up for my lack. I fear, however, you will find me a poor mistress, which is why I think it best if we proceed to the point quickly and then I can go home.'

'No.'

She glanced up at him. The anger in his face stunned her. She backed up a pace and stared at him.

His face was dark. 'I've no intention of taking you while you lie there forcing yourself to submit. I am not that base. When you come to my bed it will pleasure you as much as it pleasures me.'

'It is really not necessary.' Oh, lord. She did not want to find out what he meant by pleasure. She wanted to stay as uninvolved as possible and then, after she paid her debts, return to her quiet life.

'Oh, but it is.' The menace in his voice coupled with

the look in his eye told her he had no intention of letting this go.

With growing trepidation she watched as he sat down on the edge of the bed and removed his shoes. Then he deliberately removed his stockings. He stood and started to shrug out of his evening coat.

'Wh…what are you doing?' Surely he wasn't planning to strip in front of her? Not even Lucien had done that.

'Merely levelling the field.' He removed his coat and then his waistcoat followed. He picked them up and draped them over a chair and then picked up her gown from the floor and dropped it carelessly on top of his clothing. She swallowed as he came towards her and took a step back. Her knees hit the bed and she sat down abruptly. With a smooth movement he joined her.

'Good. This is where we start.' His thigh pressed into hers as he squarely met her eyes. 'I'll wager that by the end of this lesson you will not be so eager to quit my bed.'

'What lesson?'

'The lesson we are about to start. The lesson where I teach you what a man wants in a mistress.' A peculiar little smile touched his mouth.

She swallowed again. 'I don't really want any such lessons. I do not plan to do this again.'

'That does not matter,' he said softly. His hand lightly brushed her cheek and then he tilted her chin up. 'I am going to kiss you. We'll start there.'

'No—' Her protest was silenced by his mouth. She braced herself, expecting the same harsh assault as before, but instead his lips moved over hers in gentle exploration. One hand cupped the back of her neck, tangling in her hair. With some surprise, she realised the sensation of his mouth on hers was not at all unpleasant. Her lips parted under the light pressure and then he pulled her more firmly against him.

His tongue slipped inside. Instead of the revulsion she had felt with Lucien, she found the sensation pleasurable. She tentatively touched his tongue with her own. Justin made a sound almost like a groan in his throat and his kiss deepened. Instead of pulling away, she pressed against him.

Then his mouth left her neck and was placing a fiery trail of kisses down it to the soft exposed skin of her breasts.

He lifted his head and she opened her eyes to find him watching her with a dazed expression. 'I think you are ready for the next lesson,' he whispered. 'But first this must come off.' His hand brushed her stays. 'Turn around.'

She obeyed, wondering what she was doing. Her lips felt swollen and her body curiously languid. The touch of his fingers as he undid the laces made her feel peculiar. Her stays fell away. One arm came around her and pulled her against him and through the thin linen of her shift she could feel the hard muscles of his chest against her back. He began to kiss her neck again, but when his free hand cupped her breast, she stiffened.

His hand fell away. 'What is it?' he asked. His breath was warm on her cheek. 'Do you not like that?'

'I do not mind. Please go on.' Her face was suffused with colour and she was glad he could not see her. She supposed it was something women liked or at least were expected to tolerate but she had always felt violated.

His hand left her breast. 'Not if you do not like it. But do you like this?' He caressed her stomach through her shift in gentle, languorous circles. A slow heat began to grow in her and she pressed back against him. When his hand circled closer to the juncture of her thighs, she grabbed it. But then remembered she was supposed to let him do these things to her so her hand fell away.

He did not seem to notice. 'We can lie down now.' And then she was on her back and he was over her. She closed her eyes and waited for him to lift her shift but instead he stroked her face. And then he was kissing her again in that slow exploratory way as if he had all the time in the world.

Belle's arms came around his shoulders and she felt the hard muscles of his back through his shirt. Her hand moved up and entangled in his thick hair. Her head seemed to spin and she was kissing him back. She was vaguely aware that his hand was again caressing her stomach and hips, creating exquisite sensation. His hand moved lower and she forced herself to relax. But she could not quite help her little start of surprise when he began to caress her most private parts. 'Shh…' he said against her mouth. His fingers were stroking her and despite the barrier of her shift, she could feel a warm growing heaviness between her thighs. His tongue was teasing hers and his hand kept its steady slow rhythmic caress. She fought the urge to part her legs but the spiral of sensation seemed to be growing smaller and smaller and focused on where his hand was. She pressed against him and then cried out as the heaviness shattered into an exquisite pleasure.

He withdrew his hand and lifted his head. She kept her eyes closed, not wanting to see the triumph he must feel over her surrender. Worse, he had not even had to remove all of her clothes. Or his.

'Belle.' She felt his weight shift away from her.

She opened her eyes. Justin sat on the edge of the

bed. 'I believe that is enough of a lesson for tonight. I will help you dress and then take you home.' His voice was polite.

'Very well.' She sat up, trying to tell herself she should be grateful for his manner, that he was not rubbing in his victory, but instead she felt confused.

He helped her dress, his movements so efficient she thought he must do this often, hardly a pleasing notion.

'Damn,' he muttered.

'Is something wrong?'

'I've managed to miss a fastening. I'll have to start again.'

'No!' She turned around, not wanting to have him touch her any more than necessary. 'It does not matter.'

He scowled. 'But there's a gap in the back.'

'Since I am only going home and not out in public it hardly matters. I will be taking it off again anyway.' Although her maid would probably wonder what she had done. But it was too late for any of those considerations now.

'Always so practical.'

She had no idea whether it was a compliment or not. She followed him down the stairs and then he fetched her shawl. He had fallen into another brooding silence and she had no idea what he was thinking. He said nothing until he had helped her from the carriage. 'I will leave for Surrey tomorrow.'

'To get your horse?'

'Yes. I will return the day after. I will call on you then.'

'As it pleases you. Good night, your Grace.' She had started to leave when he caught her hand and pulled her around to face him.

'It does please me. As you did tonight. We'll finish

the rest of the lessons when I return.' He cupped her chin and brushed her mouth quickly with his. 'Goodnight, Belle.'

'Goodnight,' she whispered and turned and ran up the steps without looking back.

Chapter Six

Belle had thought that with him gone some sort of normality might return despite the loss of Maria and Chloe.

But that her life had been irrevocably altered became quite apparent the very next day when she went to find a new pair of gloves. She had made her purchase and was about to step out of the shop door when Lady Blanchard and Mrs Cunningham entered. There were no smiles on their faces when they saw her and Mrs Cunningham, who was usually quite pleasant, had a distinctly frosty look in her eye. Their acknowledgement was so brief that they might as well have cut her.

She thought it must be her imagination, however, when she was at William's Lane Library and Mrs Barry greeted her politely enough. But was there a speculation in the other woman's eye that she had not noticed before? Particularly when she asked if Belle had enjoyed last night's performance. In fact, as the conversation progressed, Mrs Barry's comments seemed to border on the impertinent. Belle finally made her escape by claiming she had another appointment.

Once in her carriage, she tried to tell herself that Mrs Barry was a notorious gossip and that she always asked questions that were a trifle presumptuous. But she could not shake off the sense that something was very wrong.

With a start, she realised her carriage had stopped in front of her house. She took her parcels and stepped down. Mrs Bates opened the door. 'Lord Ralston is waiting for you. In the drawing room.' Her mouth was puckered with disapproval.

Belle handed Mrs Bates her parcels and went directly to the drawing room. She might as well see Arthur straight away instead of putting off the unpleasant task. He sat in one of the wing chairs near the window. He looked up when she entered and stood. 'Good day, Belle.'

'Hello, Arthur. Mrs Bates said you were here.' She came into the room and removed her bonnet.

'Yes.' He clasped his hands behind his back and frowned at her. 'I have come to speak to you about last night. You cannot imagine how shocked I was to see you in Westmore's box.'

'Were you?'

'Most certainly. I would like to know why you would do such a rash and ill-advised thing. I have no doubt he has designs on your virtue.' He paced away from her and then looked back. 'I will own I was mistaken. I thought he wished to contract a proper alliance with Chloe. Instead I see he wishes an improper alliance with you.' His face showed distaste. 'You are foolish beyond belief if you think he intends to offer you marriage.'

'I do not think he intends to offer me marriage,' Belle said. She suddenly felt weary. 'Is there anything else you wanted to say to me?'

'I can think of no explanation for your behaviour other than you have developed a most unwise *tendre* for him. Why else would you risk the censure of society by appearing alone with him for all to see? Do you wish to ruin Chloe's chances?'

'No, I do not and that is why I have agreed not to see Chloe. Did Maria not tell you that?'

'Yes. Along with some ridiculous nonsense about your sacrificing yourself for Chloe.'

'You are right, that is most ridiculous.' She sighed. 'I am very tired, Arthur, and if all you want to do is scold me then I pray you will leave.'

He stared at her. A tinge of colour appeared on his cheekbones. 'I suppose you will be with him tonight,' he said tightly.

'Why would you think that? I rather thought I would remain at home.'

'You will not attend Lady Perth's rout?'

She had forgotten about Lady Perth's rout. Her first instinct was to say no, but the dowager Countess had been a close friend of her mother's and, the last time Belle had met her, had expressed the greatest desire that Belle would attend. 'I have not made up my mind.'

'Because Westmore will not escort you?'

'Westmore has nothing to do with this,' she said quietly, although she was seething with anger. 'Nor can I see what any of this has to do with you.' She started to walk towards the door. 'I am going to my bedchamber. Mrs Bates can show you out. Please give my love to Chloe and Maria.'

His mouth fell open but she was too furious with him to care. How dare he involve himself in her business? She was not related to him nor did he have any control over her affairs. None the less, he had always attempted to dictate to her just as he did to Chloe and Maria.

The whole conversation had been odd. As odd as her

encounters earlier today. Is that what the *ton* already thought? She was Justin's mistress?

Which she was in every sense of the word except for the actual consummation. Every time she thought of last night, she shuddered. She had not wanted to feel anything with him; she had only wanted to lie with him while he did what he wanted. But he had not let her remain aloof. He had brought her to an ecstasy she had had no idea she was capable of and for the first time in her life she had experienced a desire so overwhelming she had no choice but to surrender to him. Her couplings with Lucien had been humiliating and sometimes painful, but always mercifully brief. His only purpose in coming to her had been to procure an heir and he had never cared if she took pleasure in the proceedings. Her duty had been to submit. She had learned to disengage herself, to bury any emotion she might feel, and to force her mind elsewhere.

She had no idea why Justin would not allow her to remain detached. Did he, or any man, really care if the woman was pleasured as well? Or was it another way to gain power over her, make her desire him so that when they parted she would feel his rejection as strongly as he had felt hers?

Whatever his reason, she would do everything in her power to resist him.

She knew almost as soon as she set foot in Lady Perth's crowded drawing room she had made a grave error in attending. She had not wanted to come, but Belle had not wanted to disappoint Lady Perth. Lady Perth, as always, was welcoming, her kindly face wreathed in smiles when she saw Belle, but others were not so kind. More than one lady moved away at her approach and she wished more than anything she could turn tail and run, but she would not give them the satisfaction of leaving right away. She forced herself to move further into the room.

'Lady Milborne.' She turned to find Mr Aubrey behind her. 'Quite a crush. Hot as well.'

She managed a smile. 'Indeed it is.'

He looked a little uncomfortable, but before he could say more they were joined by Lord Henly and Sir Reginald Malven, a middle-aged fop with a dissipated air. Lord Henly leered at her. 'My dear Lady Milborne I am surprised Westmore did not take you with him. I would not have thought him to be so careless.'

'Indeed.' She did not seem able to move but she must, for she could not stand in the middle of a drawing room with two of London's most jaded rakes.

Someone touched her arm. 'Belle.'

For once in her life, she was relieved to see Arthur. Even his disapproving frown was welcome. He glanced at her companions, his distaste evident. 'I would like to speak to Lady Milborne. If you will excuse us.'

Lord Henly smirked. 'Taking advantage of Westmore's absence, are you?'

'Your comments are most unwelcome,' Arthur said stiffly. 'Come, Belle.'

Belle's face flamed for Henly's voice was loud. Her stomach took a sickening churn when she saw that Lady Georgina stood near them. From the malicious gleam in the older lady's eye, Belle suspected she had heard.

She followed Arthur out of the room to the hall where he stopped and looked down at her. She spoke before he could. 'Thank you for rescuing me.'

He actually looked nonplussed. 'I trust that in the future you will avoid such company. I will refrain from

pointing out that to be seen with such persons will only
do further harm to your reputation.' He cleared his
throat. 'I fear, however, there are some most unfortunate
rumours circulating. For your own sake, I would suggest
that you should return home. I will be most glad to offer
my escort. I have informed Maria that I intended to do
so.'

'You are most kind.' She really must be in a bad
dream if she was actually thinking of Arthur as kind.
But in his own odd, stiff way she realised he actually
meant to protect her.

He went off to call for his carriage while she waited
near the table in the downstairs hallway. She heard female voices and realised other guests were coming down
the stairs. The last thing she wanted to do was to face
more cold looks, so she moved into the small room off
the hall.

'I could not believe that she would actually show her
face tonight! And to think that she has always put on
such a display of virtue!'

The second voice was softer but no less censorious.
'Perhaps she thought that would erase her past.'

'Then she should not have flaunted her relationship
with the Duke of Westmore so publicly. I pity her relations. To be connected with a woman who actually
attended such…such orgies!' The last word was uttered
in a shocked whisper, but it still carried to Belle's burning ears.

She wanted to die on the spot. Whoever had said such
things about her? Humiliation seared through her and
she wondered that Lady Perth had even received her.
Except her elderly friend was nearly deaf and perhaps
had not yet heard the rumours. How could she possibly
face her or anyone, for that matter, again?

She did not want to think that Justin had spread such rumours. But if he had wanted to punish her, he had succeeded. She was, for all purposes, ruined.

Two mornings after he left, Justin returned to London. He stepped into the cool hallway of his townhouse and handed his butler his hat and gloves. 'Lady Georgina has called and is in the drawing room. She would like you to wait on her at your convenience,' Hastings said.

'How long has she been here?'

'Nearly two hours. She said she would remain all day if necessary.'

He bit back a groan. His aunt would not spend the day lying in wait for him unless she wanted something from him.

'I trust your journey was successful,' Hastings said.

'Yes. The colt is in London.' Justin saw the gleam in the butler's eye and grinned. 'As soon as he has settled down I will bring him around for your approval.' Hastings, he knew, would have preferred to be in the stables, but his father and grandfather had both been butlers, and he had not wanted to break the family tradition.

'Very good, your Grace.'

Justin's smile faded as he mounted the stairs. The colt was in excellent health, but he was high-strung and skittish. After the horse had thrown him, Chiswick had neglected the animal and the colt was more than a little wild. Justin had planned to send the colt to his estate in Devon with his head groom. But after travelling with the animal from Surrey to London he had made up his mind he must see that it reached Falconcliff himself.

Ordinarily leaving London was a matter of indifference to him but not this time. Belle was here. He did not intend to leave without her.

He entered the drawing room. 'Good day, Aunt Georgina.'

Lady Georgina glanced up. She held a teacup and saucer on her lap and the *Morning Post* lay open on the sofa beside her. She regarded him with stony grey eyes. 'I had no idea until last night that you had left London. It was very remiss of you not to inform me. I trust you have not forgotten we are expected to dine with the Blackwoods tonight.'

He frowned. 'Are we?' He'd completely forgotten. The last thing he wanted was to spend an evening in the company he was expecting would be present. Nor did he want to find Lady Clarissa under his nose at every opportunity. She currently led the pack as Lady Georgina's favourite candidate for the next Duchess.

'Yes.' Her sharp eyes were on him. 'I trust you intend to give some serious consideration to choosing a wife. I take it you have abandoned the ill-judged notion of considering Lady Chloe as a candidate.'

He folded his arms and leaned against the side table. 'Why do you think that?'

'It is quite obvious.'

He merely waited. She paused for a moment and then spoke. 'It would be extremely unseemly of you to offer for Lady Chloe after taking her sister-in-law for a mistress.'

'What do you know of that?'

'I pray you will not play ignorant. You were with her at the theatre and I doubt if there was not a soul there who did not notice that you failed to return to your box. That in itself is enough to cause a few raised brows, but coupled with the report that you were seen escorting Lady Milborne home not only once but twice late at night…it is all too obvious.'

'Is it?'

'Yes. She is lovely in a rather cool way and has a reputation for being untouchable so I can see the challenge. And she was Milborne's wife, so perhaps you cannot be blamed for wanting her although it would perhaps give you more satisfaction if he were still alive. But you can take some pleasure from the knowledge that she scarcely has a good reputation.'

He'd been listening in growing anger. 'What the devil do you mean by that?'

'Even her in-laws will not acknowledge her.' She placed her teacup and saucer on the table near her. 'I have no idea why Serena Perth admitted her...although she is rather senile, so perhaps she can be excused. One could almost feel sorry for Lady Milborne except she undoubtedly deserves it. No one spoke to her except for Aubrey, who I dare say did feel sorry for her, and Lord Henly and Sir Reginald Malven. Oh, yes and that ninny, Lord Ralston! Lord Henly was quite put out when Ralston marched her away from him. She left with Ralston, I believe.' A peculiar little smile touched her mouth. 'You no longer need to bother yourself with her. Your plot to avenge yourself was quite successful.' She rose. 'I trust I will see you at dinner tonight.'

'What plot are you referring to?'

She arched a brow. 'You know very well. I cannot think of any other reason why you would go out of your way to be seen in her company. I am surprised you can bear to look at her, much less touch her. You would be wise to extricate yourself from her before you are tainted with the same tales.'

He would not give her the satisfaction of asking what tales she was talking about. He would find out soon enough. He said coldly, 'You are wrong if you think I intended to ruin Lady Milborne's reputation. Whatever business might be between us is private.'

'You are quite wrong.' Her eyes glinted with anger. 'You are a duke and the head of one of England's oldest families. Your business is very public, which is why you cannot afford the least hint of scandal attached to your name. Your duty is to make an alliance with a woman whose breeding is equal to yours and whose chastity is unquestionable. You have a duty to produce an heir as soon as possible. You have accomplished what you wanted with Isabelle Milborne so there is no need to distract yourself any more with her.'

'No?' He met her gaze squarely. 'Perhaps I am not finished distracting myself with Lady Milborne. Nor do I intend to marry merely because you have decided it is time I do so. I will wed when I please and whom I please.' He moved away from her towards the door. 'I have not changed from my journey so I must leave you.' At the door he paused and looked back. She stared at him, her mouth tight, two spots of red on her cheeks. 'I will also send Lord Blackwood my regrets that I will be unable to dine with him after all.' He did not wait to see her reaction. He feared if he stayed a moment longer he would lose his tenuous hold on his temper altogether.

Justin stalked to his bedchamber. Hell. He had wanted to punish Belle but he realised that, despite his fury at her, he had not wanted to destroy her. He had no idea what had happened in the short time he had been away from London. Certainly the fact that she had attended the theatre with him had signalled to society they were more than mere acquaintances, but even if she was thought to be his mistress, she should not be so completely ruined.

Not to the point where her relations would not acknowledge her. Except for Ralston, whom she had left with, according to his aunt. The thought of Ralston with Belle made his blood boil and he thought if the man had touched her he would take great pleasure in putting a bullet through him.

He ran a hand through his hair and paced to the window. He scowled, angry with himself. Whatever had happened to his vow to remain indifferent? The possessive jealousy he felt had no place in his scheme to punish her. He had intended to heartlessly seduce Belle, and certainly in his most fantastic desires for revenge he had envisioned having her completely in his power. He had wanted to flaunt her relationship with him in public, both to prove she did not hold him responsible for Lucien's death and to force her to publicly acknowledge him.

His aunt was correct in one regard—her ruin would serve as the perfect revenge.

Unfortunately, he had also discovered he did not hate her as much as he thought he did.

And that he had a conscience after all.

Belle was not home when he called later that day. He called again, just before he left for a soirée, but she was still not in, according to her housekeeper. He could not tell from the woman's closed expression whether Belle was truly not at home or whether she was not receiving. Nor would the housekeeper give him any information regarding her whereabouts. He vowed if he did not see her at the soirée, he would track her down at home even if it meant he cooled his heels on her doorstep.

She was not at the soirée. Lady Ralston and Lady Chloe were present, but he suspected that approaching them would only cause further harm. Ralston was there as well, which afforded him the grim satisfaction that at least he was not with Belle.

He decided he would go to the card room and find Brandt. He had just reached the door when someone called his name. He turned and to his astonishment saw Lady Chloe behind him. He opened his mouth to say something but the white fury on her face stopped him and he found himself backed against the wall.

'I do not know what vile rumours you have spread about my…my sister-in-law, but I just want you to know that if you do anything further to hurt her I will…will…'

Good God! 'Run me through?' He almost expected her to pull out a dagger this very moment.

'Yes! And more than once! You will be very sorry.'

'This is not the time to discuss this. Unless you want even more rumours.' Her lip trembled and he knew she either planned to hit him or burst into tears.

He pulled out a handkerchief. 'Here.' To his surprise she took it. Justin scowled. 'Go sit down by the window before any of your family sees you with me. Unless you want a scene.' Sending Lady Ralston into hysterics was not something he wanted to do. 'I will join you.'

She nodded and walked towards the window seat. He waited to make certain no one was watching and then followed her. He looked down at her. 'I assure you I have not spread any rumours about your sister-in-law.'

'Someone has. And since you wish to ruin her I would think it was you.'

'I do not wish to—' He stopped. She was the last person he wanted to discuss this with. 'Where is Belle?'

'I do not know. I am forbidden to see her or even speak to her and it is entirely your doing. And she has never done a thing to you!'

'Has she told you that?' he said coldly.

'No, but she always takes your side and says you are not to blame for anything!' She glared at him. 'Even when Mama says it is entirely your fault that my brother is dead.'

He was taken aback. Belle stood up for him? He had hardly expected that.

Lady Chloe rose. She sniffed and then handed him his handkerchief. 'I am sorry I could not have it cleaned for you but I would not want anyone to know I had borrowed it. I hope you do not mind.'

'Not at all.'

Apparently her spirit was not completely crushed, however. She lifted her chin. 'I vow I will find a way to make you very sorry if you do a thing to hurt her.'

'I would watch my back if I were you, cousin,' Brandt said from behind them.

Justin bit back a curse. He turned and resisted the urge to wipe the half-amused smile from Brandt's face. 'Eavesdropping?'

'I merely wished to speak to you but since you were occupied, I decided to wait my turn.'

Lady Chloe gave him a look of cold dislike. 'It is very rude to listen to the private conversations of others. And I quite mean what I say. I will make anyone who hurts Belle very sorry, even if I must spend the rest of my life doing so! That includes you, Lord Salcombe.'

She turned and walked away, her head held high.

'I suggest you watch your back as well,' Justin said.

Brandt watched her, a bemused expression on his face. 'I would have thought her a complete mouse. I can see I was quite wrong.'

'Before you arrived on the scene she accused me of spreading vile rumours about Belle. There was some suggestion of running me through as well.'

'Good God! One would never guess she was that blood-thirsty from her demure appearance. It is a good thing, then, that she doesn't know what you have planned for Lady Milborne or I would very much fear for your demise.'

'What rumours is she talking about?'

'You have not heard?' Brandt asked carefully.

'No. I've only been in town a few hours.' He did not like the look on his cousin's face. 'What are they?' he asked softly.

'Only that Belle Milborne was a very willing participant in the orgies her husband was fond of attending.'

Justin stared at him. He gave a short, harsh laugh. 'You do not think I started them, do you?'

'She is completely ruined. It would be a very complete revenge.'

'I've no desire to destroy her reputation. Nor would I ever stoop to telling such vicious lies.'

'I did not think so, but I wonder who did. I cannot think of anyone else who would profit by doing so.' Brandt eyed him. 'But aside from the threat of death by Lady Chloe's hand, are you really concerned what becomes of Lady Milborne?'

Justin met his cousin's eyes. 'I do not want her ruin laid at my door.'

'Then I suggest you be careful. For I fear you are still very much in her thrall.'

He left shortly after that and went to Belle's house. Several lights still burned and so he trusted she had not yet retired.

He signalled the coachman to stop and jumped down. He mounted the steps to her house and rapped on the door. Belle's housekeeper opened it and regarded him with a frown. 'Lady Milborne is not receiving visitors, your Grace.'

'If she is still up, I would like to speak with her,' he said impatiently. 'It will not take long.'

She looked at him for a moment and he decided to take advantage of her hesitation, stepping past her into the dim, narrow hallway. 'You may tell Lady Milborne that I am here.'

She opened her mouth to speak, but was stopped by the sound of footsteps. He looked up to see Belle above him. She held a candle and looked at him for a moment before coming down the stairs. She paused halfway down. 'Were we to meet tonight?'

'No.' He started up towards her. 'I wanted to talk to you. It will not take long.'

She bit her lip. 'It is past midnight.'

'I know. I will not stay long.'

'Very well.' She turned and he followed her up the stairs and into a small drawing room. She set the candle down on a table.

'Do you wish to sit?' she asked politely.

'No.' He stopped in front of her. 'Are you all right?'

'Why wouldn't I be?' She looked up at him and he saw the shadows under her eyes and knew she wasn't at all.

'Brandt told me of the rumours,' he said bluntly.

'Yes. I imagine everyone knows of them.' She looked away.

'I did not start them.'

She glanced back at him and said nothing.

He took a step towards her and swore. 'I had no idea I appeared so completely despicable. First your sister-in-law and then Brandt and now you. But I vow I would not hurt you in this way.'

'My sister-in-law? Chloe? What does she have to do with this?'

'She accosted me tonight and accused me of spreading rumours about you. She also plans to make me very sorry if I hurt you.'

'Oh, dear.' Her face clouded with worry. 'I do not want her involved in this. I cannot bear for her to be hurt. I have no choice but to leave London.' She spoke almost to herself.

'Come to Devon with me.'

'To Devon?'

'I have my colt. I need to take him there but I do not want to send him with only my grooms. I swear I won't touch you if you don't want me to. At least you'll be away from here and protected.'

She stared at him. 'But our contract?'

He gave a short laugh. 'Consider it paid in full.'

'But—'

'Where else are you to go? You cannot stay with your in-laws.' He paced away from her. 'You have your house here, but I agree—staying in London is impossible. I would offer to buy you a house anywhere you wished but I've no doubt you would throw it back in my face.' He watched her. 'I have one other thing to offer you, however.' He hardly knew what he was saying. 'My name.'

She turned so white he thought she might faint. 'Your what?'

'My name. I am asking you to become my wife.'

She took a step backwards. 'No. Never!' The horror on her face suggested he had asked her to be guillotined.

Something wrenched in his stomach. 'What choice do you have? You are ruined,' he said harshly.

She caught the back of the sofa for support. 'No. I

would rather be your mistress a thousand times over than be married. I would rather die than be a wife again.'

The pain of her rejection and betrayal he thought he'd buried spilled out and enveloped him. 'Very well. I will withdraw my offer and accept yours. You will be my mistress. We will leave for Devon the day after tomorrow.' He started towards the door and then paused. 'And two nights from now you will lie with me.'

He left the room without looking at her.

Belle heard his footsteps recede and then sank down on the sofa. Had she imagined the pain she had glimpsed in his face when she refused his offer? As if she had hurt him. Surely she did not have that sort of power over him. He did not even like her so how could anything she said possibly affect him?

Then why had he cancelled their contract and then asked her to marry him in order to save her reputation? She had thought that ruining her was what he wanted.

None of it made the least sense.

She had spoken unthinkingly, for she could never marry again. Even if she was not barren, she never again wanted to turn her life, her very destiny, over to a man. But she had never dreamed that her words might wound Justin.

Belle doubted he would ever forgive her. How could she possibly go with him?

She slowly rose and knew she could no longer deny the truth to herself.

She would go with him because she still cared for him.

Chapter Seven

Two mornings later, Belle sat at her desk and finished the last of her correspondence. She had been up since dawn in an effort to finish all that must be done before she left London. She sighed and resisted the urge to drop her head into her hands. She had a slight headache and her stomach was unsettled. She only hoped it was from nerves and lack of sleep.

She shoved the last letter aside and looked up in time to see Arthur entering the study. She rose, having no idea why he should call on her. He surely must have heard the rumours by now and she could not imagine a man with his fastidious morals even deigning to look at her. 'Good day, Arthur,' she said politely.

He stepped into the room and to her surprise, he closed the door behind him. He looked at her and tugged at his stock in a nervous gesture. 'Good day, Belle. I trust you are well.'

'I am.' Puzzled, she stared at him. 'Did you have a purpose for calling?'

'Yes.' He cleared his throat. 'First allow me to express my regret for the unfortunate rumours that are circulating. Unlike many of those in Society, I believe in your innocence.'

'Thank you.' She had no idea why he wanted to tell her that.

'However, it does not mitigate the fact that you are now beyond the pale of society. I fear your rash and ill-judged liaison with the Duke of Westmore has only contributed to both the rumours and the unfortunate position you now find yourself in.' He folded his hands behind his back. 'I have heard that Westmore is leaving London today, which is no more than I would have expected from a man who is reputed to be a rake. Unfortunately, when he is gone you will have no protection. Which brings me to the reason for my visit.'

'And that is?'

'I wish to offer you my protection.'

'Your protection?' She stared at him, not certain she had understood him. 'What do you mean?'

He tugged again at his stock. 'I am asking you to become my mistress.' His face was now suffused with high colour.

'Your mistress?' She undoubtedly sounded like a parrot, but she was shocked beyond belief.

'Yes.' To her horror he suddenly advanced upon her. She backed up and found her desk inconveniently behind her. 'It cannot have escaped your notice these past years that I hold you in the highest regard. The fortitude with which you endured what must have been a situation of the most repugnant to you in your marriage to my cousin. The bravery in which you have faced widowhood. And although you have erred very gravely I cannot hold you to blame for I have no doubt Westmore seduced you. Which is why I cannot abandon you now.'

'So you wish me to become your mistress because you hold me in regard?'

'Yes. I will see to it that you are comfortably situated, perhaps in a town such as Cheltenham, which is conveniently near Braddon Hall. I would, of course, demand the utmost discretion, but there is no reason why I cannot visit you often. Of course, I would see to it that your allowance is increased and that you are provided with the little luxuries a woman wants.'

Surely she was in a bad dream? But no, Arthur was in front of her, the scent of his cologne nearly choking her. The blemishes on his skin were even more pronounced. 'I fear I must decline your offer,' she said.

He gaped at her. 'Decline?' Then he gave a startled laugh. 'My dear Belle, you have no choice.'

Everyone seemed to be telling her she had no choice. 'Yes, I do. I am turning down your offer. I have no desire to be your mistress.'

'Westmore is leaving town. You will have no protector, no one to defend your honour. You will be prey of every rake in London. At least under my protection you will be safe from their advances.'

He planned to defend her honour by making her his mistress? She bit back the inappropriate desire to burst into hysterical laughter. 'You are most kind, but I cannot accept. I—'

'She cannot accept because she is still under my protection.'

They both slowly turned. Justin stood behind them. His face held almost no expression, which was more frightening than if she had seen fury.

'Move away from her,' he told Arthur.

Arthur stared at him and then took a few steps. 'I will

own I am surprised to see you here, Westmore. I thought you had left town.'

'As you can see you are wrong.'

'But you will be leaving.'

'You are correct.' Justin folded his arms. 'And Lady Milborne is leaving with me.'

Arthur stared at him and then swung around to look at Belle for a long moment. He finally spoke. 'I see. You did not tell me that. However, I will be at your service if you should need me.'

He started towards the door only to find Justin in his way. 'She will never need your assistance. I will warn you that if I discover you have had a damn thing to do with the rumours I will ruin you. And if you come near Lady Milborne again, I will put a bullet through you.' Justin spoke with a deadly calm.

Arthur's eyes bulged, but he stood his ground. 'And if you fail to protect her I will do the same.' He picked up his hat and cane and left without looking back.

Justin crossed the room to stand in front of her. 'Did he hurt you?'

'No. He…he made me an improper offer. I am becoming quite used to them so it was nothing to signify.' She gave a strangled laugh. 'Can you imagine what Maria would say if she knew? I wonder if Arthur thought it through. How would he explain it if I actually did accept?'

She found Justin in front of her, a black look on his face. 'Don't even consider it.'

Surprised, she met his gaze. 'I assure you I have no intention of doing so. And I pray you will give up your ridiculous notion of shooting him.'

'I don't want him near you.'

The day was growing more and more peculiar. 'He

did not mean me any harm. In his own way I suppose
he wished to protect me.'

'You are amazingly naïve if that is what you think.
He wants you, my dear, in his bed, and in his power,
and that is the whole of it. I suspect he has wanted you
for some time and finally saw his opportunity. For all I
know he started the rumours in order to force you into
his arms.'

Stung, she said, 'I hardly think Arthur is capable of
that!'

'You are defending him? Is it possible you actually
have a *tendre* for that pompous idiot?' he demanded.

'Of course I do not! I am beginning to think you are
as mad as he is! I do not have a *tendre* for anyone and
if I was so foolish as to have one it would not be for
Arthur!'

His gaze locked with hers, his expression still dark. 'I
would hope you had better sense,' he said shortly. 'You
said you were becoming used to such offers. Has anyone
else approached you?'

She was still miffed at him. 'No, only you.'

'It is hardly the same thing. I did not...' His scowl
deepened. 'I trust you will be ready to leave today?'

'Yes. I have packed what I need. Mrs Bates will stay
a few days to close up the house. I am sending her to
stay with her daughter-in-law, who is approaching her
confinement.'

'If you need anything else you can tell me and I will
see to it.'

'Thank you.'

'Will you bring a maid with you?'

'No, but I have managed before without a maid.' She
had considered taking Hetty, Mrs Bates's niece, but the
girl had suffered such bouts of homesickness since com-

ing to London, even with her aunt present, that Belle had not the heart to insist she accompany her to Devon.

'Once we reach Falconcliff my housekeeper will procure a suitable girl for you.' He hesitated. 'I will send my carriage for you shortly after noon. You will travel with my secretary, Jackson. I plan to be with the colt and will most likely not see you until we stop for the night.'

'Very well.' She clasped her hands, a knot starting to form again in her stomach.

'Then I will see you later.'

She watched him go and wondered if she was doing the right thing. But she really had no choice at all now.

Shortly after noon, Belle stood by the window and watched as a carriage came to a halt in the street below her house. She was about to turn away from the window when the occupant of the carriage stepped down. Instead of the man she had been expecting, she was stunned to see Lady Georgina alight. She stifled a groan. It was too much to hope for that Lady Georgina did not intend to call here. The rap on the door told her otherwise.

She went out to the small hallway and heard Mrs Bates's soft voice and then Lady Georgina's more forceful one. 'I insist on seeing her. I do not care if she is about to depart. If you do not show me in, I will show myself.'

Oh, dear. She could not allow her to bully poor Mrs Bates. She went to the head of the staircase just in time to see Lady Georgina brush past her startled housekeeper. Then Lady Georgina spotted Belle. 'There you are. I will see you now, if you please.' She continued up the stairs. The militant look in her eye was not promising.

She followed Belle into the drawing room. Without preamble she said, 'Is it true you are travelling to Devon with my nephew?'

'Why do you wish to know?'

'Because, my dear Lady Milborne, I do not intend to allow you to go with him.'

'I see.' She had no idea whether she was angry, or curious or merely numb.

'He has certain duties that are associated with a dukedom. One of those is marriage and ensuring that the line continues. If he has no heir, the title will pass to a lesser branch of the family.'

'How very interesting.'

Lady Georgina eyed her sharply. 'You are impertinent.'

'Only because I fail to see what this has to do with me.'

'It has to do with you because as long as he is obsessed with you he will not look for a wife. I do not intend to allow this to go on. Anything can happen, accidents, an illness. He has a duty to secure the succession as quickly as possible.'

'Then perhaps you should discuss this with him.' Her temper was starting to fray.

She did not appear to hear Belle. 'Which is why I am prepared to offer you a substantial sum to disappear for an extensive amount of time. You will no longer present a distraction and he will see he must marry. When it is accomplished and his wife increasing, then you may return if you wish.'

'And where am I to go?'

'Perhaps Italy. It is very pleasant, warm and sunny. My husband's mother was Italian and I still have a villa there. I've no doubt you would be very comfortable.'

'Thank you, but I do not wish to go to Italy. If you will excuse me, I still have some business to attend to before I leave.'

Lady Georgina caught her arm. 'Do you know why he even wants you? For revenge! For the harm you and that knave of a husband did him!'

'I know that.' Belle attempted to pull her arm from the old lady's grasp but Lady Georgina's hand only tightened.

'Then why do you go with him? Do you think he will marry you? You are a fool! You would bring nothing but disgrace upon him and upon this family! You would never make him happy and he would hate you once he discovered you were barren!'

Belle felt as if she had been slapped. She stared at Lady Georgina, feeling ill. 'You do not know that.'

Lady Georgina released her arm. 'You were married for three years and there was no child. I have heard that your husband has sired more than one bastard.'

'I knew nothing of them.' She vaguely heard a rap and realised that Justin's carriage must have arrived. 'I must leave.'

'You will regret this. I will not allow you to ruin him.'

Belle did not reply or look at Lady Georgina as she walked past her. A sandy-haired young man stood in the hall. He looked at her, his gaze impersonal. 'Lady Milborne?'

'Yes.'

'I am Matthew Jackson, the Duke of Westmore's secretary. I am to accompany you today.'

She nodded. Mrs Bates had tears in her eyes when she said goodbye and a lump rose in Belle's throat as she impulsively squeezed her housekeeper's hand.

She followed Mr Jackson outside to the street where

her trunk and valise had already been strapped on to the chaise. Lady Georgina followed her. She looked at Belle for a moment and then stepped into her waiting carriage.

'Lady Milborne.'

Mr Jackson waited for her. She turned and slowly climbed into Justin's chaise and Mr Jackson joined her. The door was shut and the horses set into motion. A wave of loneliness washed over her and she fought it down. She could not allow herself to give into such feelings or she would be truly lost.

Chapter Eight

They reached the inn before nightfall. Belle had fallen into a fitful sleep and she awoke when the motion of the carriage stopped. She opened her eyes, disorientated for a moment, and then realised they had halted.

'We have reached the White Dove. We will stop here for the night,' Jackson said from the other corner.

She nodded. Her travelling companion had proved to be a remarkably efficient young man who had the amazing ability to read in a moving chaise. He had spent most of the journey with a stack of papers on his lap. He was polite but no more and she had no doubt he disapproved of her. Undoubtedly, he wondered why his employer wished to involve himself with a woman of her reputation. Or perhaps he merely disapproved of such relationships on principle. At any rate, his disinclination towards conversation suited her as she was still not feeling particularly well. She peered out and saw they were in the yard of an inn. Another coach was there and a cat sat on a bench outside the door.

Her stomach was starting to hurt again. The coachman opened the door, and Jackson stepped down first and then assisted her down. The cool afternoon air was welcome on her overheated cheeks. She blinked, not certain what to do next.

'Belle.'

She turned and saw Justin approaching them. He looked completely familiar and until she saw him she did not realise how much she needed to see him. He nodded to Jackson. 'I've bespoken two rooms and a private parlour. I would like a word with Lady Milborne and then I will escort her to the parlour.'

'Very well,' Jackson said.

Justin waited for a moment and then took her elbow. 'Was your journey comfortable?' he asked politely.

'Yes, although I will own I slept most of the way.'

'Wise of you. I've requested an early dinner. I will see you to the inn and then I must look after the colt.' He was guiding her towards the building, his touch impersonal.

She suddenly did not want to be left with only the taciturn, disapproving Jackson. For a moment longer, she wanted to be with someone who would at least talk to her. 'May I see your horse?'

He glanced down at her, slight surprise in his eyes. 'If you wish.'

'I would like to.'

'He is in the stable.' With his hand still on her elbow he guided her towards the stables at the back of the inn. He released her arm and she followed him inside, lifting up her skirt a little as she walked. The colt was in the very last stall. Justin spoke softly to the horse. In the dim light of the stable, she could see the animal was in the far corner but at the sound of Justin's voice the horse moved forward.

'He is beautiful,' she said softly. He was a bay with a dish-shaped face and dark, intelligent eyes. He tossed his head but calmed under Justin's hand. 'Have you named him?'

'Not yet.' He stroked the animal's neck. 'You could probably pet him if you wanted to.'

'If he will let me.' The colt stayed still while she touched his soft, sleek neck and then he snorted and moved away. She smiled. 'I think that is as much as he wishes to know me.'

'At least for now.' His thoughts seemed to be elsewhere, but he brought his attention back to Belle. 'I had best escort you to the inn.'

The parlour was small and dark but clean. Jackson was not yet there. She removed her cloak and bonnet and shivered a little. Justin saw her. 'I will have them build a fire for you. Is there anything else you require?'

'Not now.' He was so politely formal. She would prefer his anger over this but the façade around him was impenetrable.

He moved away then. 'I will see to the colt and then join you for dinner.'

'Yes.'

He left the room and she sat down on one of the benches. Her back was beginning to ache a little and she was glad to sit. The proprietor's wife bustled in and built a fire.

Jackson came in a quarter of an hour later and a few minutes after that Justin joined them.

But by the time the pink-cheeked maid brought in the dinner, Belle's appetite had fled. Her head was truly starting to ache and she felt rather ill. She forced a few bites down her throat and listened quietly to the conversation between Jackson and Justin. When the last of the meal had been taken away, she rose. 'I would like to retire. If you will excuse me.'

Justin and Jackson stood as well. 'Will you be able to manage without a maid? Or should I send Mrs Hubbard to help you?' Justin asked.

'I can manage.' She had deliberately worn a gown with a minimum of fastenings.

'I will be up shortly,' he said curtly.

Embarrassed, she nodded to Jackson and then fled. Of course Jackson knew why she was with Justin but nonetheless she could not rid herself of her innate modesty.

Her room was small and clean with a low-beamed ceiling. She washed her hands and face as best as she could with the jug of water. After that she pulled the pins from her hair and took out a clean nightshift. But it was when she was finishing the rest of her ablutions that she realised why she had felt slightly unwell much of the day. She sank down on the bed and wondered what she should do next. But there was really no choice; she would have to tell him.

When his knock came, she jumped, and then rose and opened the door. With more than a little trepidation, she saw he wore a dressing gown over his breeches. He stood there, dark and forbidding. 'Come in,' she said. He stepped inside and closed the door behind him. He turned the key with a deliberate motion then turned and his eyes locked on her.

'Come here, Belle,' he said softly. He took a step in her direction. His eyes had a determined glitter.

Her face must be turning a thousand shades of red. 'There is something you should know first,' she began.

He stopped. 'What?'

She prayed she would not die of embarrassment. 'I…I have begun my courses.' She closed her eyes briefly and then opened them. 'I am sorry.' She had never had to tell Lucien such a personal thing. Her abigail had always informed him when she was indisposed.

He looked taken aback. 'I do not suppose it is something you can help.'

'I suppose it might be possible to…to…that is it is not so bad at the beginning.' What was she saying? Perhaps it would be better if she did die.

'No, I am not that…' he stopped and she sensed he was as embarrassed as she was. He ran his hand through his hair and frowned. 'Do you need anything? Should I send for Mrs Hubbard?'

'No. I should be fine.'

He was still frowning. 'Are you certain?'

'It is not the first time, you know. Women do manage.'

'But you do not have a maid with you.' His face was a study in masculine bewilderment, as if such female mysteries were completely out of his realm. Perhaps they were. She had no idea how his mistresses had dealt with such matters.

'I will be perfectly fine. It is not an illness.' Despite her mortification at even having to discuss this, she felt an almost hysterical urge to giggle.

'If you are certain.' He frowned a little. 'You did not look very well at dinner. Nor did you eat much.'

'Sometimes I do not feel very well at this time.'

'I see. Should I leave you? Or do you need some sort of assistance?'

She had no idea what that would be. 'I really will be fine on my own,' she said firmly. 'I most likely will go straight to bed.'

'I will bid you goodnight, then. If there is anything you need you have only to summon me.'

'Thank you.'

He walked to the door and unlocked it then glanced back at her one more time. 'Lock your door.' He hesitated. 'Goodnight, Belle.'

'Goodnight.'

The door closed softly behind him and then she felt the tears prick her eyelids. She dashed the back of her hand across her eyes. She could not cry—she would not give into such missish behaviour. But it did not help the sudden surge of loneliness that overwhelmed her.

Oh, why must this occur now? She had thought that it would not happen for several more days if at all, for her monthly courses were irregular. She could view it as a reprieve but it did not feel like one. It felt almost as if fate had decreed she was to remain in a sort of purgatory. She would never pay her debt and thus be in his power for all of eternity.

Worse, he had been amazingly kind about the entire business. Unlike Lucien who had, at first, considered her courses an inconvenience to him, and later a sign of her infertility. He had sworn at her and she had come to dread this proof of her inadequacy as a wife. Nor had he anything but disdain for the headache and cramps that had plagued her as well.

She did not want Justin to be so solicitous. For she feared it would make keeping her heart unscathed by this affair impossible.

The painful cramping in her stomach the next morning was not promising. When she sat up, her head spun and she knew the fates were determined to punish her. If only she could crawl back in bed and stay there.

The knock on the door to the hallway caused her to jump. She found a shawl which she draped over her shoulders and padded to the door. She unlocked it and found the proprietor's daughter standing on the other side with a fresh pitcher of water. 'My Mama says I am to help you dress, my lady.'

'Thank you.' She suspected Justin had sent the girl to her. Another kindness which would only add to her debt. She was grateful for Betty's help, nonetheless and after she dressed went downstairs to the parlour.

Jackson was already there. He rose and waited until she had taken the chair across from him, before sitting back down. 'What do you wish to eat? The ham is quite good and there are eggs and toast.'

'Only toast and perhaps tea.' She asked as indifferently as possible, 'Will the Duke join us?'

'He departed a short while ago. But you are to finish your breakfast at your leisure and then we will leave.'

'I see.' She felt oddly disappointed and then told herself it was best if she did not see him. She must not grow to depend on his company.

After a piece of toast and a cup of tea, she felt a little better. By the time Jackson had helped her into the carriage, she had convinced herself she would be fine.

The jolting of the carriage did nothing for her. The familiar cramps had returned and she was beginning to feel slightly nauseous. She sat stiffly upright on the cushions and debated whether she would be better off if she closed her eyes or kept them open.

Perhaps if she concentrated on something else. 'Have you been with the Duke many years?' she asked Jackson.

'Two years,' Jackson said stiffly.

'And where are you from?'

'Manchester, my lady.'

His polite, formal replies did not encourage further comments. She did not want to force conversation on someone so obviously unwilling, so she turned to look out of the window. The scenery passing by only made her feel more ill. She looked quickly down at her lap and closed her eyes.

'Are you ill, my lady?'

She opened her eyes. 'No. Sometimes the motion of a coach can make me feel a little unwell, but it is certain to pass.' At least she hoped so. But the dull cramp in her abdomen reminded her that she was not over the worst of it.

'We can stop if you wish. There is an inn in another five miles.'

'That will not be necessary.' She did not want to hold Justin up. He would regret bringing her more than he undoubtedly already did. But the swaying of the carriage combined with her nearly empty stomach and the pain contrived to work against her. She held on as long as she possibly could, but a mere two hours into the journey she was finally forced to open her eyes. 'I am sorry, but I must ask you to stop the carriage now.' She swallowed. 'I fear I am about to be quite ill.'

Surprise replaced Jackson's stolid expression. 'Er, of course.' He leaned out and rapped sharply on the roof of the carriage. By the time the carriage rattled to a halt, she was starting to retch. Then the door was flung open and she stumbled outside.

Kneeling in the muddy road and losing the contents of her stomach was one of the most humiliating experiences of her life. But suddenly Jackson was beside her and a handkerchief was thrust into her hand. She took it. 'Thank you. I am very sorry.'

'There is no need, my lady. I have assisted on such occasions several times in my life.'

'Have you? Surely not by a roadside?' She sat back.

'Even by a roadside.' He peered into her face. 'Can

you stand? I will help you back into the carriage and then we will head for the inn. You may have me stop the carriage again if needed.'

She allowed him to help her to her feet. 'You are kind, but I do not wish to hold the Duke up. I know he wants to get his horse to Devon as quickly as possible. I am certain to feel much better now.'

He appeared unconvinced. 'We will stop nonetheless. The Duke wished me to watch over you.'

'I pray you will say nothing to him about this.' She resolved she would do anything in her will-power to not be sick again. She was almost convinced that things would be quite fine now that she had lost everything but a mere half-hour later she knew it was not. She closed her eyes and prayed she would not humiliate herself again.

She nearly died of gratefulness when the coach halted and she saw they were at another inn. The fresh air made her feel better and as she followed Jackson to the building she was certain she would be perfectly fine. The innkeeper came to meet them and to her surprise, greeted Jackson as if they were old friends. He showed them to a private parlour and promised to procure refreshments.

Belle sank into a chair, the thought of eating making her feel unwell. She forced herself to speak. 'I will be fine after I rest for a few moments. Please promise me you will not tell the Duke.'

She thought he nodded before he left the room. She closed her eyes, resisting the urge to curl up on the sofa. Her head was now hurting as well and the thought of slipping away into oblivion was becoming more appealing by the moment.

She must have dozed off for the next thing she knew someone was saying her name. Dazed, she opened her eyes and then was completely confused when she saw Justin bending over her. She sat upright. 'What are you doing here?'

'Jackson sent the groom for me. We were not far in front of you. He said you are ill. Why did you not send word earlier?'

She must still be dreaming. He actually appeared worried. 'I did not want him to send word to you at all. It is nothing really. I will be quite fine after I rest.'

'You don't look well. I will procure a room for you and then send for a physician.'

'No! Please do not. I am not ill.'

'Then what is it?' He frowned down at her. 'Is it because of your courses?'

'Yes.' She had no reason to deny it. 'Sometimes on the first day or two I feel out of sorts. Then it passes.'

She waited for his disgust or impatience. 'You should have told me last night,' he said abruptly.

Her cheeks heated. 'It was humiliating enough that I had to tell you such a thing. I had hoped that perhaps I would be fine.'

'You do not need to feel humiliated by telling me.' He still frowned. 'After you are settled in a room I will send Mrs Clarke to assist you. We will halt here.'

'Surely not you as well. You must continue with your colt.'

'I am hardly about to leave you here by yourself.'

'I am quite used to travelling by myself when necessary. I am, after all, five and twenty.'

'A great age,' he said drily. 'You are, however, my responsibility and under my protection. I've no intention of leaving you here while you are ill and without so much as a maid.'

She stared at him. 'I am not your responsibility.'

'You most certainly are.' He straightened. 'One I have no intention of delegating.' He strode to the door. 'Mrs Clarke will be in shortly. By the way, she is a distant cousin of Jackson so I've no doubt she will take good care of you.' He left before she could say a word.

He considered her his responsibility? Certainly not one he wanted if his curt manner and grim expression was any indication. Why had he even brought her with him? She had thought it was only for revenge but then she recalled his offer of marriage. Despite everything between them, he still felt responsible for her. There was no pleasure in the thought.

Justin ran his hand down the colt's sleek neck. Instead of trembling, he now stood still. The animal was doing much better than he had anticipated as if he now did not mind the travel and unfamiliar accommodations quite so much. The Hare and Hart's were certainly luxurious compared to most inns and undoubtedly due more to Jackson's connections rather than to his ducal title, his colt had been given the best stall. He gave the horse a final pat and left him to his hay. He had best return to the inn. And Belle.

He had no idea what he was going to do with her. His anger and bitterness towards her had died the moment she had told him, her face flushed and vulnerable, that she had her courses. Her cool reserve was gone, instead she had looked like a mere girl, her mortification over confessing such a feminine and personal thing apparent. She had looked so fragile in her nightrail with her hair down her back that it had taken all his will power not to pull her into his arms and comfort her.

He'd never thought much about this particular functioning of a woman's body except that it had occasionally inconvenienced him. Certainly he had never thought of it as enhancing a woman's femininity. Or a woman's desirability. So, the surge of protectiveness combined with sheer lust he'd felt had stunned him.

And confused him. Nothing in her behaviour since that one night at Greystone had proved her to be the heartless creature he thought her. Even her rejection of his rash offer of marriage had not been in keeping with the adventuress he wanted her to be. Should she not have accepted him and all the advantages of his title and wealth? He was beginning to think he had been mistaken about her after all. But why then, would she have participated in her husband's plot to kill him? Had Milborne some sort of hold over her? Or had she been telling the truth when she had told him that Milborne would have killed him if she had not said she was part of the trap?

Even after three years, he could still recall her face when he had told her he loved her. She had looked stricken, as if he had mortally wounded her by his declaration. He had not understood her anguish and had only known that she had thrown his love back in his face. But if she had not known of the plot, she had believed he had just purchased her favours for two thousand pounds. She must have felt as betrayed by his apparent treachery as he had felt, a few minutes later, by hers.

If she did tell the truth then, his actions towards her were unforgivable. He had stripped her of everything; her reputation, her family, all but her chastity which he had vowed to take as coolly and deliberately as possible.

He knew he was no longer capable of such callousness because he no longer hated her. If indeed, he ever had.

Jackson accosted him almost as soon as he stepped inside the inn. 'Lady Milborne is awake. Susan has just brought her a bite to eat. She still insists she can continue with the journey.' He looked reproachful as if it were Justin's fault she wanted to continue.

Didn't she have an ounce of sense? 'I will talk to her.'

He knocked and entered when he heard her soft reply. She was in her room sitting in a chair near the bed. A cup of tea sat on a near by table. Soft colour stole into her cheeks when she saw him and he cursed the surge of desire that shot through him.

He scowled. 'You should be in bed.'

'Why?'

'Because you are obviously not well.'

'I feel much better.' She looked discomfited. 'I am sorry. I did not wish to delay your journey by such… such female weakness. I am certain we could continue on if you wish.'

'Which I do not.' He came towards her and stopped. 'And you do not need to apologise. I do not consider this a female weakness.'

'Don't you? You are very kind. Which is more than I deserve—I know I have ruined your life in every way possible.' She did not look at him.

Hell. She was about to cry. It was so unlike the cool, remote woman he knew that he was completely stunned. Just as he had been last time in his carriage. Without thinking, he reached down and took her hands and pulled her up. 'Don't do this,' he said roughly. He pulled her to him, his arms going around her soft, warm body. She felt perfect in his arms, her curves melting against his. She pressed her face into his chest and then gave a little sniff. He groaned and then tilted her chin up. Her lips parted slightly, her eyes questioning and then his mouth came down on hers.

She offered no resistance this time. Her hands tangled in his hair, inflaming his desire. He rained kisses on her

mouth and then on her neck. His hands cupped her
breasts and although she stiffened for a moment, she
made no protest when his fingers circled the hard nipples
beneath her gown. His hand splayed her soft belly. The
realisation she wore no stays threatened to drive him
over the edge.

It was only when he realised he was about to push
her down on the bed that sanity returned and he pulled
his mouth from hers. She was breathing hard and when
she opened her eyes, he saw his own desire reflected in
her hazel eyes. That she returned his desire stunned him
for he had thought she would resist him to the end.

He felt a brief surge of triumph at finally breaking
down her resistance, but the victory was short-lived. He
wanted all of her, not just her body and the thought
terrified him.

He took a step back. 'I should let you rest.'

'Yes.' She pulled her gaze away from him. He could
almost feel her inwardly retreating from him.

'Then if you are well enough we will leave in the
morning.'

'Very well.' The distance in her voice was there.

He wanted to swear. Instead, he pulled her around to
face him. 'Goodnight, Belle.' He kissed her again
roughly, and then left.

They reached Falconcliff three days later.

Belle had her first glimpse of it as they rounded a
bend in the road. The carriage had been travelling a route
that followed the winding cliffs along the coast. She had
been fascinated by her glimpses of the water pounding
against the shore and Jackson spoke to her twice before
she realised he had addressed her. She looked up and
saw the house. It sat on the edge of a promontory, a

square sprawling structure of grey stone, silhouetted against the clear blue sky. It looked rather romantic and frightening all at once. She tore her gaze away and fought down the unexpected bout of nerves that suddenly hit her. 'I do not suppose there are any ghosts,' she said to Jackson.

He smiled. 'I have not heard of any. Although there are certain passageways where one might expect to see a spectre. Two decades ago, however, you might have encountered a smuggler or two.'

'They were actually in the house, I believe.' She could still recall the teasing glint in Justin's eye when he had told her about the smugglers and how, as a boy, he had actually watched them bring a boatload of goods ashore. Instead of being properly frightened, however, she had turned the tables on him and declared she could think of nothing more interesting than seeing such a thing. She fought down the wave of sadness. She doubted Justin would ever tease her again in such a way.

'Only in the cellars,' Jackson said. 'The current Duke's grandfather did not care for the property and left the running of it solely in his steward's hands. His steward was nicely bribed to turn a blind eye to the more illegal activities taking place on the estate. However, the next Duke chose to put a stop to it. Some of the passages leading to the cellars were starting to cave in and he feared there would soon be a loss of life.'

She smiled at Jackson. 'So at least there is something romantic about the house.'

They had become quite companionable. She had discovered he was the youngest son of a rector and he was also much more to Justin than a secretary; he often acted as an adviser, and even more than that, he was a friend. She had increasingly come to view him as her friend as well. She hardly counted Justin in that category. Since that night he had kissed her, she had scarcely seen him except at meals. He had returned to the stiff formality he had shown most of the trip and she would have thought he was completely indifferent to her, but once or twice she had caught a look almost of longing in his eyes when they rested on her.

Her marriage had taught her that it was possible for desire and contempt to co-exist and Justin could want her without even liking her. But she could not forget his kindness in a situation that had only filled Lucien with contempt.

She had no idea what would happen once they reached Falconcliff. In fact, she had no idea what he expected of her at all.

Chapter Nine

The housekeeper, Mrs Keith, was tall and very stout, with a walk that looked exactly like a duck's. Belle followed her up the winding staircase and down a narrow hall that seemed to go on forever. Mrs Keith finally stopped in front of one of the doors. 'This will be your chamber, my lady. I hope you will find it suitable.'

Belle stepped inside. It was an enormous room with a carved wooden mantelpiece on one side and tall windows. The bed was huge and old-fashioned and there was an old chest in one corner. 'It will be very suitable,' she said, although in truth she found it rather daunting.

Mrs Keith opened a door on the wall opposite the bed. 'This is the sitting room.' She seemed to be waiting for Belle's perusal so Belle obediently looked at the room. It was smaller than the bedchamber and at first glance, appeared much more cosy.

'His Grace said you did not bring a maid with you. I will send Ellen in to help you unpack. Perhaps you will wish to rest before dinner. His Grace keeps country hours.' Mrs Keith paused. 'Is there anything else you need, my lady?'

'No, not now.' Belle waited until the housekeeper had

bustled out before sinking down on the wing chair near the window. Her head ached a little from the coach journey and she felt tired and rather homesick. She missed Chloe terribly. And even Maria, despite everything.

She clasped her hands together and refused to give into the desire to burst into tears. On the journey, as uncomfortable and disconcerting as it had been, she had felt suspended in time. Her time in London seemed ages ago and what awaited her at the journey's end had been enveloped in a foggy future. Her headache and cramps had subsided by the third day and she had almost looked forward to sitting in the carriage and watching the countryside pass. There had been a certain predictability in her days. But now she had arrived, she had no idea what would happen.

She rose and looked out of the window. Her room faced a rather tangled garden with an old wooden arbour and a bench. Beyond the garden she could see an expanse of lawn bordered by trees and shrubs. And beyond that a glimpse of sparkling blue water. The sun was shining although huge white clouds drifted overhead.

She was tired but too restless to lie down. Perhaps a walk would take her mind off other things. Justin had briefly greeted her, but after he saw her into the house had departed again. Apparently she was to be left to her own devices.

So it hardly mattered whether she stayed in the house or not.

The scratch on the door made her turn. A young maid entered. She looked rather hesitant. 'I am Ellen, my lady. Mrs Keith sent me to help you. She said you would like to rest. Should I help you undress?'

'Thank you, Ellen, but I have decided I would like to walk instead.' Belle smiled at the girl. 'Perhaps you could tell me if it is possible to view the sea from the grounds.'

'There is a path that leads from the garden. But it is overgrown.'

'Could you show me from the window?' Belle asked.

Ellen walked to the window. 'See? It is the one by the bench.'

There was indeed a path that led into the trees on one side of the house. 'That is what I will do, then.' She smiled again at Ellen, liking her sweet, round face. 'Can you show me the best way to get to the garden?'

Ellen returned her smile a little shyly. Belle tied the ribbons of her bonnet and then drew on her gloves. She finally decided she would take a shawl and draped it over her gown and was glad of Ellen's direction for the passages in the house seemed long and confusing. They finally came to a drawing room where French windows led to a terrace with steps down to the garden. She left Ellen and stepped out on to the terrace. The sun touched her cheeks and she could smell the tantalising scent of the sea.

Ellen had not been wrong; the path was overgrown and after catching her shawl twice on branches, she finally came to an opening. The path opened to a cliff and spread before her, sparkling like the bluest gem, was the sea. She caught her breath, never having imagined it to be so blue. Or so expansive that she would feel like a mere speck. The air smelled wet and salty and wonderful and Belle suddenly felt a surge of happiness.

She pulled off her bonnet, wanting to feel the breeze and the sun on her face and knowing perfectly well she would freckle by tomorrow. She started to walk, not really caring where she went, only that she wanted more of the treasure in front of her.

She finally came to an old wooden bench and sat down. Far out from shore she saw the sails of a vessel, and closer in, a few smaller craft bobbing on the water. Seabirds circled in the sky and occasionally she could hear their cries. Absorbed in the scene before her, she jumped when she heard a shout.

'Belle!'

She jerked around. Justin was striding towards her. He was hatless, the breeze ruffling his dark hair. He halted in front of her. 'What the devil are you doing here and by yourself?'

Her pleasure was abruptly shattered. 'I wanted to view the sea. I have never seen it before.'

'Alone? When I was informed you had left the house without a word—' He stopped and ran a hand through his hair. 'Damn it, Belle! I thought….' He scowled.

'You thought what?'

'Nothing,' he said shortly.

With sudden insight, she saw his dark looks actually hid worry. 'You thought that I had left?'

'I've no idea what I thought. Don't ever go from the house again like that.'

He had really thought she would just leave him. Belle stood. 'I won't. I promise I will always leave word with you where I am. It was only that I wanted to see the water and I thought you were probably occupied with other matters and would not notice if I slipped away for a little while.'

'You should not be here alone. You do not know your way.'

'I thought I would follow the exact path back. Since there is only one I have no doubt I would have made it safely back to the house.'

'I don't want you wandering around by yourself.'

She should be angry at his arrogance, instead she wanted to touch his face and kiss away the stubborn look. 'Very well, your Grace. I promise I will not wander about by myself. Will that satisfy you?'

'No.' His eyes locked with hers for a moment and then he gave a short laugh. 'Yes.' He moved a little away from her. 'So you have never seen the sea?'

'No, not until today.' She smiled at him. 'It is so big and so endless. I think I could sit here for hours and just look and never have enough of it!'

His mouth was beginning to relax. 'You have decided all of this in less than half a day?'

'Yes. I knew from the moment I saw it from the carriage. Which is why I decided straight away to come here.'

'Then your effort should not be wasted. We can go to the shore if you'd like.'

'Oh, I would! If you do not have something else you would rather do.'

'No, I do not.' He ran his eyes over her. 'You should put on your bonnet.'

She had forgotten about it. She put it on and quickly tied the ribbons.

'This way,' he said. They walked for a short distance to where another path branched off down the slope. He started down first and then held out his hand. 'It is a bit steep. I would not want you to slip.'

She placed her hand in his and he helped her down the path. It was steep and rocky in places and she was glad she had worn her half-boots. She nearly slipped at the bottom and then she forgot about the path when she reached the end and found herself in a small cove with a sandy beach. He led her towards the shore and they stood there for a moment, watching the waves lap. His hand felt warm and strong around hers and, for a moment, she felt completely safe with him.

It was an odd sensation, one she had so rarely experienced since her marriage, that she was stunned.

She looked up at him, taking in the strong lines of his jaw and nose, the dark lashes that surrounded his dark eyes. Certainly he was handsome, but it was the strength of his personality that made him so devastatingly attractive. Too attractive. She caught her breath and looked away. It would be too easy to fall in love with him. She could not allow that.

Justin released her hand. 'We can get closer if you'd like. You can remove your boots and stand in the waves.'

She looked back up at him and his eye held a distinctly devilish gleam, as if he expected her to refuse such a scandalous idea. She smiled. 'I would like that.' She looked around and saw a large piece of whitish wood she could use for a bench. She sat and then reached down and began to unlace her half-boots.

The next thing she knew he was kneeling at her feet and his hand stayed hers. 'I can do this.' His eyes locked with hers, the devilish glint still there. She felt breathless when she realised he was flirting with her. As he had at Greystone.

She gave a little laugh. 'I really do not think it is at all fitting to have a duke at my feet.'

'Why not?' His mouth curved in a wicked smile. 'I am at your service, my lady. As I always have been.'

Her cheeks heated. 'I do not think I need your services.'

'No? You might change your mind.' His gaze went to her mouth.

'I…' The most wanton thoughts filled her head.

Thoughts that had to do with lips, and tongues and heat. She jerked her hand out from under his and straightened. 'I…I have changed my mind about wading.'

He finished unlacing her first boot. 'Afraid? There is no need to be. I will make certain you won't be hurt.'

She had no idea whether he was talking about the water or something else entirely. Her body felt hot and prickly as he untied the laces to her other boot and then gently removed it from her foot. But when his hand moved up her ankles to her calf, she yelped. 'Wh…what are you doing?'

His brow shot up. 'Removing your stockings. I would not think you would want them to get wet.'

'Actually I do not mind at all.' His hand still rested on her calf, burning through the thin silk.

'They will be ruined. Besides, you will not experience the full pleasures of the water lapping over your feet. Or the sand between your toes.'

'Then I will remove them myself.'

'But I insist.' His voice was polite as if he was merely offering to allow her to go first through a doorway.

'No! It would not be at all proper. We are in a…a public place and anyone could come along. Please, I would rather do it myself.'

His hand slid down to her ankle. 'So, you are saying that if we were somewhere more private you would not object?'

'Of course I would.' Why had she ever even thought about doing this? No lady would ever even consider baring her ankles to wade in the sea and particularly in front of a man to whom she was not related. But then, she thought with more than a little despair, she was no longer a lady. Not in anyone's eyes. So, what did it matter?

Justin's eyes were on her face and he removed his hand from her ankle. 'There is no need to look so blue-devilled. I promise I won't do anything you don't like.' He stood. 'Remove your stockings. I'll turn my back while you do so and take my own boots and stockings off. There is no need to worry about someone seeing you. This is my property and, for the most part, is quite private.'

She nodded and waited until he walked away from her. She did not glance his way as she peeled off her stockings and placed them carefully with her half-boots, then rose. The sand felt cool and grainy between her toes.

She glanced at Justin. His feet were bare as well, as were his strong, muscular calves. She swallowed but before she could look away, he saw her. 'Ready? Then come.'

He waited for her to join him and together they walked to the edge of the water. 'I should warn you it is cold,' he said.

'I won't mind.' She stepped daringly close and a wave lapped at her feet. He was right, it was cold but the feel of the water was so delightful she hardly cared. She picked up her skirt and stepped further out. A gurgle of laughter escaped her when the water washed over her toes. 'This is wonderful! How can you bear to be in London when you have this?'

She turned to look at him and his expression wiped the laughter from her face. 'But of course, you must be used to it. I must sound like the most idiotic of school-girls.'

'No.' His eyes were on her face. 'I have never seen you laugh before. Not like that.'

'Oh.' She felt ridiculous under his scrutiny and self-conscious that she was standing in the sea, her ankles exposed, the hem of her skirt wet and dirty and laughing in a way she had not since she had left school. 'I must look extremely foolish.'

'You look beautiful. I would give you the sea if it were possible, just to see you laugh in such a way.'

'Justin…'

But he had already caught her up in his arms. His mouth descended on hers in a kiss that made her forget she stood at the shore of the sea. Her skirt dropped from her hands and she did not notice that it trailed in the water. She only knew him: the taste of his mouth, the feel of his chest against hers, the beating of his heart.

He lifted his mouth and stepped away from her. 'That was not what I intended to do. I vowed I would stay away from you.'

'Why?' The day felt a little less bright. 'Or perhaps I do not need to ask. I imagine you must despise me.'

'You think I would kiss you like that if I despised you?' He caught her hand. 'Come with me. I don't want to stand in the sea and talk.'

He led her from the water to the wood she had used before as a bench. 'Let's sit here.'

She sat on one end and he sat next to her, his thigh pressing against hers. She could feel his warmth through her thin skirt. He turned to look at her. 'I don't despise you, Belle.'

She glanced at him. 'I can't imagine why you don't. After what I did to you.'

'Did you do anything to me?' he asked softly.

She was puzzled. 'What do you mean?'

'Did you conspire with your husband to kill me?'

'No, I never did.'

'I believe you.'

Stunned, she stared at him. 'But why would you believe me now? You did not before.'

'Because, except for that one moment when you told me you knew of your husband's trap, I have never found anything to indicate you are other than what you appear. I was determined to find some evidence that your lovely face and sweet smile hid the soul of a wicked seductress. But there is no evidence and so I was wrong.' His eyes were on her face. 'I have no right to beg your forgiveness, but I will hope that some day you will forgive me. I've no doubt it is you who must despise me for participating in a wager which must have seemed the worst betrayal of a friend and then, three years later, setting out to seduce you.' He looked away from her towards the water.

'Why did you wager for me?'

He glanced back at her and a wry smile touched his mouth. 'I had some idea that I might be able to save you from your husband. I had no idea how, but at the very least I intended to make certain you did not fall into the clutches of Banbury or Farley.'

'I see.' So he had wanted to protect her after all. She should have known that.

'Do you?' he asked. 'I have destroyed your reputation, your life, based on my own blindness. You do not know how damnably sorry I am.'

She touched his arm. 'Then I will repeat your words and tell you that I don't despise you. How can I when Lucien hurt you so terribly? I cannot blame you for wanting revenge for I would have as well. And I must ask your forgiveness for I hurt you as well by doubting you.'

'There is nothing to forgive.'

'But there is.'

'You are too good.' His mouth curved in an odd smile. 'I always considered you too far above me—I suspect you still are.'

'But I am not.' She caught his hand. 'I could not understand how someone like you would even notice the dull mouse I thought myself to be. But you did not mind when I had nothing to say and you made me laugh and I did not feel so stupid. Except when you attempted to teach me to play billiards.'

This time his smile held amusement. 'I would not have called you stupid. Merely unskilled.' His smiled faded and she dropped his hand. 'So what do we do now?' he asked. 'I've no intention of forcing you to my bed. I've torn up my copy of the contract and I trust you will do the same.'

She suddenly felt cold but it was not only from the clouds that had covered the sun. 'I can leave tomorrow, then.'

He stared at her. 'That is not what I meant. I would have you...' He frowned and looked up at the sky. 'It is going to rain. We need to leave the beach and then we can finish the conversation at the house.'

She nodded and sat back down on the log to pull on her stockings and boots. He handed her a handkerchief.

'You'll need to remove the sand from your feet first.'

She nodded and bent her head, her cheeks still warm. As she finished, she saw clouds had blown in and the wind had whipped up. The atmosphere suddenly felt as whirling and charged as her emotions.

They walked back to the house in silence. By the time they reached the terrace, the wind was blowing in strong gusts and large drops of rain had started to fall. He caught her hand, pulling her up the steps. Justin pushed open the French door and then stopped abruptly.

He muttered an oath and dropped her hand. Belle caught her breath, almost careening into him. It was then she saw the visitors. If she could have run then, she would have.

The man was tall and broad-shouldered and, despite his elegant appearance, she had no doubt he was very powerful. The woman who sat on the sofa was equally elegantly dressed and quite beautiful.

Justin drew in a breath. 'Giles. Marguerite. I will own I was not expecting you. Otherwise I would have been here to welcome you in a more suitable fashion.' For one of the first times since Belle had known him he sounded flustered.

The woman rose. 'We had heard you were to be here a day or two ago, but when you did not arrive, we were rather worried. So we decided we would stop and see if there was word of you. Mr Jackson informed us you were home although out, but we decided we would wait.' Her smile was warm, but when her gaze fell on Belle, the warmth faded. 'I do not believe I have met your guest.'

Justin took Belle's hand and brought her forward. 'Lady Milborne, may I present Lord and Lady Haversham? Their estate borders on Falconcliff.'

'I am pleased to meet you,' Lady Haversham said coolly.

'And I am pleased to meet you.' She met Lady Haversham's gaze with as much aplomb as possible under the circumstances. The name of Haversham was vaguely familiar and then she recalled why. Lord Haversham had been Justin's superior, the man he had rescued during Waterloo.

'Lady Milborne,' Lord Haversham said politely. His expression was no less cool and she knew very well that they were well aware of who she was. And why she was here. And they did not approve.

She could not fault them. 'My lord.' She managed to meet his eyes.

She turned to Justin. 'I...I imagine you must wish to converse with your friends in private. And I must change. If you will pardon me.'

She left before he could say anything. She feared it she stayed much longer, she would burst into tears.

Ellen had just finished helping Belle dress for dinner when Mrs Keith bustled in. 'His Grace wished me to inform you that Lord and Lady Haversham will be dining with him tonight as well.'

'Thank you.' The possibility of pleading a headache had crossed her mind, but she decided it would only be cowardly. She had no idea what he had told them, if anything to explain her presence, but if any of the rumours had reached their ears, she wondered that they would even consent to sit at the same table with her.

She entered the drawing room with a great deal of trepidation. Lord and Lady Haversham were already present as well as Justin. Lord Haversham and Justin were conversing near the mantelpiece and Lady Haversham was standing near the window. In profile, her belly was slightly rounded, and Belle saw she was with child. Unexpected envy and longing hit her with such force she was stunned. Then she saw everyone look at her and she forced herself to move into the room.

Justin came to her side. He had changed as well and wore a dark coat and pantaloons. They all looked very elegant and she felt plain and dowdy in her simple cream gown. His expression was polite, with none of the pas-

sion she had seen in his eyes at the shore. The afternoon
had begun to seem like a dream.

'We will dine shortly,' he said. 'Come and talk to
Lady Haversham.'

She was doubtful that Lady Haversham wished to
converse with her, but she crossed the room with him.

'At least the rain has stopped,' Lady Haversham remarked when they reached her. Her gaze fell on Belle.
'Justin told me that you have not seen the sea before.'

'No. It is very lovely.' She knew she must sound stiff.
Justin moved away and she resisted the urge to grab his
arm and force him to stay with her. 'I had no idea it
would be so grand. I suppose that is why I decided I
must wade in it the very first thing, which is why I
looked so dishevelled when I met you.'

Lady Haversham seemed to unbend a little. 'I quite
understand. I did the very same thing when I first saw
it. I insisted that Giles stop the carriage so I might get
out and touch it. He would not allow me to remove my
slippers so I fear they became quite ruined.' She smiled
a little and then it faded. 'How long will you be at Falconcliff?'

'Perhaps a few weeks. I have not decided.'

'I see.' Her clear blue eyes studied Belle as if she
could not quite make up her mind about her. But before
she could say more, dinner was announced.

Belle might have enjoyed the dinner if the circumstances had been different. Both Lord and Lady Haversham were excellent conversationalists. Lady Haversham
had been with her husband at the Congress in Vienna
and later at the Duchess of Richmond's ball on the eve
of Waterloo. She learned, as well, that Lady Haversham
and Justin had grown up on neighbouring estates in
Kent. She realised she knew very little about his life

during the years he had been away from England. The camaraderie between them left her in no doubt that they cared deeply for Justin.

She was a complete outsider.

Belle was relieved when the dinner was over. Her relief was short-lived when she realised that she and Lady Haversham were to withdraw and leave the men to their brandy. She had no idea what she would say to the cool and elegant Lady Haversham.

The other woman apparently knew the house very well. She led Belle to the drawing room with the confidence of one who had been there many times before. She indicated one of the sofas near the mantelpiece. 'Please sit down, Lady Milborne.'

Belle sat and Lady Haversham took the chair next to her. The gaze she turned on Belle's face held no warmth. 'As you perhaps gathered, I grew up with Justin and I consider him a brother. He was nearly killed and then forced to leave England because of your husband. I do not know all the details, but enough to know that you hurt him badly. I do not intend to let you hurt him again. He saved my husband's life at Waterloo and I owe him a debt I can never repay.'

'I do not intend to hurt him,' Belle said quietly.

'Then why are you here?'

'Because I too have debts I must repay.'

'I see. And what debts are those?'

'Justin was merely a pawn in my husband's scheme for revenge. He had to pay for my husband's madness. My husband paid nothing and so I am paying his debt for him. And my own. That is why I am here.' She was too tired to dissemble. Let Lady Haversham make of it what she wanted.

'You are repaying your debt to him by becoming his mistress?' Lady Haversham appeared incredulous.

'That was our original agreement. We signed a contract that outlined the terms. At the end of the Season my debt will have been paid.' She looked at Lady Haversham. 'Or would have been. He changed his mind and does not want me after all. So you need not worry as I will no doubt be leaving shortly.'

'Good heavens! A contract? That is so…so cold!'

'It was only to be a business arrangement.' Belle found her cheeks were heating despite her effort to sound cool. 'We were not entering into it for any other reason.'

'Indeed!' Lady Haversham stared at her. 'So Justin offered you *carte blanche* and you accepted merely for business purposes?'

'Something like that. My husband owed him two thousand pounds. He did not want the money so we came to another arrangement.' She felt her cheeks grow even hotter.

To Belle's surprise, Lady Haversham's brow snapped down. 'He forced you to become his mistress in order to pay your husband's debt? Why ever would he do such a despicable thing?'

'My husband set out to destroy him and he nearly succeeded. I, too, hurt him. I cannot blame him for wanting payment. But his behaviour has not been despicable at all. For you see that, despite our agreement, I am his mistress in name only. He informed me today that he has torn up the contract. I do not think you need to concern yourself that he will be hurt by me because there is nothing between us.'

'I am beginning to think that I should worry about you as well. So he has not seduced you, despite your agreement. And you think there is nothing between you.' Her coldness had disappeared and she stared at Belle with fascination.

Belle flushed. 'Of course there is not. I would not have told you any of this except that I wanted to reassure you that Justin is in no danger from me. I will leave here as soon as possible.'

'Without paying your debt?'

Belle looked away. 'He does not want payment. He made that very clear.'

Lady Haversham suddenly smiled. 'Oh, but I think you are wrong. He is very interested in your fulfilling your obligation. I suspect that now that he has you here, he will chivalrously refuse to take advantage of you under his roof.' Her smile faded. 'I will own I was not pleased when Brandt sent word that Justin meant to bring you here. I was determined to defend him against you. But I do not think I am wrong when I say that you care for him.'

'No, you are not wrong and that is why I must go.'

'I think,' Lady Haversham said, 'that is why you must stay.'

They both looked up as the men entered the drawing room. Lady Haversham touched Belle's hand for a brief moment. 'If you need anything, you have only to send for me.' She rose and smiled at her husband. 'My love, I rather think we should depart. I am tired and I've no doubt Justin and Lady Milborne are fagged as well from their journey.'

Her husband's answering smile left no doubt of the strong bond between them. 'If that is your wish.' He grinned at Justin. 'I fear that I am reduced to obeying her every whim.'

'Hardly.' Lady Haversham made a face and caught

Justin's hands. 'We will expect you very soon at Haversham Hall. And Lady Milborne.' She suddenly kissed his cheek and stepped back.

Haversham bowed over Belle's hand. 'Goodnight, Lady Milborne.' He looked at Justin. 'I will see the colt tomorrow, if I may.'

They made their departures and suddenly the house seemed all too quiet. She turned and saw Justin was staring at the mantelpiece. He turned his gaze to her. 'I imagine you are fatigued as well. You may retire if you want.'

His voice was polite. That he was dismissing her was clear. She looked at him for a moment. 'Goodnight, then.'

'Goodnight, Belle.'

She made her way to her room and closed the door behind her. The lamp had been lit and the room was warm, but it did not erase the sudden loneliness in her heart.

And why had she bared her soul in such a way to Lady Haversham? And confessed why she was here? Lady Haversham had been kind, more than kind, but she should not have told her all those things.

And how could Lady Haversham think Justin still wanted her to fulfil her contract terms? He had made it very clear he did not want her here. And certainly not in his bed.

She would tell him tomorrow she intended to leave as soon as possible. Despite Lady Haversham's words, she could think of no reasons for staying.

Chapter Ten

She woke the next morning to another clear blue sky and to the sound of quiet footsteps. For a moment, she had no idea where she was and then she remembered. She was at Falconcliff. Her stomach fluttered and she resisted the urge to crawl back under the snug, warm bedclothes. She opened her eyes and sat up. Ellen had just set a fresh pitcher of water on the dresser. She turned and gave Belle a shy smile. 'Good morning, my lady.' She came to stand by the bed and folded her hands neatly in front of her. 'Mrs Keith says to ask you if you would like a tray brought to you or do you want to take breakfast in the dining room?'

'The dining room, I think. Is the Duke up as well?' she asked.

'He has already gone to meet Lord Haversham,' Ellen said. 'Should I help you dress now?'

'Yes, if you please.' So he had already left the house. Disappointment washed over her. She told herself it was only because she wanted to tell him as soon as possible that she intended to leave. But she knew the real reason was because she wanted to see him.

* * *

After she had dressed and breakfasted on toast and coffee, she wandered into the hallway and wondered what she should do with herself. Jackson was just coming out of one of the doors. He saw her and then crossed to her side. 'Good morning, Lady Milborne,' he said politely. 'I trust you slept well.'

It was nice to see a familiar face. She smiled at him. 'Yes, thank you. How are you?'

'Very well. I am glad to be back at Falconcliff.' He cleared his throat. 'The Duke wished me to inform you that he will see you when he returns from Haversham Hall. Meanwhile, you are to explore the house or grounds as you please, although if you want to venture beyond the gardens I am to accompany you. He also has an extensive library which you might like to visit.'

She suspected Jackson was very busy and so she did not want to bother him with the garden. 'The library would be nice. I can find my way there if you wish to tell me.'

'I will be delighted to take you there myself.' She followed him across the hallway and down a short wing. No longer reserved in her presence, he talked the entire way. 'The library was built in 1786. The fourth Duke was a collector of books and did not consider the current library adequate. He consequently decided to add on this room. His Duchess then insisted that he add on a music room as well and thus the room grew to a wing.'

He stopped and allowed her to pass him into the room. It was magnificent. Tall windows on the far side revealed a glimpse of the sea. The walls were lined with books and in the middle was a table with chairs, a globe and heavy books of maps. Wing chairs and a sofa were grouped around a mantelpiece and near the window was another group of chairs. 'What a wonderful room!' She turned to Jackson with a smile. 'I have no doubt I will entertain myself very well in here.' She could hardly wait to sit in one of the chairs by the window.

He hesitated. 'Are you certain? I would be happy to show you the house or the gardens.'

'Oh, no. I will be more than happy in here.' She was already starting across towards the window.

He followed her. 'As you wish. If you need anything you have only to send for me. Should I have tea brought in to you?'

'That would be nice,' she said absently. She already stood at the window. The water reflected the deep pure blue of the sky and she felt a surge of happiness.

Jackson glanced at her face. 'Then I will leave you. You may borrow any of the volumes as well.'

'Thank you.' She gave him another smile and he returned it with one of his rare ones, before he quietly left the room.

She watched the water and thought that she would like to find a cottage by the sea. A small one, with a view if possible, but if not, at least with a path near by that would take her directly there. Or she could rent rooms, if she must. After a while, Mrs Keith came in with a steaming pot of tea and a cup and saucer, and Belle finally took one of the chairs. Perhaps if she lived some place like this, the loss of Chloe would not be so hard to bear.

For after she left Falconcliff, she did not expect she would see Chloe again.

Or Justin.

She thrust the thoughts aside. She would not think about that. She would think about her cottage. And living by the sea. She turned her gaze to the water again.

She was so engrossed she did not notice when someone entered the room. It took her a few moments to sense she was no longer alone. She glanced up. Justin stood behind her.

He was dressed in buckskin breeches, a plain coat and boots. He still carried his crop so he must have come directly from outside.

Belle set her teacup and saucer awkwardly down on the small table next to the chair and rose. 'Good day, your Grace.' At least her voice was steady, although her knees felt shaky at the sight of him.

His brow shot up. 'Yesterday you called me "Justin". I prefer that over "your Grace". At least from you.'

'Do you?' She felt flustered. He looked relaxed and there was a little smile on his mouth, almost as if he were pleased to find her there. She could not let that distract her from what she needed to say to him. 'I need to talk to you.'

'And I need to talk to you.' His eyes swept over her face. 'I rather think I will let you go first. What is it?'

'I wanted to tell you that I will, of course, leave Falconcliff as soon as possible.'

'Amazing how our minds run along the same lines. I wanted to tell you that you are to stay at Falconcliff with me until I return to London.'

She stared at him. 'But why? I thought that you would want me gone since we no longer have a contract.'

'Why would you think that?' He sounded merely curious, but his gaze remained on her face.

'If I am not to be your mistress then I can think of no reason why you would want me here.'

'Can't you? Aside from the fact that I am not about to ruin you and then cast you out into the cold, you might consider that I want your company for reasons other than bedding you. Of course, if you should decide you would like my company for that particular purpose I would be more than happy to oblige you.'

Her cheeks heated. 'I do not think so.'

'But you are not certain.' His smile was rather wicked. 'You may think about it and then let me know if you change your mind. Just because we no longer have a contract does not mean I am not amenable to the terms.'

From the glint in his eye, she knew he was teasing her, but her gaze went to his lips and she suddenly recalled yesterday's kiss. She pulled her gaze away from his mouth. 'For what other reasons do you want my company?'

'For a picnic, for one thing.'

'A picnic?'

'A picnic by the sea. I rather thought you might enjoy that.'

'Oh, I would!' She was too revealing again. 'I would very much enjoy a picnic. Thank you,' she said more primly.

He raised a brow. 'You are most welcome.' He glanced down at her feet. 'You will want to put on shoes that are sturdier than those you are wearing. And a gown you will not mind getting wet.'

'Oh, yes.' She could not help smiling at him. His gaze suddenly darkened and she caught her breath. Her pulse leapt at the awareness in his eyes and she knew Lady Haversham was right.

Justin shifted away from her. 'Can you be ready within the hour?' His voice was carefully polite again as if he wanted to hide his emotions.

'Yes.'

She watched him leave the room. The thought of spending a day with him filled her with happiness, but mixed with it was a sort of despair. She could not deny that she was already half in love with Justin. And there was no future in it at all.

Belle stared down at the pool below her. Tiny creatures moved about in their own watery world. She had never seen a tide pool before and she was fascinated.

They had to climb over some rather large rocks to reach the pool. She had not cared that her skirt was wet or her half-boots were probably ruined at least for purposes other than this, or that her hair had fallen out of its pins. She had felt as if she was on an adventure into unknown lands and such untidiness only came with such journeys. She bent down to get a closer view of the round creatures that looked like a large pincushion. 'What are those?'

'Anemones,' Justin said. She glanced up at him. He leaned against a larger rock, arms folded. He looked rather like a pirate with his open-necked shirt and buckskin breeches and bare feet. She was still rather resentful that he could climb on the rocks without shoes but forced her to wear hers. She grudgingly accepted his explanation that he had been doing such things since boyhood and so his feet were toughened, whereas her feet were only used to carpeted rooms and smooth bare floors.

An indulgent smile played around his mouth. 'We should go back. The tide is starting to come in.'

'Must we?' She hated to go. He had been remarkably patient with her questions and exclamations over every new discovery. And surprisingly knowledgeable.

'Yes, unless you want to be stranded on these rocks.' He unfolded his arms and pushed away from the rock. He held out his hand and she placed hers in his, a tingling going down her arm at his touch. Justin pulled her to her feet and she stumbled a little so that he caught her against his chest. His chest was strong and warm and he smelled of sea and wind and his own unique scent. She wished she could stay there forever. His arms tightened around her for a moment and then he released her. 'We need to go.'

Belle nodded. He stepped down to the next rock and held out his hand. She took it and gingerly climbed down. He helped her across the rest of the rocks to the sand and when she turned to look she saw the water had already risen over the lowest of the rocks.

Justin dropped her hand. They were at the same sheltered cove he had shown her yesterday. 'Are you hungry? We can eat now if you would like.'

She had forgotten there was to be a picnic. 'But where is the food?' They had not brought anything with them.

He grinned. 'Look behind you.'

She turned and saw the two baskets by the cliff overhang. 'How did they get there?'

'Magic. I merely wished for them and they appeared.'

'How ridiculous!' But she smiled back at him. He looked relaxed and confident and so much like the young man she had known that she had almost been swept back in time. He had teased her and made her laugh then as he had today. But her happiness was just as bittersweet today as it had been three years ago.

He frowned a little as if sensing her mood had changed. 'What is wrong?'

Belle smiled again. 'Nothing is wrong. Should we eat?'

'Yes.' He still frowned a little as he took her hand and led her across the sand to the baskets. A rug had been laid across the top of one of them. He took it and spread it on the sand. He refused her offer to help him

and she found herself sitting cross-legged on the rug
while he laid the food out.

She felt rather awkward having him wait on her. Except for male servants, she had never had a man do such
a thing for her. He finally gave her a plate full of food
and then took his own and sat beside her. They ate in
silence for a few minutes, then she glanced at him. 'I
did not mean for you to wait on me.'

'I wanted to.' Justin leaned back against the rock behind him. 'Before you tell me that dukes should not do
such things I will inform you that I did not sit around
idle while I was in the army. I did not consider myself
above serving my men.' He smiled a little. 'Or Giles,
who happened to be my superior.'

'Was it very bad? The army, that is?' She did not
know what to say. War and its horrors were something
she could only imagine.

He shrugged. 'I do not think war is ever pleasant. But
to answer your question, yes, it was very bad.'

She looked at his strong profile and the way a lock of
hair had fallen over his forehead, making him look rather
boyish, and thought of him in the middle of a battle.
What if he had not come home as so many others had
not? The thought was unbearable. 'I am sorry,' she said.

He turned to look at her. 'Why?'

'For all of it. And because I do not think you would
have gone if it had not been for Lucien. And for me.'

'You consider yourself responsible for my joining the
army? My dear Belle, I would have undoubtedly gone
anyway.'

'But you might have been killed.' She knew she was
not making much sense.

'Yes, but that is not something one dwells upon.' He

looked more closely at her. 'Would you have felt responsible for my death as well?'

'Yes.' She blinked back tears.

'Are you crying?' He set his plate down. 'Don't.'

She shook her head and looked down at her plate. A tear trickled down her cheek and she dashed it away. Justin removed the plate from her lap and placed it next to his own, then his arm came around her and he pulled her against him. 'Why are you crying?'

'I…I would not have wanted you dead.' She pressed her face into his shirt front.

'Because you feel responsible for me or because you would miss me?' he asked.

'I would miss you,' she whispered.

He stilled for a moment and then his hand cupped her chin. He tilted her face so he could look at her. 'Everything is becoming very complicated,' he said and then he kissed her.

Her arms came around him and pulled him closer. She did not protest when he lowered her to the rug. She revelled in the feel of his weight on her, pressing her into the soft sand. Her hands tangled in his hair and she met the urgency of his kiss with her own need.

He finally lifted his head and braced his hands on either side of her. Belle opened her eyes. His face was above hers and she could see the faint shadow of his beard. She had never thought of a man's eyes as beautiful but his were. She reached up and touched his face and he caught her hand and gave a strangled laugh. 'My dear Belle, you are in grave danger of being seduced.'

'Am I? I am not certain that I would mind.' At this moment she wanted nothing more than to pull him back down on her and finish what they had started.

'But I would want you to be completely certain.' He kissed her hand and then rolled off her, sitting up.

She sat up as well, feeling hot with unfulfilled need. Not at all like her cool, practical self. The self who would never dream of allowing herself to be seduced in such a place. Or in any place at all.

'Belle.'

She looked at him. She could not read his face. 'I did not intend to take advantage of you, but by now it must be quite obvious that I want you.'

'Yes.' Her cheeks heated and she felt vulnerable under his gaze.

'Does that scare you?'

'Yes. It does.' She glanced away. For myriad reasons, but most of all because she feared losing herself to him.

'It scares me as well,' he said softly. 'Which is why I will not give into my very real desire to take you now without regard to the consequences. In fact, I will not touch you again unless you want me to.'

Oh, she wanted him to, but she could not throw all of her cautions away so easily. But why not now? She had been willing enough when she had signed the contract.

The answer was not difficult. Under the terms of the contract she had been paying a debt and she had told herself that it mattered little whether she gave him anything more than her body. Without the contract, she would come to him freely and he would truly be her lover. She could no longer pretend her heart was not involved as well.

'I suppose you are about to tell me you want to leave Falconcliff.' His voice was careful, too careful and she knew he did not want her to go.

'No.' She met his eyes and smiled a little. 'You said

I was to stay with you until you left for London. Of course, if you want me to go, I will do so.'

His gaze locked with hers. 'No, I don't want you to go.' He rose. 'Do you want more to eat? There are still apricot tarts and strawberries.' His voice was matter of fact.

'I would like that.' She kept her own voice calm.

After that, they treated each other with diffidence, careful to avoid touching one another unless absolutely necessary. They walked back to the house in silence. In the hallway, he turned to her. 'You will want to change. I will see you at dinner.'

'Yes.' She watched him walk away and then went to her bedchamber.

After Ellen helped her into a fresh muslin gown, she curled up in the chair next to her window and looked out at the garden below.

She had no idea what she was going to do. They could not stay under the same roof and pretend there was nothing between them. Whatever it was had nothing to do with contracts and everything to do with the smouldering attraction that had been there from the very beginning.

An attraction neither of them had dared act upon.

But there was nothing to stop them now, which was what frightened her. She did not want to completely lose her heart to him. But would one night be so wrong? She had never had a lover in the true sense of the word. He would not hurt her and there was the possibility she might take some pleasure from the act. But more than that, she wanted to lie in his arms and give what she could of herself to him. Perhaps, in some way, she would finally atone for the past.

But he would not come to her, so she would have to go to him.

She would have to seduce him.

Chapter Eleven

Her resolution nearly failed during dinner. He still maintained a polite reserve and she would have thought their earlier conversation a dream if she had not found his eyes on her, his expression almost brooding. They had retreated to the drawing room after dinner and played a hand of piquet. She could hardly concentrate and lost badly although she was generally a good player. Her only consolation was that he seemed equally distracted. She brushed against his hand twice and each time he jerked it back and the flare of desire in his eyes sent her pulse racing. She finally escaped upstairs where Ellen helped her undress and change into her nightrail.

She rose from the chair by the window and her stomach started to churn. It was time for her to seek him out. She would start with his bedchamber and, if he was not there, corner him wherever he was. She glanced down at her high-necked cotton nightrail. It was hardly enticing—she felt as chaste as a schoolgirl in it. The plain dressing gown she had thrown over it was exactly that— plain and sensible. Hardly items a mistress who hoped to please a lover wore.

Well, she could do one thing. If she was going to go

through with this she might as well do it completely. She undid the sash of her dressing gown and let the garment slide to the floor. She pulled her nightrail over her head and laid it across her bed, then picked up her dressing gown and slipped it back on. As she tied the sash again her fingers quaked. Then she left the room.

Justin pulled his shirt from his breeches and started to unbutton it. He had dismissed his valet early, wanting to be alone. He scowled. He did not think he could make it through one more dinner with Belle sitting across from him, her eyes large and luminous, and her skin soft and glowing in the candlelight. Although her white gown was still modest, the neckline seemed to be lower than that of most gowns she wore and he could hardly keep his eyes off of the creamy expanse of silky flesh above the bodice.

Even the card game he had suggested had not distracted him. Each time her hand brushed his he was jolted with such desire, he could hardly keep from pulling her against him. He never should have torn up the damn contract. For some reason it had kept his lust in check. But now the paper was gone, he could not longer deny that his reasons for wanting her had nothing to do with revenge.

The knock on his door startled him.

He undid the last of the buttons and shrugged out of his shirt. 'Come in,' he said curtly.

He looked up and his heart slammed against his chest when he saw Belle step into the room. Her eyes fixed on his face, she closed the door behind her and leaned against it. She wore a dressing gown and her wavy chestnut hair was loose around her shoulders. Confused, his eyes slid down her body and he saw her feet were bare.

His mouth went dry. 'What are you doing here?' he managed.

'I still have a debt to pay.'

'If you recall, I changed my mind.' He swallowed as she took a step towards him. 'I have torn up my copy of the contract.'

'But I haven't torn up mine. According to my contract I haven't fulfilled the terms.'

'You've done enough. We've shared a number of kisses which were quite satisfactory.'

'That is not what the contract specified.' Her voice was calm and her eyes remained on his face. 'It said I was to become your mistress until the end of the Season.'

'You have, for all purposes and intents.' He gave a short laugh. 'The world thinks you have at any rate.'

'Do you usually just exchange kisses with your mistresses?'

He frowned. 'That, my dear, is none of your concern.'

'It is, actually.' She started to move slowly across the room towards him.

He watched her, mesmerised. She had an oddly determined look on her face. He took a step back and found himself against the bedpost. She stood in front of him, far too close, and his eyes strayed to her lips. He had an image of crushing them beneath his. 'What the hell are you doing?' he demanded hoarsely.

'I believe I told you, I wish to repay my debt.' She moved closer to him. 'Do you wish to co-operate or not?'

'No.' Every part of his body made his denial a lie. 'I've no desire to take from you what you do not want to freely give. It was wrong of me to coerce you into becoming my mistress.' He had no idea what he was saying.

She smiled then, a little secretive smile that nearly sent him over the edge. 'Then you will be glad to know that I plan to coerce you instead.' She started to untie the sash of her gown. He could not tear his eyes away as the sash undid and the gown parted. She wore nothing underneath. He groaned, desire surging through him so powerfully he nearly keeled over.

She looked up and the glimpse of uncertainty in her eyes broke through all of his defences. He caught her to him, his mouth finding hers. His hands went to her shoulders beneath the material of her gown and he slid it from her shoulders. It fell to her hips and his hands followed, curving round the naked flesh and then cupping her buttocks. He pressed her to him, his erection hard against her. He heard her soft moan and he lifted his mouth from hers. Her cheeks were flushed, her eyes heavy with desire, her lips swollen from his kisses.

Justin scooped her up in his arms and carried her to the bed. The robe had completely fallen away and she was exposed to him, her slender legs, the soft curve of her belly, her small, perfect breasts, the thatch of dark hair at the juncture of her pale, smooth thighs. He drank her in, wanting to worship her with his body. Her eyes were on his face, wide and vulnerable, and she made a move to cover her breasts with her hands.

He reached out and caught her wrists. 'Don't. You are beautiful. Every part of you. Let me look at you and then I will touch you.'

She swallowed and nodded and lay quietly under his gaze. He undid the fastenings of his pantaloons and found his own hand was shaking as he peeled them off. Then he stretched out beside her. He lightly kissed her and then began to stroke her hips. His hand moved over the sensitive skin of her belly and felt her tremble. Then he touched her breast, his hand lightly circling the nipple. She stiffened.

'You do not like that?' he whispered.

'No. Lucien sometimes hurt me when he…he touched me.'

A blaze of anger and jealousy shot through him. 'I will be gentle. If I hurt you, you can let me know.'

'Yes.'

He watched her face as he caressed her breasts. She sighed and closed her eyes, and he bent his mouth to tease her nipple with his tongue. His hand splayed across her belly and then moved to tangle in the dark curls below. He felt her body arch against his hand and knew he could no longer wait. He positioned himself over her and gently parted her thighs with his knee.

Her eyes shot open and he saw the panic in her face. Despite his aching need, he could not take her like this. He bent and kissed her and then lowered himself so he lay next to her again. 'What is wrong?' she whispered.

'I do not think you are ready for me,' he said softly. He kissed her again, his mouth gentle and coaxing until she opened her mouth to him in response. His hand slipped between her silken thighs and his fingers found her core. He began to caress her in slow, rhythmic strokes. She gasped and stilled and then she moved against his hand. He kept his mouth on hers, his tongue imitating the movement of his fingers until he heard her soft moan. He quickly rolled on top of her. Her eyes opened again but this time they were heavy with unfulfilled desire. 'Justin. Please.'

'In a moment, sweetheart.' He eased himself between her thighs and then pushed into her. She was tight and hot and moist and enveloped him so perfectly he nearly exploded there and then. He paused, allowing her to adjust to him before he began to move in slow, measured thrusts, wanting to take her with him. His mouth was on hers, cajoling and seducing her into surrender. His movements became more urgent and finally her hips rose to meet his. He heard her cry out and felt her shudder before he was lost in a world of pleasure and sensation and oneness. His seed spilled into her and then he collapsed on top of her.

Her eyes were still shut, her breathing hard. Swift protective possession shot through him. He cupped her face with his hand. 'Are you all right?'

Her eyes fluttered open. 'Yes. Is…is this what it is supposed to be like?' She sounded as wonder-struck as she had by the sea earlier.

'This is precisely what lovemaking is supposed to be like. It can be even more pleasurable, in fact.'

'Can it?' The delicate colour in her cheeks only deepened.

'Yes. Which is something I intend to demonstrate.' He realised he still had her pressed into the bed. As much as he craved the feel of her beneath him, he did not want to hurt her, so he lifted away from her.

To his surprise, she sat up, and he frowned. 'What are you doing?'

'Did you want me to return to my bedchamber?' She did not quite meet his eyes.

'Why would I want you to do that?'

'Is that not what usually happens after…after this?' She bit her lip. 'At least with Lucien, when he was finished, he…'

Justin sat up and caught her chin so he could see her face. 'Your husband was a damnable cur in every way

possible including this. No, you are not to return to your
bed. You will stay in mine. Not the least because I intend
to show you some other pleasures that can be between
a man and a woman.' He was already easing her back
against the pillows. 'And when I am done, when we are
done, you will not even think of Lucien.'

Belle woke to find Justin's arm draped over her. At
first, she could not recall where she was. Then she remembered; she was in his house, in his bed and in his
arms. She did not move for a moment, hearing his soft,
even breathing, feeling the warmth of his arm across her
bare flesh. She had crossed the final barrier—she was
now his mistress in every sense of the word.

Not only that—she had behaved as wantonly as any
mistress could, first seducing him and then partaking of
the pleasures of the flesh to the fullest. He had brought
her to the pinnacle of ecstasy not once, but twice more,
until they had finally drifted into a deep slumber. Even
now, despite the slight soreness, she felt the heavy, warm
pit of sensation between her legs and knew if he wanted
to take her again, she would welcome him.

She refused to regret it. She could not. She had come
to Justin with the intention of doing exactly what she
had done. Except she had not expected one night to so
devastatingly sweep away the person she thought she
was. Calm, collected, passionless. She had thought she
knew from her marriage what to expect. She should have
been warned from her response to his kisses and that
one night in London, but it had only been a mere prelude
to the ecstasy she had found in his arms. And she had
been wild and passionate and everything that she had
not thought herself. A self she was not sure she wanted
to know.

Belle slowly opened her eyes. Faint light crept through the cracks of the heavy drapes. She thought it might be just after dawn. She shifted a little and although he moved, he did not wake. She managed to scoot out from under his arm and gently eased it to his side. Then she sat up, careful not to disturb him. A lock of dark hair fell over his forehead. Despite his strong profile, he looked vulnerable and almost boyish and a swift desire to brush his hair back and kiss him shot through her. She wanted to lie with him again, not for love-making but because she wanted to feel his warmth and strength. Feel part of another person.

But she could not allow that. She could not lose herself in him. She could not fall in love with him for she would truly be lost.

She slipped from the bed. Her dressing gown lay on the floor and she picked it up and put it on, suddenly finding her nakedness disconcerting. She wanted to escape to the privacy of her bedchamber and recover her sense of self.

Justin still did not waken as she quietly left his room and closed the door behind her.

Chapter Twelve

Justin found her in the library again. She sat in the same chair as she had yesterday, her gaze on the sea below. He watched her for a moment, the perfect outline of her cheek, the way her hair curled about her face, the soft curves of her breast beneath her lavender gown. He could almost feel their rounded softness in his hands and his groin tightened in response.

'Belle.'

She turned and soft colour filled her cheeks. 'Good morning, your...that is, Justin.'

She looked adorable. 'You still want to address me as "your Grace"? After last night, I would think the need for such formality between us was annihilated.' His eyes swept over her face. 'Don't you?'

Her colour deepened. 'I suppose so. Although in front of others I would prefer to preserve a certain amount of formality.'

'But, my sweet Belle, there are no others present at this moment.'

'But there could be. A library is not very private. Anyone could walk in.'

'Anyone?'

'A servant. Or a guest, that is.'

The prim note that had returned to her voice made him want to kiss her. 'There are no other guests that I am aware of. And my servants would hardly be shocked if you addressed me by my given name. Or perhaps you fear something else might happen.'

Her eyes widened. 'Such as what?'

'Such as this.' He caught her around the waist and pulled her to him. Before she could protest he kissed her. Her lips parted under his and then she moved her head away. 'No.'

He lifted his head for a moment. 'No, what? Say my name,' he whispered against her mouth.

'No. Justin.'

He released her. 'That was not too difficult. Nor did anyone interrupt us.' He touched her cheek. 'Why did you leave me this morning? I awoke and you were gone.'

'I...' She flushed. 'I did not want to be seen in your bed.'

'Still so modest?' he murmured. He smiled wickedly. 'I look forward to unmasking you again. And very soon at that. I wasn't quite finished with you, you know.'

'Justin!' She took a step away from him as if she feared he was about to have his way with her at that moment. He was tempted, but he did not want to shock her. However, he intended to seize the next appropriate opportunity.

'I need your company for something else,' he said.

'And what is that?'

'Billiards.'

'Billiards? Why would you want me for that? I can hardly hit the ball.'

'You will, by the time I am finished with your lesson.

This time there will be no interruptions and we can spend the entire day on your lesson if we want.'

'Do you not have something else you would rather do?'

He allowed his eyes to linger on her mouth. 'I do, but I somehow doubt you would agree to it.'

Instead of the blush he had expected, she eyed him calmly. 'I do agree a horseback ride would be rather uncomfortable. Perhaps when the sun is out.'

He laughed. 'That is not quite what I meant as I suspect you know very well.' He picked up his gloves. 'I will change and then we can go to the billiards room. We can also tour the house if you'd like.'

'I would like that.' She smiled at him.

He was stunned at the happiness on her face. Was it merely at the prospect of seeing the house or at spending time in his company? He had experienced a moment of panic when he had awoke and found her gone and for a moment had wondered if he had dreamed the whole night. But the faint scent of her that still lingered in the bedclothes told him the night had not been a dream.

He had not known why she had left him and had half-expected she would have returned to her cool, composed self. Had she only come to him in order to atone for the wrongs she thought she had done to him? Or had it been because she desired him as much as he did her?

He could only hope it was the latter. The alternative was worse than nothing at all.

The billiards room was in the older wing of the rambling house. They passed through a long gallery of portraits and finally came to a dark panelled room with long windows and an old carved mantelpiece. A fire already crackled in the fireplace and warmth had started to seep into the room. There were several comfortable chairs and a sofa as well as the billiard table which occupied one corner of the room. Belle walked to the window. The sea was visible from this room as well. The rain now beat against the window and the sea was as grey as the clouds—wild and untamed and she was utterly fascinated. She hardly noticed Justin was behind her until he spoke. 'Have I lost you again?'

She jumped and whirled around. 'I beg your pardon?'

'You seem to go into a trance every time you catch a glimpse of the water.' His voice was dry but his face held amusement. 'Jackson said you went directly for the window in the library and hardly knew when he left the room. I doubt you moved until I entered.'

'I am sorry. It is just it is so entrancing and it changes colours with the sky. Perhaps when I grow used to it I won't care so much.'

'I suspect you will. I think it has enthralled you. It did me the first time I saw it, which is why I prefer this house, much to the dismay of my relations.' His mouth lifted in a half-smile. 'I have already instructed Mrs Keith to have your possessions moved to a chamber with a view of the sea. I should have thought of that earlier, but it never occurred to me you would be so fascinated. The chamber is smaller than the one you occupy, however.'

'That does not matter.' She smiled at him. 'Thank you.'

'I am glad it pleases you,' he said softly.

She gave a shaky laugh. 'You do not need to please me.'

'But it is my pleasure to do so.' His eyes met hers and the intensity of his expression made her catch her breath.

She forced her voice to remain light. 'I am ready to start the billiards lesson. But I should warn you that I have not done this since the last time you attempted to instruct me. If I recall, I was an extremely dismal pupil. I am less than hopeful about the results.'

'But the lessons themselves can be enjoyable.'

She felt the telltale blush steal to her cheeks. 'I suppose so, although I have found most lessons rather tedious.' She had no idea what she was saying.

The lazy smile still curled his mouth. 'I assure you these won't be.'

She gave up. Fencing with him was impossible—that he was a master at it was obvious.

'Should we begin?' she asked.

He took her hand. 'Yes, but first I must drag you from the window.' He gave her hand a gentle tug. She followed him to the baize-covered table where he released her hand and moved to a rack of cues. 'Would you prefer a mace or a cue?'

'A cue, I think.'

He pulled one down and tested its weight. 'This should work for you.' He took another stick down and then gave her the first one. He set his aside and shrugged out of his coat. It was hardly suggestive but her mouth went dry none the less. He wore a waistcoat over his fine linen shirt. She watched him set the balls, his movements graceful and expert, then he turned to her. 'Are you ready? Come here and I will help you position your stick.'

She moved to the table and took the cue from his hand. She pointed it at the ball only to find Justin's arms closing around her. 'Like this,' he said into her ear. He moved her hands into position and then moved away from her. 'Now try to hit it.'

Whatever was he talking about? Her body still tingled from where he had touched her.

'Do not worry if you make a mistake. You can try it as many times as you wish,' he said.

Oh. She was supposed to hit the ball. She took aim and brought her arm back, then forward. Her stick contacted with the ball and it slowly rolled towards the middle of the table and then stopped. 'Oh, dear. It hardly did anything.'

'At least you hit it,' he said kindly. He retrieved the ball and set it back in place. 'Try it again. Do you want me to help you?'

No! Then she'd never have a chance of concentrating. 'Perhaps if you showed me first.'

'Very well.'

She stepped aside and he positioned himself in front of the ball. He leaned forward, the movement stretching his shirt and waistcoat across the taut muscles of his back. A sudden recollection of how they felt under her hand hit her and she jerked her gaze to his fingers. They were strong and lean around the stick, the signet ring he wore on his left hand catching the light from the window. Unfortunately, watching his hands proved no less distracting.

He finally hit the ball in a swift, sure movement. It rolled directly into the pocket on the opposite side. He straightened up and glanced at her, male satisfaction at such a neat hit evident. She found herself smiling at him. 'Very good. How did you do that?'

'Practice. And concentration. I do not allow myself to be distracted.'

Evidently, her presence was not having the same effect on him as his was having on her. Well, she would just have to put aside her lustful, immoral thoughts and focus on the task at hand rather than on him. 'Let me try it again, then.' She picked up her stick with resolution.

He made no move to physically help her this time, but she was quite aware his eyes were fixed on her. It was almost as bad as having him touch her. She tried to ignore him and vowed she would at least hit the ball hard enough so it would reach the other side of the table.

She slammed the stick into the ball which bounded across the table and leapt off with such force she feared it would crash through the floor.

Mortified, she forced herself to look at Justin. His brow shot up. 'I should hate to have you angry at me with the stick in your hand. I suspect you would be lethal.'

Her hand went to her mouth. 'I am sorry. Do you think I damaged your floor? Or the ball?'

His mouth twitched. 'I doubt it very much.'

'I will retrieve it.' She moved around the side of the table. The ball had rolled across the floor and come to rest near the fireplace. She was relieved to see no holes in the floor and find the ball in one piece.

She picked it up and walked back to the table. 'I would like to try again,' she said. All signs indicated that she should acknowledge defeat and give up, but she was determined she would get at least one ball in a pocket. Particularly since he was laughing at her.

'Good girl.' His eyes danced. 'Perhaps I should help you this time.'

'No, I wish to try it myself again. However, I think I could concentrate better if you would look at something besides me.'

'Most certainly, although you will deprive me of the pleasure of watching you.'

She cast him a baleful look. 'It is hardly kind of you to take pleasure in watching me make a sad botch of this.'

'Ah, but that wasn't what was giving me pleasure.'

He was flirting with her, and no matter what she said he would twist it. She marched to the table and glanced back at him. 'I really would like to try this without any spectators.'

'Of course. I will stand near the window, although I would be grateful if you would warn me before tossing any more balls off the table.'

'I have no intention of doing that again, your Grace,' she said with dignity. She turned back to the table and gritted her teeth. She would conquer this.

The first shot went wide of the mark, but the second was solid. By the third try she had managed to at least move a ball in the direction she wanted. And by the eighth shot, a ball finally wobbled into a pocket. She nearly shouted with joy.

'Very nice.'

She whirled around and nearly hit Justin, who stood directly behind her, with the stick. He stepped back and then gently took it from her hand. 'You are dangerous with this thing,' he remarked.

'I had no idea you were behind me. I thought you were not going to watch.' Her heart was thudding rapidly although she couldn't tell if it was from his nearness or excitement over her victory.

'I could not help myself,' he said with an apologetic air, but she doubted he was the least bit apologetic. 'I own I was bored so I thought I would see how you were progressing. I arrived in time to see your victory. I had no doubt you would finally manage to corner one of the balls. You are very determined when you want something.'

'You may still laugh but I will get better and then I will challenge you to a match.'

He grinned. 'I look forward to it. However, a few more pointers might be in order.'

She frowned at him. 'Such as what?'

'The position of the stick when your ball is here, for instance. This angle can make it rather difficult. Allow me to show you.' He neatly demonstrated and then hit the ball. He then re-spotted the ball. 'You can try it now.'

The stick would not quite line up and she felt awkward. He moved to her side and put one arm around her so he could guide her hand. Then he shifted her other hand into position. His light impersonal touch made her feel almost weak. 'I'll help you hit the ball,' he said. He spoke almost impersonally, but she heard the slight huskiness in his voice.

'All right,' she said. Her own voice sounded very peculiar.

But he made no move to hit the ball and he suddenly stepped away from her. 'This is impossible,' he said.

Belle managed to speak. 'I fear I am a poor pupil at such things. I could never throw a ball properly or…or shoot an…' Her voice trailed away as he drew her back against him.

His hands splayed over her stomach, his breath warm on her cheek. 'No, my sweet Belle, that is not what I meant.' And then his mouth found the hollow at the base of her neck. Her head fell back and she could feel the hard muscles of his chest against her, then his hands moved up to cup her breasts through the soft muslin of her gown. She made a little sound.

'I do not think I can wait,' he murmured. 'I want to love you now.' He pulled her more firmly against him, leaving her in no doubt of his desire.

'Justin…' But he had turned her and his mouth covered hers silencing her protest. She was backed up against the billiard table and he was kissing her with a wild passion that sent her spiralling into a vortex. He lifted her and she was on the table. He braced his hands on either side of her, his mouth still on hers. She clung to him but when he lifted her skirt and his hand began to stroke the soft flesh of her inner thigh, she pulled her mouth away. 'Justin…we cannot…'

His smile was wicked. 'But we can. I told you these lessons would not be tedious.'

'No, they are not.' Her body was trembling with anticipation and heat. When his hand went to the fastening of his breeches, she thought she would explode then. His eyes were fixed on her face as he bent over her, bracing his arms on either side of her on the table. 'Where were we?' he asked.

'I think…' She looked up into his dark face, his eyes heavy with passion and need for her. With astonishment she saw that although she was for all purposes at his mercy, that was only an illusion. She was not powerless, instead, he was in her power, a feminine power she had never dreamed she possessed.

She surrendered then, both to him and to herself. Her arms came around his neck and her hands tangled in the thick, silky hair at his nape. She drew his head slowly towards her. 'I think we were here,' she whispered before bringing his lips to hers.

Chapter Thirteen

'Lord Salcombe.'

Startled, Brandt spun around. He had just sauntered out of the Harringtons' ballroom towards the card room. He was stunned to find Lady Chloe behind him. She had made it quite clear she held him in dislike, a novel experience, since most females seemed to find him attractive whether he wanted them to or not. To his annoyance he found it irked him that the lovely Lady Chloe proved the exception. 'Lady Chloe,' he drawled. 'Should I be flattered that you have deigned to speak to me?'

'Why?' She frowned a little. 'I want to ask you about my sister-in-law. Do you know where she is?'

It was his turn to frown. 'She is with my cousin, I believe. At his home in Devon.'

'Do you know if she is well?' Her large expressive eyes were filled with concern.

'I have not heard from my cousin but I presume she is. You have heard nothing from her?'

'No. Both Mama and Arth…Lord Ralston have forbidden me any contact with her, although I think Mama is now very sorry. But I had hoped you might have heard something.' She looked so crestfallen, he felt a twinge of conscience.

'You are very fond of Lady Milborne?'

'She is the best person in the world,' she said softly. 'I miss her terribly. I do not want her to be hurt any more than she already has been.'

The twinge was turning into a full-blown attack. 'My cousin is not cruel. She will be safe with him.'

'Will she be?' She looked doubtful. 'But he forced her to go with him.'

'What do you know of that?'

'She did not look very happy when she was with him at the theatre so I cannot imagine she went with him willingly, which is why I worry about her.'

'Yes.' He should be shocked that an innocent young lady would not only observe such things but comment on them. Instead, he found himself admiring her for her loyalty to someone she cared deeply about.

He said, almost reluctantly, 'I had planned to make a short visit to Devon. I will make certain Lady Milborne is well. Will that reassure you?'

'Oh, yes.' She suddenly looked hopeful. 'Can you deliver a note to her?'

'If you can get it to me by tomorrow. I will leave the day after.'

'Thank you.' For the first time, she smiled at him and he nearly reeled under the impact.

'Very well,' he said curtly, taken aback by his own reaction.

She turned to go, then paused and looked back at him. 'Belle has done nothing wrong, no matter what you believe. My brother used her just as badly as he used your cousin.'

Before he could utter a word, she was gone. Brandt

watched her make her way back to the ballroom, a slender auburn-haired girl with an unexpected strength under her demure appearance. A wry smile touched his mouth. He'd intended to go to Devon to make certain his cousin was protected from Lady Milborne, but now he had just promised to make certain Lady Milborne was protected from his cousin.

Brandt realised as soon as he finished the sentence that he had made a tactical error in telling his aunt he was to leave for Falconcliff. Her eyes took on a speculative look. 'Splendid. I will accompany you.'

'I doubt Justin will be pleased when I show up. He will be even less pleased if both of us do.'

Her mouth tightened with displeasure. 'If you do not escort me then I will be forced to travel alone. I have no intention of remaining in London when he is under that creature's influence. What if she attempts to force him into marriage? It is bad enough that she has enticed him away from London and in the middle of the Season.'

'In all fairness to Lady Milborne, it was Justin who enticed her away.'

'Which makes it worse,' Lady Georgina snapped. 'I will not allow this little affair to go any further. He has duties, one of which is to marry and produce an heir, but since he has been caught in her toils, he seems to have forgotten this. He needs to be reminded.'

He knew that once she made up her mind to do something, dissuading her was impossible. If he escorted her, he could at least keep an eye on her. 'Very well, we will leave tomorrow.'

'Splendid.' The triumphant little smile on her face did not reassure him. He did not have solid proof, but he was beginning to suspect Lady Georgina was behind the slurs on Lady Milborne's reputation. He had no more desire to see Justin caught in Lady Milborne's claws than his aunt did, but his sense of fair play would not allow him to resort to malicious slander.

He now needed to protect both Justin and Lady Milborne from Lady Georgina.

The rain fell for the next few days. Belle found she did not mind. The sea continued to fascinate her and she spent hours in the library reading or watching the water or practising her billiards when Justin was occupied with other matters. They dined together and sometimes played cards and billiards after dinner. They had few visitors, the heavy rains making travel difficult. Lord Haversham stopped by twice. His manner towards her had warmed a little, although she knew he did not completely approve of her presence.

The nights she spent in Justin's arms. He taught her about the pleasures of lying with a man and she learned that she was not the cool dispassionate woman she had thought. Sometimes in the aftermath as she lay, naked and spent, against his chest, she thought she did not know herself at all, which frightened her more than a little.

During the day, by herself, she felt once more the cool, sensible person she had tried to become after Lucien's death. But she had had a sense of suspended time, as if she were living in a fairytale castle in a sort of dream. The world that she had left, her quiet life with Maria and Chloe, and more recently, London with its balls and parties and gossip, seemed far away. She tried not to think of what would happen when she left Devon.

The rain fell for over a week. Exactly ten days after she arrived, the sun feebly shone through the clouds. She had gone down to breakfast in the dining room when Justin came in. He was dressed in leather breeches and a plain coat and riding boots, as he was most mornings. He rose early and rode, even when the weather was less than ideal, unless there was a particularly nasty storm. Then he went straight to his study to meet with his estate manager or Jackson.

He flung himself down in the chair opposite her. 'I thought we could go riding today if you wish.'

She had learned the 'if you wish' was merely a formality. He had made up his mind she would go riding with him. She supposed she should take exception to his heavy-handedness, but underneath his imperiousness she sensed he truly desired her company. And she wanted nothing more than to be with him. 'Yes, if that is what you would like.'

He frowned at her a little. She could see he was in one of his impatient moods and something was distracting him as well. 'Would you like coffee?' she asked.

'Yes. If you please.' He rose and paced towards the window, before turning to look at her, hands clasped behind his back. 'Marguerite, Lady Haversham that is, has invited us to dine with them tonight.'

She poured his coffee and stirred in the two lumps of sugar he always took. She looked at him, a little startled. 'That is very kind of her.'

He still wore a frown. 'I can decline if you would rather not accept.'

'Why would you think I would not want to accept?'

'Because she overset you when they dined with us that very first day,' he said bluntly. 'I could see that from your face when Giles and I returned to the drawing room.'

'No, she did not overset me. Not really.'

'What did she say to you then? We have known each other since childhood which she considers a licence to meddle in my affairs.'

'She said nothing to me that I would not have said if our situations had been reversed. She merely wished to make certain I would not hurt you.'

He frowned. 'That is none of her concern.'

'It is. She cares about you. She is your friend, as is Giles. She knows something of what happened three years ago and that I hurt you. I cannot blame her at all for her questions. And I will not come between you and your friends, so you must promise me you will say nothing to Marguerite.'

He looked at her for a moment. 'Very well. I will not say anything. However, we are not obligated to dine with them.'

'I would like to,' she said firmly, although she had felt more than a little trepidation about the invitation under the circumstances. It was beyond kind of them to invite her because she doubted there were very few other married couples who would extend an invitation to her. But she meant what she had told Justin—she would not force him to choose between her and his friends.

'If you are certain.' He still wore a slight frown. 'Then I will send a message for them to expect us.'

'Yes. Come and sit down and have your coffee. It is probably cold, however. Should I pour you another cup?'

'No. This will do.' He took his place across from her again and she handed him the cup and saucer.

She resumed her chair and stared down at her own full cup, then glanced at Justin. He was sipping his coffee, his attention now caught by *The Times*. The scene was unbearably domestic, as if they were man and wife rather than temporary lovers. No, she had never had such an occasion with Lucien, but this was what her parents had done. What she had dreamed her marriage might be like.

A lump rose in her throat and she pushed her cup away. It felt so comfortable and so right to be sitting with him like this and she knew it could never last.

The sun still shone by the time they returned to the house in late afternoon. Justin had taken her over the entire property. He rode a large grey gelding and she had been mounted upon a smaller horse, a bay by the name of Gawain. She saw his horses and then the colt, who looked completely at home in his new paddock. After that they had ridden down a narrow winding path to the sea. They spent a considerable time by the water and then he had pulled her down beside him on a bleached log which she now knew was driftwood and had kissed her thoroughly.

It had been a happily spent day and now, back in her bedchamber, as she readied for dinner, she wished she could remain in this private world. But she could not for it was not reality.

The journey to Haversham Hall took a mere quarter of an hour. The house was red-bricked and graceful and sat at the back of a huge lawn. The carriage halted in the circular drive and Justin alighted first, and then helped Belle down. He released her hand and she smoothed the silk of her grey gown in a nervous movement and wished she did not suddenly feel so apprehensive.

The hall was large and cool and much more modern than anything she had seen at Falconcliff. The stout butler showed them to an elegant drawing room where Lady

Haversham waited for them. She rose from the chair and came forward to greet them. Her smile was wide and warm, and any doubts Belle felt about her welcome vanished.

She kissed Justin lightly on the cheek and then clasped Belle's hand. 'How nice to see you again. We have seen Justin a few times when he has ridden over to discuss business with Giles and he has said you were well. I feared the rain would never let up and it would be an age before I could invite you, which is why I sent off an invitation straight away as soon as I saw the merest hint of sun this morning. I hope it did not inconvenience you.'

Belle returned her smile. 'No. It was very kind of you to have me,' she said.

'Oh, not at all. Giles should be here shortly. And Caroline and William have been clamouring all day to see Justin.' She cast him a mischievous glance. 'I fear they plan to keep you very well occupied until they go to supper.' She looked back at Belle. 'My son and daughter. He is their godfather.'

'I did not know that.' She had no idea Lady Haversham already had children.

The other woman made a face. 'How disappointing! I would have thought that he would brag to everyone about them. I suspect he has been occupied with other matters so I will forgive him this time.'

Just then a small boy and a girl burst through the doors, followed by a harried-looking young lady. 'Uncle Justin!' the boy cried. He launched himself across the floor at Justin and then suddenly noticed Belle. He stopped and stared at her with large blue eyes.

'William,' his mother said, 'how often have I told you not to dash across the room in such a way? You must

learn to enter a room like a gentleman.' The rebuke was
gentle and it was apparent from the softness in her face
she truly doted on him.

'Yes, Mama,' he said, but the mischief in his eye was
not repressed.

'I beg your pardon, my lady,' the young woman said.
She and the girl had reached them. 'I had reminded him
he must not run but he was so anxious to see his Grace
that I fear he quite forgot.'

'I've no doubt the lesson will some day make an impression,' Lady Haversham said. 'You may go now, Lucinda. I have promised them they may stay with us for
a short time.'

'Thank you.' Lucinda made a brief curtsy and hurried
out of the room.

William had grabbed Justin's hand. 'Do you want to
see my puppy? He is very fat and licks my face and his
name is Lion because he is very fierce.'

'Which is a very silly name,' his sister said scornfully.
'I do not think he will be at all fierce. He is afraid of
Betsy. I would have named him Mouse.'

William gave her a quelling look. 'Some day he will
eat Betsy! Do you want to see him, Uncle Justin?'

A slight smile quirked Justin's mouth as he looked
down at the boy. 'Yes, but not at this very moment.'

'And first you must greet Lady Milborne,' Lady Haversham said. 'She is Justin's guest at Falconcliff.'

Belle found two pairs of solemn blue eyes trained on
her. They greeted her politely but with a trace of wari-
ness, as if they were not quite certain what to make of
her. She guessed that Caroline must be about eight and
William looked to be no more than five. They were
beautiful children with their mother's startling sky-blue
eyes and their father's dark hair.

She smiled and said very politely, 'I am glad to meet two more of the Duke's friends. How do you do?' She held out her hand and they took turns shaking it.

Lord Haversham entered the room at that moment. The children ran to him and he embraced them. She felt another tug at her heart as she watched the domestic scene. Her own parents had loved her in such a manner and she had thought that was how she would be with her own children. She glanced at Justin and found his eyes were on her, his expression unreadable. She gave him a little smile and then looked quickly away.

Lord Haversham turned to Justin. 'Have you been invited to see the puppy yet?'

'Not only once, but twice. Would there be time before dinner?' Justin glanced at Belle. 'If you have no objections.'

She shook her head. 'No, of course not. I think visiting a new puppy is of prime importance. I only hope he will not prove to be too fierce and try to eat you.'

William had clutched Justin's hand again. 'He won't,' he told her with grave reassurance. 'He will only eat my enemies.'

'I am glad to hear that.'

'So am I,' Justin said. He grinned at Belle, and she found herself smiling back at him.

She realised Lord and Lady Haversham were watching them, so she tore her gaze away from Justin. It was decided Giles would visit the puppy as well, and Caroline, with a great show of bestowing a favour upon them, said she would also accompany them.

Belle was left alone with Lady Haversham, who smiled at her. 'Would you like to sit down or would you care for a stroll in the garden? I fear this might take more time than one might expect. They adore Justin and would monopolise him completely if possible.'

'I can see that and that he returns their sentiments as well.'

'Yes, he does. Should we go to the garden?'

'I would like that, but only if you would not be too fatigued.'

Lady Haversham laughed. 'No. I am one of those fortunate females who actually feel quite well once I pass the first few months. I am quite sick at first and then I make the most amazing recovery.' She led Belle through the French windows and to a small terrace. The garden was directly outside. 'I suspect you are fond of children as well,' Lady Haversham remarked.

'I am.' Belle's smile trembled a little.

'Justin will make an excellent papa some day, although I fear he will be like Giles and spoil his children dreadfully. His own father was very strict and not very affectionate, at least not outwardly, although I believe he loved his son very much. He was devastated when Justin left for the army and I think he suspected he would not see him again.'

'You are speaking of Lord Haversham?' Belle was puzzled at this confidence.

'No, of Justin.' Lady Haversham's expression was apologetic. 'I do tend to cross my lines even in conversation and wander off in the most odd directions. I only meant to say that I think it would be the best thing for Justin to set up a nursery.' She paused near a rose bush.

'Yes.' Belle focused on the rose. 'I think so, too.' She did not believe Lady Haversham intended to hurt her, but her words pierced her as swiftly as any sword.

'Justin seems happy,' Lady Haversham said softly. 'I do not think I have seem him so for a long time.'

Belle glanced back at Lady Haversham. 'Does he?'

'I think so. Even Giles said so and he almost never notices such things. But are you happy as well?'

'Yes. I am. Falconcliff is lovely and Justin is…is very kind.' That did not begin to describe it but she could not think of what to say.

'And an excellent lover, if the rumours are true.'

Belle's cheeks flamed. 'Lady Haversham, I…'

Her eyes sparkled. 'You must call me Marguerite. I did not mean to embarrass you but since I am married and obviously know about such things…' she cast a look at her gently rounded stomach '…and you have been married before, we can be frank. But you do not have to tell me a thing if you don't wish. I've no doubt Justin would be appalled if he knew we were discussing such a thing. As would Giles. Not that they would ever think about discussing the subject themselves.'

Belle thought of the less than respectable conversations she had heard between Lucien and his acquaintances concerning the female sex. 'No, I have not noticed they have the least interest in such things. Yes, he is very good in that regard—not that I have had much experience,' she added hastily and then wondered what it was about Marguerite that inspired such confidences. Perhaps it was the laughter in her eyes or the sense that she truly cared and would not use the information against her.

'Merely very good?' Marguerite gave a whoop of laughter. 'I am not certain he would be at all flattered. But then it is his other sterling qualities you undoubtedly admire.'

'Yes, those, too.' She smiled at Marguerite.

'I am very glad of that. He needs someone who admires him for the other things he is, such as kind, not just for his title and wealth.'

She was not quite certain what Marguerite meant to tell her. The sound of voices and childish chatter interrupted any further conversation. She saw Justin, Giles and the two children were striding across the lawn towards them. This time a child held each of Justin's hands and his head was bent as he listened to Caroline.

The scene tore at her heart. Marguerite was right—he looked happy and natural as if he were perfectly at home. With a sort of despair, she knew she had fallen in love with him. And, because of that, she must go because she would never be able to give him all he needed to make him happy.

Justin watched Belle as she sat on the sofa in the drawing room of Haversham Hall. Caroline sat beside her, their two dark heads bent over a picture book. They had dined early and, after dinner, William and Caroline had been allowed to join the adults for a short time before a protesting William was whisked up to bed. Caroline had been allowed to stay up a little longer and she had somewhat diffidently brought out a book and asked if Belle would like to see it. That Belle had been more than pleased to be asked was evident from the warmth that had leapt to her face, but she had just as courteously told Caroline she would be very happy to do so. Belle had been perceptive for Caroline always withdrew when undue fuss was made over her.

Caroline said something, and Belle's face was very serious as she replied. He had a sudden vision of Belle at Falconcliff, their own small daughter at her side doing exactly the same thing. In a blinding flash, he knew he had no intention of ever letting her go.

Justin was still reeling under the thought when Marguerite appeared at his side. 'I like her very much.'

He looked down at her, rather dazed. 'Who?'

'Your Belle, of course.' She smiled up at him for a moment and then sobered. 'I was certain I would detest her and when Brandt said you were bringing her to Falconcliff, I was determined I would put a stop to any machinations she had. But then I saw she was not at all what I thought and that she is kind and generous.'

'She is.' And much more. The nights she spent in his arms had been an union that went beyond that of the physical and he knew he would never tire of her.

'So, what are your intentions? I worried at first that she would hurt you, but now I worry that you might hurt her.'

'My intentions? I intend to marry her.'

Her smile was wide. 'Very good. I would suggest as soon as possible.'

'That is my intention as well.'

'That would be wise. Before Lady Georgina gets wind of it. I've no doubt she will endeavour to stop you.'

'She won't.'

'But she will try. She has always attempted to interfere in your affairs. She wants you to marry Lady Clarissa Blackwood, does she not? I daresay she thinks Lady Clarissa will be quite amenable to her influence.'

He frowned. 'What do you know of that?'

'It is amazing what gossip one learns even this far from London. My sister-in-law keeps me very well informed.' She glanced at the pair on the sofa again. 'I must ring for Lucinda and have her take Caroline up to bed. I suggest you propose to your Belle soon. You really should not waste any time in these matters. Besides, I look forward to being a godparent to your first child.'

He was too startled to make a reply, although he wanted to tell her to cease her meddling. But she had already flitted off to ring for the nursemaid. He scowled. As much as he hated to admit it, she was probably right. He should not let the matter go on. The only thing that gave him pause was that Belle had refused him before. He knew she was skittish about marriage—he could hardly blame her. But things had changed between them since then. That she was not indifferent to him was obvious. He had no idea whether she was in love with him or not, but he intended to use every argument at hand to persuade her, including that she might already be with child.

But he did not propose after they left Haversham Hall. She was quiet, more so than usual, and, from the droop of her head, he thought she must be tired. As much as he wanted to secure her consent, he had at least developed a measure of self-control over the years. So he would wait.

But not for long.

Chapter Fourteen

Lord Salcombe and Lady Georgina arrived in the late afternoon of the next day. Belle had just come around the side of the house from the garden when she saw the carriage in the drive. She stopped. She did not recognise the crest, but she recognised the tall, brown-haired man who alighted. He turned to help another occupant down and her heart took a sickening dive when she saw Lady Georgina.

Justin had said nothing about visitors. But then she had not seen him today except for a brief moment at breakfast. Last night had been the first night since she had arrived that she had spent in her own bed. To her chagrin she had developed a slight headache and had nearly fallen asleep in the coach on the trip home from Haversham Hall. Justin had helped her up to her bed and sent Ellen in to look after her. He had been solicitous, but had seemed as preoccupied as she was and, after dropping a quick kiss on her forehead, had left her.

She had awoken this morning, her headache gone, but unable to quite shake the melancholy she had felt since last night.

Lord Salcombe had seen her. His eyes were fixed on

her face and she could almost imagine their look of thinly veiled disapproval. She forced herself to go forward and he moved to the side of the carriage to wait for her. By now, Lady Georgina had spotted her as well.

She forced a smile to her face. 'Good day, Lady Georgina, Lord Salcombe.'

Lady Georgina's cold grey eyes met hers. 'I see you have made yourself quite at home.' Her gaze went briefly to the flowers she had picked.

Belle lifted her chin, refusing to buckle under her disapproval. Salcombe's expression was harder to interpret. 'These are for the drawing room. Justin is out on the estate. I am not certain he knew exactly when you would arrive, otherwise I feel sure he would have been here to greet you. You will have to make do with me instead.'

'He did not know we were coming,' Salcombe said.

'Which undoubtedly explains why he is not here.' She knew she was not being very cordial, but she felt edgy and defensive. 'You must come in.'

Lady Georgina ignored her and took Salcombe's arm. 'I do not wish to stand out here all day.' She started up the steps without waiting for Belle.

Belle trailed them into the hall where Mrs Keith stood. While Belle had been talking with Salcombe and Lady Georgina, the footmen had brought in the luggage which was now in the hall. Mrs Keith's austere face lit when she recognised Salcombe. 'My lord, 'tis good to see you.' Her expression was merely polite when she turned to Lady Georgina. 'My lady. I fear the Duke said nothing about your arrival.' She cast Belle a puzzled look.

'It is a surprise,' Salcombe said. 'We did not send word we were coming.'

'I see. Well, then you will be wanting your usual suite, I imagine. It is the one at the far end of the west wing.

Should I ready the blue bedchamber for Lady Georgina, my lady?' she said to Belle.

Lady Georgina's mouth had tightened with suppressed fury. 'The blue bedchamber will not suit me at all. I would like the one at the south corner.'

Mrs Keith turned dismayed eyes to Belle. 'But…'

'That will be fine,' Belle said. 'You can prepare that bedchamber for her.' She was not about to argue that she already occupied the room for she feared it would only cause more distress for everyone.

Lady Georgina had already started up the staircase to the drawing room. Salcombe and Belle followed, but just outside the drawing room door she was stopped by Salcombe's hand on her arm. She looked up at him, puzzled that he would touch her. Salcombe removed his hand. 'I have a message for you from Lady Chloe,' he said quietly.

She was startled. 'Do you?'

'Yes.' He pressed a note into her hand. 'She is concerned about your well-being.'

'Thank you,' she said and wondered how such a thing had come about when it was so apparent he held her in no esteem at all. 'You are very kind.'

'Not at all.'

'You have spoken to Chloe, then? Is she well?'

For the first time a smile touched his mouth. 'I think so.'

Good heavens. He actually liked Chloe and more than just a little, if she was not mistaken— Which explained why he had delivered Chloe's message.

She realised she was staring at Salcombe. 'I am glad,' she said softly. 'Thank you for letting me know.'

He inclined his head and waited for her to pass into the drawing room. Lady Georgina had already removed her bonnet and pelisse and had seated herself on one of the sofas. 'I will ring for refreshment. What would you like, Brandt?'

'Nothing at the moment.'

She looked at Belle. 'I trust you intend to put those flowers in a vase before they wilt. Then I want to speak to you.'

Belle went to the vase that sat on one of the tables and thrust the flowers in the water. She took a deep breath in an effort to suppress her anger. She should be more charitable towards Lady Georgina and understand that it was only concern for her nephew that prompted her hostility. Instead, she sensed there was something other than Justin's well-being that motivated Lady Georgina to involve herself in his affairs.

She finally turned around.

'Brandt, I suggest you find Westmore and let him know we have arrived,' Lady Georgina said.

Salcombe frowned. 'I thought you would prefer to rest after the journey.'

'I am not the least bit fatigued.' She smiled thinly. 'Go. I wish to speak to Lady Milborne in private.'

He looked over at Belle. 'Do you know where Justin is?'

'I am not certain. I know he meant to see one of his tenants and then was to go to Haversham Hall.'

'I'll find him.' He hesitated and seemed about to say something more, then changed his mind. 'I will return shortly.'

His footsteps echoing in the hall left Belle feeling adrift. She forced herself to look at Lady Georgina. 'I believe you have something to say to me.'

'Oh, I do. I do not know what game you are playing, but I've no intention of allowing you to ruin my nephew's life. You may consider yourself the mistress of this house, but you are not. Nor will you ever be. I will see to that even if it means I completely ruin you in the process. And your family.'

Belle met the woman's gaze, not wanting her to know how much her threats frightened her. She had no doubt Lady Georgina would do exactly as she said. 'You may rest assured that I will not be mistress of this house or of any house in Justin's possession, either now or in the future. Is there anything else you wish to say to me?'

'I suggest you make plans to leave here as quickly as possible. Tonight, preferably. There is no reason for you to remain. There is an inn in the village. You can stay there and then you can go in the morning. I will, of course, loan you the funds.'

Belle felt heat rise to her cheeks. 'I do not need your money.'

A footman entered with the tea tray. Lady Georgina directed him to set it on the table near her. She rose and picked up the teapot in a movement that was still grace-ful. 'I will have some tea. I would ask you to join me but you will, of course, want to pack your things.'

Belle stared at her for a moment and then turned on her heel without saying a word.

'Is that not Brandt coming up the drive?' Marguerite asked. 'On one of your horses?'

'Brandt?' Justin's brow shot up but he turned to look anyway. He was about to leave Haversham Hall and had just stepped out of the front entrance. She was not mis-taken—the horse cantering up the long winding drive of Haversham Hall was from his stable and the rider was indeed his cousin.

What the devil? He ran down the steps leading from

the front entrance to the drive and waited for his cousin to halt the grey gelding next to him. From his cousin's dusty appearance he thought it was unlikely Brandt had changed from his travelling clothes. 'What are you doing here?' he demanded, although he suspected he knew very well.

'Looking for you. Lady Milborne thought you might be here.'

Justin scowled. 'I trust you were civil to her.'

'Civil enough, although I cannot say the same for Aunt Georgina, which is why I thought it prudent to fetch you home as quickly as possible. As well as to warn you.' He looked over Justin's shoulder. 'Good day, Marguerite.'

Justin had not heard her approach. She stood next to him. 'Lady Georgina is here?' she said, her expression dismayed. 'Why ever would you bring her?'

'I trust you have a reasonable explanation,' Justin said coldly.

'I don't. She either came with me or by herself. I suggest you return home and rescue Lady Milborne.'

'I intend to.' Justin started towards his horse.

Marguerite caught up with him. 'I am coming to Falconcliff as well.'

'Why?'

'Because Belle will need a friend. A female friend. You must go now, but I will be over as soon as I change into my riding habit.'

He glanced down at her slightly rounded belly. 'I doubt if Giles will be pleased to have you cantering all over the countryside.' He could tell from the stubborn look in her eye that she would not listen to him.

'Hardly all over the countryside, just next door. I'll leave a note for him and let him know we have been invited for dinner.' She smiled. 'Besides, Dr Moore has emphasised that exercise in moderation is quite good for ladies in my particular condition.'

'I'll leave Brandt to escort you. Don't argue,' he said before she could open her mouth. He doubted Dr Moore knew Marguerite's definition of moderation. He took the horse's reins from the groom and mounted in a swift, easy movement.

'Don't let her canter,' he said to Brandt.

'Have no fears on that score. I've no desire to incur Haversham's wrath. I will see you shortly. Don't do anything rash.'

'I won't make any promises.' He urged his horse into a trot and started down the drive. He had no idea what his aunt hoped to accomplish by coming here. No, that was not true, he knew exactly what she wanted to accomplish.

Belle folded a pair of silk stockings and placed them in the valise. She and Ellen had almost finished packing her clothes and only her jewellery and a few other small items remained. She stared down at the valise for a moment, and tried to think what she was to do next. Her mind seemed to be completely blank.

She supposed she should ask for a carriage to be sent around. She was loath to leave without telling Justin, but she feared he would try to stop her. Or perhaps he wouldn't. Surely he would see how awkward it would be to have his mistress under the same roof as his cousin and aunt. She was undoubtedly a hypocrite, but she still could not feel it was right to conduct an illicit liaison when one's relations slept down the hall.

But, oh, how she would miss him.

'What are you doing?'

Justin's snarl jerked her out of her trance. She spun around. He stood in the doorway of the bedchamber, dressed in riding breeches and coat, specks of mud on his boots, his crop still in hand.

'I…I am packing.'

He advanced into the room. 'What the devil for?' His gaze fell on Ellen who stood near the wardrobe, a pair of gloves in her hand, her eyes wide. 'I would like to be private with Lady Milborne.'

'Yes, your Grace.' Ellen set the gloves down on the dresser and scurried out.

Without taking his eyes from Belle, Justin closed the door behind him and came across the room. 'Why are you packing?' he asked softly.

Her eyes must be as wide as Ellen's. 'Because I cannot stay here with your aunt and cousin. It…it would not be proper.'

'Did my aunt put that idea into your head?'

'No, not exactly.' She swallowed at the look in his eyes. She might not need to find a room at the inn because he might strangle her first. 'It would be very awkward for everyone. Perhaps I am rather prudish, but I do not think it is at all the thing to have a mistress under the same roof as one's family.'

'Indeed. And why not? Do you worry they might guess what we do when you come to my bed at night?'

'Well, yes. And it is immoral.'

'Do you feel immoral when you are in my arms each night?'

'That is not the point.' Her face was heating and she felt flustered. 'I cannot stay any longer. And your aunt would like this room.'

'I suppose you said you would give it to her.' A brief

sardonic smile crossed his face. 'Then you may share my room with me.'

'Will you please be reasonable?'

'No.' His hands went to her shoulders. She heard his crop fall to the ground before he hauled her to him. Her heart slammed against her ribs at his expression and her knees started to shake. She should resist him, push him away, but instead her arms crept around his neck. When his mouth met hers, her arms only tightened and she returned his kiss with an equal passion. She would not be in his arms like this again.

They were alerted by the knock on the door. Belle lay with her head on his chest and his arm encircling her. She had closed her eyes, wanting to pretend they could be like this for an eternity. She opened her eyes just as Justin stirred.

'Belle.'

Marguerite's voice brought her firmly back to reality. She moved from his embrace and sat up. 'Yes. I…I am here.' Although the door was closed and locked, her cheeks heated and she felt as self-conscious as if Marguerite had actually come into the room.

'I merely wanted to let you know that Giles and I have arrived. After you have dressed I would like to talk to you.' There was a pause. 'You can let Justin know we have arrived as well.'

'Yes.' Her voice was shaky. She waited until she heard Marguerite move away from the door before looking down at Justin.

His mouth curved in a wicked smile. 'See, that was not so bad. You sounded quite calm as if having people knock on your door while you engaged in an immoral activity is a common occurrence.'

She gave a little laugh. 'I could not see that having hysterics would serve an useful purpose.'

'Probably not.' His gaze roamed her face. 'Should we engage in another round of immorality before dinner?'

'No! Most certainly not!' This time her cheeks flamed. She climbed out of bed. 'It is very rude to leave your guests to entertain themselves while we are up here doing...doing this. I still have not moved from this room and I must finish packing.'

He sat up and caught her wrist. 'I won't let you leave.'

She looked into his face. 'I have no choice. You must see that.'

His eyes were serious. 'Then I leave with you.'

'Justin...'

'Stop arguing with me.' He released her wrist and rose to a sitting position. He was naked and she tore her gaze away from the sight of his lean, muscular body, a body she knew more intimately than her own. She found her shift on the floor and picked it up.

He came up behind her and turned her to face him. 'I will see you at dinner.' He touched her cheek with a gentle finger. 'Don't worry, Belle. Everything will come out right.'

She nodded and wished she could believe him.

Chapter Fifteen

Marguerite was not alone when Belle paused in the doorway of the drawing room. Lady Georgina was already there, as were Giles and Salcombe. Marguerite sat on one of the sofas near Lady Georgina, who was seated in a stiff chair. The two men stood by the windows. As she moved into the room, silence fell for a moment, and then Lady Georgina turned to Marguerite. In a loud voice she asked if she had heard from her eldest sister.

'I have,' Marguerite said. She rose and went towards Belle, her hands outstretched. 'Dear Belle, how nice it is to see you again!'

Belle took Marguerite's hands. 'Thank you,' she said and hoped Marguerite knew how much she meant it.

Marguerite smiled. 'Come and sit by me on the sofa.' She had a gleam in her eye and Belle could see she intended to challenge Lady Georgina.

Lady Georgina's mouth tightened when the two women sat down. Oh, dear. Belle did not want Marguerite to fall victim to Lady Georgina's wrath because of her.

Marguerite smiled at Lady Georgina. 'How nice it has

been to have Belle in the neighbourhood! We have become very dear friends, you know.'

'Have you?' Lady Georgina glanced at Belle. 'Then you will be most disappointed to know Lady Milborne is to leave. Tonight, in fact. Is that not so, Lady Milborne?' Her expression dared Belle to contradict her.

'I...' Belle began.

'But she will not be going far.' Marguerite smiled again, this time her smile held more than a little triumph.

'No, not far at all,' Justin said from the doorway. He had changed into pantaloons and a black coat. His face was grim. 'In fact, she will not be going anywhere.'

'Oh, but she is.' Marguerite met his eyes. 'She is coming to Haversham Hall.'

Belle wandered into the library and stood at the window. In less than half an hour she would leave for Haversham Hall. She had sought out Jackson and thanked him for his kindnesses and had been touched when he said, rather hesitantly, that the household would miss her.

The water blended in the darkness of the night. The magic was not there tonight—she felt cold and alone, despite knowing she would be with a friend tonight. The arrival of Lord Salcombe and Lady Georgina had smashed the illusion of being in a faraway, safe place where all things were possible. The real world had intruded again and any hope that there would be a magical ending had gone.

She turned when she heard footsteps. Justin stood a little behind her. 'I thought I might find you here,' he said.

She moved towards him. 'I came to bid the sea farewell.'

'You are not leaving forever,' he said. 'You will be back.'

'I hope so.' She did not think she would, but she did not want to argue with him now. 'It is probably time for me to go. I do not want to keep your friends waiting since they are kind enough to have me.'

'They are your friends now as well.' He frowned a little. 'I have something I want to say to you, but now is not the time. I will call on you tomorrow.'

'I would like that.' She would brace herself to say goodbye. Perhaps it would be easier away from Falconcliff. 'We should return to the drawing room.'

'Yes.' He still frowned, but said nothing more as he followed her from the room. He was preoccupied even as he handed her into the Havershams' carriage and she already felt as if the beginnings of a chasm had started to crack between them.

Belle was sitting on a bench under an arbour in one of the gardens that surrounded Haversham Hall when Justin called late the next morning. Caroline had been with her for nearly an hour but had just been summoned by her governess to finish a lesson.

She looked up when she heard footsteps on the gravelled path. He strode towards her and she slowly rose and waited for him.

Justin stopped in front of her. He was dressed much as he had been yesterday when he came to her bedchamber and she wanted nothing more than to throw herself in his arms again. Instead she said, 'Hello, Justin.'

'I want to talk to you.' He ran his hand through his hair and she knew he was tense.

'I know.' Her eyes searched his face. His expression was hard to read. 'What is it?'

'I want you to marry me.'

Her heart hammered against her chest and for a wild moment she wanted to tell him 'yes'. She shook her head. 'Justin, I…I cannot.'

'Why not?' He frowned. 'Is it because of your marriage to Milborne? God only knows, I could not blame you for being reluctant, but I promise you marriage to me will not be like that. I will draw up a contract outlining your rights if you wish.'

'No. It is not that.'

'Then what is it? The past? Do you think I hold it against you? I told you I believe you. The past does not matter.'

Tears sprang to her eyes. 'Doesn't it? How can you say that?'

He caught her hand and brought it to his lips. 'Because it does not. You have proved yourself to be warm, and generous and brave, and that is all that matters to me now. I want you, Belle. I want you to be with me, I want to wake up with you each morning. I want you to bear my children. Our children.'

'That is why I cannot!' She felt more anguished than she had ever thought possible. 'I cannot have your children.'

'You do not want children?' He drew back a little. 'I rather thought after seeing you with Caroline and William that you were fond of children.'

'I am.' She took a deep breath. 'But I cannot have children. Not yours. Not Lucien's. I…I am barren.'

He stared at her for a moment. 'How do you know that?' he finally asked.

'Because more than anything Lucien wanted an heir. He was most…most diligent in his efforts to ensure there would be one. But after three years of marriage I never conceived. So, you see, marriage between us is impossible.'

'How can you be certain that it was not Lucien who was at fault?' he asked quietly. His eyes were on her face.

'He called in a physician who dealt with such things. He put me on all sorts of regimes but in the end he said that it was his opinion that I was barren.' She could not bring herself to tell him Lady Georgina's contention that Lucien had illegitimate children.

'It does not matter to me. I want to be with you.'

'It may not matter now, but it will in the future.' She saw he was about to protest and she took his hand. 'You must listen to me. I can tell you all the things you know about your responsibility to your title and your family and your lands. That you need an heir to carry your bloodlines. But even more than that, you need children of your own. I saw how you were with Caroline and William—how much you love them and how happy you are when you are with them. Marguerite said so herself, that you will be an excellent father. I cannot deprive you of that. You would grow to resent me and I would carry the guilt of not giving you what you most desire.'

'I desire you. Nor would I resent you because of such a hand of fate. My title and the entailed properties would pass out of the direct line but they would go to Brandt so I cannot be too bitter. I have every intention of becoming an exemplary godfather.'

'It will not be enough.' She pressed his hand tighter. 'There is your family as well. They resent me with good reason, but if I marry you it will drive even more of a wedge between you. I am not completely stupid—I could see even last night that relations between you and your cousin were not as they should be.'

'That does not matter. I cannot live my life to please my relations.' His mouth was set.

'But it is one more thing. And when there are no children, they will resent your marriage even more. There are the other things as well. The rumours that circulated in London about me and about you. I cannot accept your offer. I cannot allow you to sacrifice all that matters to you to marry me.'

She had no idea if he'd even heard her. 'Do you love me?' he demanded fiercely.

She closed her eyes. If she told him the truth, she feared he would never accept her answer. She opened them. 'I…I am very fond of you. I care for you and will always wish you well.'

His face was grim. 'I think you are afraid to love. Otherwise, you would see that all of your objections are not insurmountable.'

'The fact that I am barren is not,' she said quietly. 'It precludes me from ever marrying.'

'So you will live your life without love.' His eyes bore into hers. 'You spoke of guilt. Do you think I will live my life without regard to the knowledge that you are outside the pale because of me? Think of that, my dear.'

'I do not hold you responsible for that. I chose freely to become your mistress.'

'I must correct you. You chose to become my mistress because I forced you. Do you not recall that it was either your virtue or your sister-in-law?'

'I always knew that some day I must redress the wrong done you. I was willing to pay whatever price you asked.'

'So, you came with me, a martyr who was prepared to sacrifice body and virtue in payment for her sins? Or your husband's? Was that the only reason? I had thought you were without guile, but how much of the pleasure and giving when you lay in my arms was an act?'

'None of it was.' She spoke quietly and tiredly.

'That only makes it worse, then. You gave me part of your soul as well. That, my dear, was hardly sporting of you. You have put me at a complete disadvantage. I will leave you now. I have no desire to find myself further in your debt.' He executed a short bow and then left her.

This time she did not watch him walk away.

Chapter Sixteen

Marguerite waited for her on the terrace that led from the drawing room to the garden. Her face was filled with concern. 'Are you all right?'

'I am, thank you.' To Belle's chagrin, her voice trembled.

'Oh, my dear!' Marguerite dashed forward and caught her hands. Her face held such compassion that Belle nearly broke down then.

'I pray you will not say anything kind to me or I will probably burst into tears.'

'Then I will have to abuse you! How could you refuse Justin?'

'He told you that?'

'No, but I knew he meant to offer for you. He looked so despondent when he left a little while ago, that I knew you could not have accepted him. Whatever prevented you? Was it Lady Georgina? She is a truly terrible old lady and has always meddled in Justin's affairs, but you cannot let her frighten you!'

Belle drew away. She could dissemble, but as always when faced with Marguerite's forthright kindness she found herself wanting to tell her. 'No, it was not Lady

Georgina.' She forced herself to meet Marguerite's eyes. 'I am barren. After I saw him here with the children I knew I could never accept him.'

Marguerite's face was troubled. 'Are you certain you are barren?'

'I am certain. He tried to tell me it did not matter, but I know it does. Perhaps not at the moment or even a year from now, but it will. And it already matters to me.'

'I see.' She studied Belle's face for a moment. 'Then you have made up your mind.'

'Yes.' She was puzzled by the odd note in Marguerite's voice, almost as if Marguerite did not quite see that it was the only choice she could make. That, in fact, there really was no choice at all.

Lady Georgina cornered Justin as he stalked to his study. 'I want to talk to you,' she said.

'I fear I am occupied at the moment.' He reined in his temper. She was not to blame for the reason Belle gave for refusing him, but he resented her presence all the same. Most of the time he tolerated her, but barely. She had been his father's only sister. In her own way she had loved his father, which was why he did not completely wash his hands of her. And because he was the head of the family he was responsible for her.

'You have hardly given me a moment since I arrived. I dare say you are angry with me for sending Lady Milborne away but you must see it was for the best.'

He stared at her. 'Did you send her away?'

'Not directly, perhaps, but she did understand that it would be impossible for her to stay any longer now that we have arrived.' Her lips curved in a little smile.

'Then I hope you will understand that if she had not

gone to stay at Haversham Hall and been forced to go elsewhere, that I would have gone with her.'

The smile disappeared. 'You are very foolish. She has no reputation. Have you heard the tales? Her husband forced her to participate in his little parties, which were no better than orgies.'

'The person who started the tales had better hope that I do not discover his or her identity. Because if I do, I will see that person never sets foot in society again.'

Justin did not wait for her answer. He moved past her into his study and closed the door. He was beginning to feel sure he knew exactly who had started the rumours.

He knew his aunt would stop at nothing to destroy Belle as long as she perceived the younger woman as a threat.

He could not allow her to do that. His aunt wanted him to wed a woman of her own choosing. She saw Belle as a hindrance that must be removed.

Very well. He would marry where his aunt wished. But only under certain conditions.

He watched the sea below him. The clouds had rolled in and the sea reflected the greyness of the sky. He doubted very much that he would bring his unknown bride to Falconcliff.

In fact, he doubted that he would return to Falconcliff at all.

Justin called on Giles and Marguerite the next morning. He was shown into the small parlour where they were still at breakfast. Giles had just said something that made Marguerite smile and she touched his hand. An envy that was almost painful pierced him.

Marguerite glanced up and saw him. 'Justin.' Her face sobered and she rose. 'How are you?'

'I had wanted to talk to you today. You and Giles.' He paused, not certain how to begin. 'I have something to ask of you.'

Giles frowned. 'What is it?'

'You have often told me that you are in my debt. I am about to call in my vouchers.'

He confronted Lady Georgina next. She was in his drawing room, seated on one of the straight-back chairs she favoured. A cup of tea sat on the table next to her.

'Good morning, Westmore,' she said. She was elegantly dressed as usual and perfectly composed. 'Please sit down.'

He leaned against the arm of the sofa instead. 'I have a proposal to put before you.'

'What is it?' She looked at him, her eyes narrowed a little. 'I pray it has nothing to do with that creature.'

'What creature is that?'

'You know quite well.'

'Perhaps you will enlighten me.'

'Lady Milborne, of course.' She laughed a little. 'Oh, do not look at me like that! You know quite well I dislike her and would do anything to keep you out of her clutches. As long as you are besotted with her, you will not do your duty and marry.'

He smiled coldly. 'I am quite willing to do my duty, but there is something you must do in return.'

'You are willing to marry? My dear Westmore, I…but who do you have in mind? Is there someone?' Then she stared at him. 'No! It cannot be Lady Milborne! I swear if it is…'

He interrupted her. 'It is not Lady Milborne. Nor do I have a specific candidate in mind.'

'Lady Clarissa, then. I have always thought she would

be most suitable. She has the breeding, and is certainly considered a diamond of the first water! She is most accomplished and I've no doubt will be a most admirable Duchess.'

Since that description could fit any number of eligible young ladies, he found her qualifications a dead bore. 'I suggest you listen to what I want you to do before you plan the wedding.'

'Very well. What is it?' she asked impatiently.

'You will leave for London the day after next. As I will. Giles, Marguerite and Lady Milborne will travel to London as well. You will hold a soirée a week after your arrival.'

'Really, Westmore, you are dictating in a remarkably high-handed fashion. But if it pleases you, of course. I can invite a number of eligible girls—'

'You will invite Lady Milborne as well as Giles and Marguerite.'

'Invite Lady Milborne? You are mad! I would never do such a thing! Have you completely lost your sense of propriety?'

'Not at all.' He kept his gaze on her. 'If you do not invite Lady Milborne, there will be no marriage to Lady Clarissa or to any other eligible young lady. But that is not all I require. You are to acknowledge Lady Milborne in public. In fact, if you fail to acknowledge Lady Milborne on any occasion, I will not only make no offers of marriage, but I will refuse to acknowledge you in return.'

She gasped. 'You cannot be serious! You are mad!' She gave an odd laugh. 'No, you're not mad, you are still besotted! I suppose I should be grateful you only intend to keep her as your mistress instead of as your wife!'

His eyes locked with hers. 'She is not my mistress. I trust there will be no rumours to that effect.'

'I have no idea why you are doing this! After what she did to you!'

'She did nothing to me. So, do I have your word?'

'Very well. If only to see that you are safely married and with an heir on the way. I hope that will cure you of this obsession.'

He moved away from the sofa. 'I intend to put these terms in writing so there will be no misunderstanding about what I want from you.'

'Good heavens, Westmore. I am a relation, not some sort of merchant you are dealing with!'

'None the less, there will be a document. I will leave you now as I've other business to attend to before we depart for London. By the way,' he added, his voice deliberate, 'the only reason I am not to wed Lady Milborne is because she refused my offer.'

Her mouth fell open but Justin left the room before she could say a word. He had one last call to make.

Belle pulled her shawl more firmly around her shoulders. She sat on a bench at the far end of the Havershams' property. The estate was further from the sea than Falconcliff but she could still see the water in the distance.

She supposed she should return to the house. She had been out here nearly an hour and Marguerite would worry if she was gone too long.

She rose and started back down the well-kept path that ran along one edge of the grounds. She had just passed the summerhouse when she saw a man coming towards her.

Justin. Her heart pounded. Her first impulse was to

dodge into the summerhouse and hope he did not see her, but it was too late. He had already spotted her. She stopped and waited for him.

He came to a halt a few feet from her. 'Good day, Belle,' he said. His expression was cool and reserved, as it had been that night when she had first seen him again.

'Good day.' At least her voice did not tremble.

'Are you going back to the house?'

She nodded. 'Yes.'

'I will walk with you. I have some matters to discuss with you.'

'And what are those?' She started to walk.

He fell into step next to her. 'I have come to the conclusion that you are correct. I have certain responsibilities in my position. So when I return to London I will heed your advice and find a wife.'

She kept her voice calm, despite the sick feeling in her stomach. 'I think that is wise of you.'

'Do you? I am glad.' He slanted a look at her. 'I do not suppose you would consider continuing our liaison.' His voice was completely indifferent.

She stopped. She had no idea whether it was a question or a statement. Or whether he meant to insult her or hurt her or both. She met his gaze without flinching. 'I would not do something so despicable to your future wife. I lived with an unfaithful husband, and even when there is no love between husband and wife, it is still painful to know your husband considers you of less value than his mistresses.'

Something flickered in his eyes. 'Belle…' he began.

'I would prefer to end our conversation, your Grace.' She began to walk again.

He easily caught up with her. 'Wait. I promise I'll

hold my damnable tongue. There is something else. One more duty I have.'

'I've no desire to be your confidante in these matters.'

'This concerns you.'

'You have no duty towards me.'

'I do. I have taken away your good name, I will see to it that it is restored.'

'That will be impossible.'

'Not at all.'

'I do not wish you to even attempt to do so.' She did not look at him.

'And allow you to continue to martyr yourself while I escape unscathed? No, my dear Belle, you will at least grant me this.'

She was stung. 'I do not consider myself a martyr! I have only tried to do what I thought was right!'

'Which is precisely what I am doing. I've already spoken to Giles and Marguerite. I will leave for London the day after next and you will leave with Giles and Marguerite the following day.'

She glanced at him. 'I don't wish to return to London.' They had reached the lawn just behind the house.

He caught her arm. 'Let me go,' she said.

'Not until you listen to me.'

She turned to face him. 'Very well. I am listening.'

He dropped his hand from her arm. 'You will return to London because I intend that you will be restored to society. There are still a few weeks left in the Season, which will enable you to be seen in Giles and Marguerite's company as well as my cousin's. Once you reach London, you will stay with Marguerite and Giles as their guest. They will host a small party shortly after your arrival. You will attend as many public functions as possible and we will make it clear that anyone who does not receive you will be deprived of our company as well.'

'All of this is not necessary.'

'It is. You have been staying at Haversham Hall for the past three weeks as a guest. Brandt will vouch for that. As well as my aunt.'

'She must loathe that.'

He smiled, but there was no amusement in his face. 'Not at all. She realises it would be to her detriment to have rumours of our liaison leak out.'

'I see.' She could not imagine how he managed to bring that about.

'Are you in need of funds?'

She flushed a little. 'No, I have what I need. Thank you.'

He inclined his head. 'Not at all.' He paused for a moment and then spoke. 'I will bid you farewell, then. I will undoubtedly see you in London.' He was as cool and impersonal as if they were strangers. Which was for the best. Otherwise she would be devastated.

'Yes.' She hesitated and then held out her hand. 'Goodbye, Justin.'

He took it, his hands briefly clasping hers before releasing it. 'Goodbye, Belle.'

She did not watch him walk away.

Chapter Seventeen

'Lovely!' Marguerite said. She turned Belle towards the looking glass. 'I do not think you should ever be allowed to wear grey again.'

'Most certainly not.' Madame Celeste adjusted the sleeve of the peach-coloured silk gown. She stepped back and surveyed Belle. 'Perfect. You will rival any lady present tonight.'

The colour was lovely. Her skin glowed and her eyes seemed darker. But the bodice appeared to be nothing more than a band of silk and there seemed to be an excessive amount of bare flesh showing above it. She glanced at Marguerite. 'Is it not rather low?'

'It most certainly is not! You cannot continue to dress like a Puritan and hide away your assets.'

'I would like to keep at least some of my assets hidden.'

Marguerite laughed. 'Do not worry. No one will be shocked.'

'Perhaps a fichu of some sort?'

'No!' Marguerite exclaimed.

Madame Celeste pursed her lips. 'It would quite ruin the effect.'

She gave up. She had discovered Marguerite intended she would re-enter society with a flourish. The three days she had been in London had been spent in a whirl of visits to nearly every fashionable shop in London that dealt with a lady's needs. Tonight would be her first foray into society. They were to attend the opera and Marguerite had insisted she must have a new gown.

Madame finished the fitting and promised the gown would be delivered in good time for tonight's affair. Just as Belle and Marguerite were about to leave, the door of the shop opened. Maria and Chloe entered. Belle stopped, her heart pounding. She hardly knew what to say.

Chloe saw her first. 'Belle!' She flew at Belle and Belle's arms closed around her.

She scarcely heard Marguerite's, 'Good day, Lady Ralston,' and Maria's rather flustered answer.

She released Chloe, who stepped back. 'Oh, Belle, you are back! I have missed you so!'

'And I have missed you.' She looked over Chloe's head at Maria, whose own face was confused. 'Hello, Maria.'

Maria's lips tightened, and for a moment Belle did not think she would answer, but then she said,

'Belle.'

'Belle is staying with us,' Marguerite said.

'Is she? I did not know that,' Maria said. She cast Belle a confused look. 'I did not know she was in London.'

'She returned with us from Haversham Hall.'

'From Haversham Hall?'

'You did not know she was there?' Marguerite managed to make it sound as if everyone knew that. 'She was our guest there as well for the past few weeks. But we decided to return to London for the remainder of the Season. I will be having a very small party next week. The invitations will go out today. I do hope you and Lady Chloe can attend.'

Maria made a little sound. 'I suppose…I do not know…'

'Of course we will attend,' Chloe said firmly. 'Won't we, Mama?' Never tractable, Chloe looked exceedingly stubborn and Belle knew she intended to have her way.

'Yes,' Maria said helplessly. 'Thank you.'

Marguerite smiled. 'We must go now. We have several errands to attend to. So delightful to see you, Lady Ralston, Lady Chloe. We will call on you in the next few days.' She took Belle's arm. 'Good day.' She sailed out the door and Belle had no choice but to follow.

Once on the street Belle gave a shaky laugh. 'I never thought Maria would be persuaded to speak to me again. And truly, I understood why she did not want to, but I felt so wretched at not being able to see Chloe.'

'Well, now you shall.' Marguerite looked quite pleased with herself. 'This is only the first step. Between us, we will see that you will be considered completely respectable.'

'Us?'

'Justin and me. Of course, Giles as well and Brandt, but Justin is mostly responsible.'

'I see.' The happiness she had felt at seeing Chloe faded. Some day the mention of his name would not hurt so much, but for now the ragged tear in her heart was still raw and open.

Belle sat in the Havershams' box and tried not to think about the last time she had been to a performance. Of course, it had been the Theatre Royal and not the opera.

But… She must think of something else, such as the fact she and Marguerite were to call on Maria and Chloe tomorrow.

Or that Marguerite and Giles had become her friends. That was the one good thing that had come of this entire affair. She glanced at her companion. She had come to love them; Marguerite with her lively spirits and kind heart and Giles, although reserved and not much inclined to idle talk, had welcomed her to his home. And the children. She had treasured the time she had spent with them at Haversham Hall. They had made her promise she would return soon to see them.

She glanced out at the boxes. Chloe and Maria were seated with Arthur a row down. And then her heart slammed into her throat when she saw Justin just entering a box. He was with Lady Georgina and an older couple. But it was the young lady with them who caught her attention. Her pale hair and slender figure were vaguely familiar but she could not quite recall her name. He solicitously helped her into the box and bent his head to speak to her and she knew, without a doubt, that he intended to court her. She yanked her gaze away but not before Marguerite saw her.

'I see Lord and Lady Blackwood and their eldest daughter have joined Justin and Lady Georgina tonight,' Marguerite said quietly. 'She is Lady Clarissa.'

'She is very lovely.'

'She is considered one of the Season's beauties. She is an heiress as well as the daughter of a Marquis. Rumour has it that her father has turned down a number of offers already, some of them quite eligible. He is believed to be holding out for higher stakes.'

'A duke, perhaps.' She would not pretend ignorance. 'I think so.'

Belle drew in a breath. 'There is no need to spare my feelings. Justin told me that he would find a wife when he returned to London.'

'You do not mind?' Marguerite asked carefully. 'You seem so calm sometimes.'

'Only because the alternative would be for me to go mad.' Her hands tightened around her reticule. 'And I mind. I mind terribly but there is nothing I can do.'

'You could tell him that you will marry him.'

She shook her head. 'That is the one thing I cannot do.'

Justin had tried to keep his gaze from straying to the Havershams' box, but despite his best efforts he had finally given in and looked up. At first he had thought she had not come after all and wondered whom Marguerite had brought in her stead. He'd felt a quiver of shock when he realised the dark-haired beauty in the peach gown was Belle. Desire, jealousy and anger shot through him. What the hell was Marguerite up to? She looked nothing like his demure Belle. He did not need a quizzing glass to see that her gown exposed every inch of her creamy breasts that was possible without causing a scandal.

He dragged his gaze away. She was not his Belle. Nor would she ever be. He turned his attention to Lady Clarissa who sat next to him, hands folded in her lap. She was a beauty with narrow patrician features, although her chin receded a trifle too much for his tastes. Her eyes were large blue and her mouth a rosebud shape that was appealing. Beneath her well-cut silk gown, her breasts were high and full. He did not think bedding her would be an unpleasant task, but he doubted there would be much passion involved. But then, he neither wanted nor expected passion from a marriage he considered a business arrangement.

He could not complain she talked too much. Conversation with her seemed to consist of his questions and her responses in a clear, polite voice. She was not overly bold and her responses were exactly what were deemed acceptable for a well-bred girl. She deferred to his aunt, proving herself to be precisely what Lady Georgina wanted in his wife.

When the interval arrived he asked Lady Clarissa how she liked it. She turned her blue eyes on him. 'I fear I do not much care for this particular opera,' she said politely.

Ah, an opinion at last. 'And why not?'

She merely looked at him. 'I do not know,' she said finally.

The conversation did not seem destined to go any further. He rose. 'I am going to the lobby. Do you wish to join me?' he asked her.

'No, thank you.'

At least he could escape from the box for a few minutes. Alone. First he needed to remind his aunt of her duty. She was talking with Lord and Lady Blackwood. Unlike her daughter, Lady Blackwood was an animated conversationalist. Brandt had just arrived along with two of Lady Clarissa's admirers and Lady Blackwood turned her attention to them. Justin touched his aunt's arm. 'You have a box to visit,' he said in a low voice.

She looked far from pleased. 'Not now. I am going to visit Harriet Collings.'

'Then I am leaving for White's.'

She locked gazes with him before finally giving in with ill grace. 'Very well.'

'Brandt.' He turned to his cousin. 'Aunt Georgina wishes to pay a call to Giles's box. Perhaps you will escort her.'

Brandt promptly held out his arm. 'Of course.' Lady Georgina laid her gloved hand on his arm, her mouth in a tight line.

A quarter of an hour later, Justin was about to return to his box when he heard his name. Eliza Pomeroy stood behind him.

'Good evening, Eliza.' He had not seen her since the night of the duel. She was plumper than she had been, but was still a striking woman with her auburn hair and vivid blue eyes.

He was about to walk past her but she stopped him. 'There is something I have wanted to say to you for a long time. Perhaps this is not the best place, but I must tell you this before it is too late.'

'What is it?'

'I…' she began and stopped. A peculiar expression crossed her face.

He half-turned and felt as if he had sustained a blow. Belle and Marguerite were strolling towards them. Belle had just smiled at something Marguerite had said when she saw him. All animation drained from her face. She turned away but not before he saw the anguish in her eyes. Marguerite inclined her head towards him before they passed through the doors that led to the boxes.

Justin jerked his attention back to Eliza. 'What did you want to say to me?'

She drew in a breath and for the first time he saw her composure was shaken. 'I have wanted to tell you that Lady Milborne had nothing to do with her husband's plot to kill you. Lucien saw you were attracted to her

and decided he would use that against you. But when he
realised his wife had come to care for you, he decided
he would punish her as well. I should have told you this
years ago. Perhaps it would have changed things for you.
And for Lady Milborne. I do not think it is too late for
either you or Lady Milborne to find happiness.'

He wished she were right.

Chapter Eighteen

Marguerite's small party turned out to include nearly fifty guests. Belle had been taken aback by Marguerite's energy but her efforts to persuade Marguerite that she could see to all the arrangements had been waved aside. 'It is only at the very beginning when I feel ill most of the time and fatigued but after that I have an amazing amount of energy and can hardly bear to sit still until the very end.'

Giles's look had been wry when Belle had expressed her concern. 'I cannot stop her once she makes up her mind. As long as she is not ill or overly tired, her physician has said she can do as she pleases.'

The drawing room had been decorated with pots of plants and silk vines. The violin and viola players were in one corner. Maria and Chloe were among the first to arrive and Belle now sat in the small room directly off the drawing room with Chloe.

Chloe had just finished telling her about a shopping expedition to Grafton House when Belle looked up and saw Sir Lionel Garrick standing in front of them. He was a pleasant-looking man in his fifties, a widower with a grown son and two daughters. She had met him at the

opera and he had called the next day. He smiled at them.
'Good evening, Lady Chloe, Lady Milborne. I did not
wish to interrupt, but Marguerite said I might find you
here. Might I persuade both of you to walk in the garden
with me? The evening is especially fine.'

'Thank you, that would be very nice,' Belle said. She
glanced at Chloe.

Chloe smiled. 'I would like that as well.'

They both rose and followed Sir Lionel. They had just
reached the door when they came face to face with Justin
and Lady Clarissa.

Belle's equanimity shattered. He looked equally
stunned, his gaze going to Sir Lionel, and then to where
her hand rested on his arm. His eyes narrowed and his
voice was coldly civil when he spoke. 'Good evening,
Lady Milborne, Lady Chloe. Garrick.'

Sir Lionel glanced briefly at Belle before inclining his
head towards the other two. 'Lady Clarissa. Westmore,
heard you were back in town. Haven't seen you at
White's recently.'

'No.' He sounded distracted, Belle thought. His gaze
had gone to Belle's bodice which suddenly seemed too
low, before returning to her face. He appeared about to
speak when Lady Georgina bustled up beside them. 'Ah,
there you are.' She looked directly at Belle. 'Lady Milborne, have you met Lady Clarissa?'

'No, I have not been introduced.' She forced herself
to meet Lady Georgina's gaze.

'Then you must do so now,' Lady Georgina said with
a hint of malice. She performed the introduction.

Belle smiled at the young lady, determined she would
not let anyone know how her heart sank. 'I am delighted
to meet you.'

Lady Clarissa did not smile. 'How do you do, Lady

Milborne?' Her voice was well-bred and clear, but that she did not particularly relish the introduction was evident. No doubt she had heard rumours of a possible liaison between her and Justin.

What a horrible muddle. Belle suddenly wanted to escape and find a quiet corner where she could be alone, where she did not have to pretend that nothing was wrong and her heart was not broken. But she could not. Instead, she smiled up at Sir Lionel. 'Shall we continue to the garden?'

'Of course.' He smiled back at her. She was relieved when they finally were outside on the darkened terrace. She turned her attention to Sir Lionel and Chloe and chattered brightly, not wanting them to guess that anything was amiss.

But when she finally was alone, the solitude she had thought she craved felt only like a prison. She climbed into bed and, for the first time, she knew for a certainty Justin would never lie beside her again. She would never feel his warmth next to her, gaze upon his face while he slept. Never laugh with him. Or argue with him. He would, instead, lie with the cool, lovely Lady Clarissa. For the first time since she had left Devon, she wept.

The next two weeks passed in a flurry of balls, routs, soirées and performances. The campaign to restore her to some measure of respectability had worked and the gossips had found more entertaining prospects. One of them was whether the Duke of Westmore was to marry at last.

Belle threw herself into the activities and tried not to think of anything much. She drove out with Sir Lionel three times and stood up with him twice at one ball and then worried that she was encouraging him falsely, for

she had no desire to marry at all. So when he called to
ask her to drive with him again, she sent word that she
was not well.

Which was the truth. She had awoken that morning
and felt tired. Her head hurt a little and her stomach was
uneasy. In fact, she had felt under the weather for several
days and had developed a light case of the sniffles as
well. Marguerite had insisted she stay in bed because
they had been out so late the night before and they had
another ball to attend that evening.

She felt better when she woke and by the time she
dressed for the ball, she had convinced herself she was
quite recovered.

The ball was held in honour of the youngest daughter
of the Earl of Litchfield. She was a tall, rather athletic
girl who appeared uncomfortable in her white muslin
and pearls. She was also one of Lady Clarissa's friends
and Belle had no doubt that young lady would be present. Which meant Justin would most likely attend as
well.

She would do as she had on every other occasion—
try her best to avoid him without appearing to do so.

She could not help but notice that Lady Clarissa arrived with her parents and that he arrived just before the
third set. Angry with herself for paying attention, she
accepted Sir Lionel for the next dance although it was a
waltz.

He was an excellent partner, but the whirling had
made her head ache again and her stomach uneasy. She
was relieved when the dance was over. He led her to the
side of the ball room and asked if he could procure her
refreshment. She shook her head. 'No, thank you. I think
I will just rest for a few moments.'

'I do not think you are still quite well,' he said.

She managed a smile. 'It is just the headache. I fear I am rather prone to them.'

'Should I find Lady Haversham for you?'

'No, I will be fine.' She wanted to be alone for a few minutes.

He hesitated and then, after again offering to find Marguerite, took his leave. She looked after him and, with some regret, thought he was far too nice. She slipped from the ball room and found a smaller room near by. Thankfully, only a few other people occupied the other side of the room. She found a vacant chair near the door and sat down. She fanned herself, feeling hot and a little dizzy and hoped she was not coming down with an illness. She closed her eyes for a moment and realised someone stood before her. She opened them and found Arthur directly in front of her. She had not spoken to him since the day she had left and she stifled a sigh. She was in no mood for one of his pompous lectures.

He tugged at his cravat. 'Dear Belle, I have been wanting to talk to you ever since that rather unfortunate conversation we had.'

'Please, not now.'

'I fear I spoke rashly. I have wished to apologise ever since.'

Of all times to accost her with this, why must he choose now? 'You are undoubtedly right. But I must ask you to speak of this another time.' For some reason, she was quite aware of the odour of his body as well as his breath, and it was making her feel rather nauseous.

'I cannot let this rest until I tell you that I adore you. I would be most honoured if you would consent to be my wife.'

Surely he had not just proposed marriage to her in the

middle of a ball? But the heated look in his eye told her she had not misheard. 'I cannot, Arthur,' she said faintly.

He knelt beside her. 'I see I have taken you by surprise, my love.'

She glanced over at the three ladies on the other side of the room. They seemed to be elderly and she prayed they were partially deaf as well. 'Indeed. But I must refuse.'

'My dear…' He possessed himself of her hand. He started to bring it to his lips while she frantically tried to tug it out of his grasp. He suddenly halted when he realised they were no longer alone.

She glanced up and her heart slammed to her throat. Justin stood there and the look in his eye was murderous. 'I suggest you release Lady Milborne's hand.'

Arthur started and then frowned. 'You are interrupting a private conversation, sir.'

'One she does not seem to welcome.' His jaw was set and he looked fully capable of mowing Arthur to the ground. 'Perhaps you do not recall our last conversation. Let me remind you, then. I said if you came near her again I would put a bullet through you.'

'Justin, please. This is not necessary,' she said and then prayed Arthur had not noticed the use of his given name.

Arthur stood, his face flushed. His own mouth had tightened in a stiff, resentful line. 'You have no rights over her. And when she becomes my wife, it is I who will order you to stay away from her.'

'Your what?' Justin said softly.

Belle rose, now feeling truly ill. 'I am not going to be your wife, Arthur. Or anyone else's for that matter. I do not care what either of you do but I must ask you to do it away from me.'

They both looked at her then. Justin's face changed. 'Belle, damn it. You are ill.'

'Yes, rather. Which is why I wish you would leave me.'

'No.' He scowled at her in his familiar way. 'Sit down. Why the devil are you here at this affair in the first place?'

She lifted her chin. 'Because I did not feel like this until I was annoyed by unwelcome attentions.'

'I beg your pardon,' Arthur said stiffly. 'I think, Westmore, it would be best to fetch Lady Haversham.'

Justin fixed him with a cold stare. 'I agree. You can find her in the card room.'

Arthur opened his mouth and then shut it, walking stiffly off. Belle looked at Justin. 'You may leave me as well.'

'I am taking you to St James's Square.'

She gasped. 'You are not.'

'I am. You look as if you are about to swoon. I should ring a peal over Marguerite for running you this ragged.' He held out his hand.

How dare he treat her in this arrogant manner as if nothing had changed between them? 'I am not going with you, your Grace. Think of the talk.'

'There will be even more talk if I carry you from the ballroom. So, will you come with me willingly or must I force you?'

Had he gone mad? He had a peculiar glint in his eye as if he were barely reining in his temper. 'I will go with you if only to keep you from doing something exceedingly rash.'

'Good. I'm glad you intend to be reasonable.'

Reasonable? She did not feel that way at all. She ignored his hand and rose. Her head was hurting and she did feel overly warm and a little sick. He took her arm and escorted her down the stairs to the entry hall below. He gave no sign that he noticed the interested looks cast their way and then he stopped in front of an old-fashioned chair. 'Sit down. Did you bring a shawl or cloak of some sort?'

She sat. 'A shawl. Really, you do not need to escort me. You should not. If you will find Marguerite or Giles, please.' He couldn't possibly be serious about this! Could he not see that it would be a mistake?

But he had already left her to speak to a footman. She did not feel well enough to protest and only hoped Arthur had managed to find Marguerite.

But there was no sign of Marguerite by the time Justin returned to her side with her shawl. 'My carriage is here,' he said.

She looked up at him. His face still had that odd determination and she doubted he intended to leave her alone. 'But I should at least inform Marguerite. I cannot leave without telling her.'

'I have sent a message. She knows.' He draped the shawl around her shoulders, his fingers brushing the nape of her neck sending a shiver down her spine.

'Belle!'

She looked up to see Chloe coming down the steps. She reached Belle's side, her face concerned. 'Arthur said you were ill and then someone said they saw you leave with Westmore but I could not believe it.'

'She is ill and I am taking her to Lord Haversham's house,' Justin said.

Chloe started and stared. 'Oh.' Her eyes were fixed on Justin before looking back at Belle, her expression oddly speculative. 'Will you be all right?'

'Of course.' She caught Chloe's hand. 'Please do not worry. You must return to the ballroom.'

'In a moment.' She hugged Belle and then turned and dashed back up the stairs.

She was glad to lean back against the squabs. He said nothing during the short ride to St James's Square for which she was grateful. It was only when they halted that he spoke. 'I trust you are not contemplating marriage to Ralston.' His voice was low and rough.

She shuddered. 'No, of course not. I could not think of a worse fate.'

'But perhaps to Garrick?'

'That is not your concern.'

'Your happiness concerns me. It always will.'

Her hands tightened in her lap. 'It should not. You will have a wife and children that will be your concerns. I will be but a memory and I pray that what has passed between us will not affect your happiness.'

'I do not think human emotions are as easily regulated as you want to believe.'

'They may not be, but if emotions are not governed by other means such as reason, and duty and honour, then they are capable of tremendous destruction.'

'My dear, as usual I must bow to your superior logic. You are right of course, civilisation would be in a sorry state if everyone allowed their passions to govern them.' The sarcasm in his voice made her flinch.

He assisted her from the carriage and accompanied her up the steps to the house. He paused and looked down at her. 'I will be leaving the day after next for Lord Blackwood's house in Kent. So, it is unlikely I will see you again.'

It was so final. She wanted to fling herself in his arms and beg him not to go, but she could not. Instead she held out her hand. 'I wish you all happiness, your Grace.'

He hesitated and then took it. 'Then you must allow me to wish you all happiness as well.' He brought her hand to his lips and pressed a brief kiss on the back before releasing it. 'There is one thing I will leave you with, however. Duty and honour must be tempered with emotion or they will be nothing but hollow gestures. And reason is a very cold companion in one's bed. They can destroy happiness as effectively as any human emotion. Goodbye, Belle.' He left her and did not look at her again before he climbed into his carriage.

She turned and slowly entered the cool hallway. She knew that this time she would not see him again.

Chapter Nineteen

Belle entered the dining room the next morning to find Marguerite already up. Dressed in a pale yellow gown, she looked bright and cheerful. She smiled at Belle and then her expression changed to one of concern. 'You still look rather peaked. I should have insisted you stay home last night.'

Belle took the chair across from her and fought back the urge to sneeze. 'I did not feel so bad until after I stood up with Sir Lionel.'

'He does have that effect on one, doesn't he?' Marguerite said with a teasing look.

'Just the opposite, actually. He is very kind.'

'But that is not enough, is it?' Marguerite looked at her with sympathy. 'I take it that nothing changed at all between you and Justin?'

'There is nothing to change. He is going to Kent to stay with Lady Clarissa and her parents.' She reached for the coffee but the smell was not appetising. Perhaps tea would be better. She took up the teapot and poured herself a cup.

'Oh, Belle! I wish it did not have to be like this!' Marguerite suddenly burst out. 'Lady Clarissa will not make him happy and he is only contemplating marriage to her because of some stupid sense of duty! Do you think they can possibly be happy together?'

'I do not know,' Belle stammered, taken aback by the vehemence in her voice. 'Surely if they try and if there are children…'

'But how can children be happy if their parents are not? You do not know what it is like if one's parents barely tolerate each other. My father and mother hardly spoke to one another; they were civil, of course, but it was plain their marriage was only one of duty and there was nothing between them but ill-concealed contempt. I cannot remember ever seeing a genuine smile on Mama's face and Papa could hardly stand to be home. I knew then that I would only marry if I could love!' She sniffed and a tear ran down her cheek. 'I am sorry, I…I did not mean to say so much!'

Belle rose and went to her side, putting her arm around her shoulders. 'Don't be. I had no idea. Dear Marguerite!' She hugged her tight and after a few moments Marguerite pulled away. She wiped her eyes with a handkerchief and attempted a watery smile.

'I suppose that is why I want so badly for Justin to be happy. His parents were, you see, and I used to spend so much time there they teased me about becoming a daughter. He was like a brother, more so, for my own brother was so much older and was as remote as Papa. I…I had hoped that last night when he sent word he was to take you home that it might be different, but when he returned to the ball I saw it was not.'

'I am sorry, Marguerite.' Belle looked helplessly down at her friend. Nothing seemed right. She had never dreamed that refusing Justin would affect Marguerite as well. But she had never thought that striking that bargain with him in the first place would have so many repercussions. She wondered if there would ever be an end to the unhappiness that had started so many years ago.

'Do not be,' Marguerite said. 'Please sit down. Would you like some eggs? I can ring for a fresh plate.'

'No, I think tea and toast will suit me.' She took her chair.

'Marmalade, then?'

'No, dry.' If she could manage that.

Marguerite gave her a wry smile. 'Poor thing. Dry toast and tea. Those are the only things I was able to tolerate for months when I was first increasing. Thank goodness, I have an appetite again.'

Belle's hand stilled over the plate of toast. Dear God, that couldn't possibly be what was wrong with her! She dropped her hand. No, it was quite impossible. Her courses had not come again, but then, they sometimes did not. She had a slight cold and had been out too many late nights, that was all.

'Belle, is something wrong?'

Her head jerked up and she smiled. 'No, nothing. I was just thinking of something, but it is of no importance.' She took a piece of toast. 'I think I will have some marmalade, after all.'

Brandt looked across the table at his cousin. 'You don't have to do this, you know.'

'But I do,' Justin said coolly. 'It is my duty to marry and produce an heir. The sooner, the better, would you not agree?' He downed the remainder of his port and set the glass on the table, then lounged back in his chair.

They were seated in a corner of the morning room at White's where he had met Brandt an hour earlier.

'No, I would not,' Brandt said. 'Not when you're in

this damnable state. I doubt you even like Lady Clarissa particularly.'

'I do not dislike her. She is well bred, accomplished and well mannered. I have no doubt we will suit very well.'

'I wonder what Lady Clarissa would think about such an assessment.'

'I've no idea. She rarely expresses an opinion on anything.'

'I am beginning to think I would rather you wed Isabelle Milborne after all,' Brandt said slowly. 'I will not deny I was pleased when she left Falconcliff. Hell, I was delighted despite the fact I could see she cared deeply for you. I still cannot forget how badly she wounded you before.' He frowned. 'So what the devil happened between you at Falconcliff?'

'She refused my offer.'

'Why?'

'She says she is barren.' His mouth curled. 'She refused to let me sacrifice my duty for her, although I tried to persuade her I had no objections if you were my heir. Nor did she want to create a rift between me and the rest of my family. I could not, of course, object to such noble arguments.'

'So you will sacrifice yourself anyway on the altar of duty,' Brandt said softly. 'I do not think that will serve either.'

'Ah, but at least I will have the satisfaction of fulfilling it.'

'She will not be your mistress?'

'She does not want to injure my future wife in the same way Milborne injured her. So, no, she will not be my mistress.' He rose. 'I have some business to attend to before I leave town. By the way, the reason she agreed

to come with me to Falconcliff was not only to protect
her sister-in-law, but because she wished to redress the
great wrong Milborne did me.' He looked at Brandt with
a cynical eye. 'Which hardly eases my conscience at all.
Promise me you will watch after her until she leaves
London. I don't trust Aunt.'

Brandt stared at him and then nodded slowly. 'Very
well.'

'One more thing. Eliza Pomeroy finally told me that
Belle had nothing to do with her husband's plot after
all.'

He left Brandt staring after him.

Belle finally found an empty chair in one corner of
the crowded room Lady Willoughby had designated as
the card room. A number of small tables had been set
up to accommodate the guests who wished to play cards.
The room was hot and only added to her feeling of faint-
ness, but at least she could sit.

She sank gratefully into an upright wooden chair.
Thank goodness. She had feared, for a moment, she
would either swoon or become ill when she was in the
drawing room, which was the last thing she wanted to
do.

She did not want anyone to think something was
wrong with her. Certainly not Marguerite.

For she was starting to think it was quite possible she
was with child, and nothing could be more disastrous
than having Marguerite suspect.

So, for the past five days, ever since that morning at
breakfast, she had forced herself to smile and go on as
if nothing was wrong. She managed to eat and drink at
least something at mealtimes and thankfully had not yet

vomited, although there were times when she was certain she would.

She closed her eyes for a moment, allowing the conversation to swirl around her. How could this have happened? She had been so certain that a pregnancy was impossible—that she was barren—that even now she wondered if she were making up the symptoms in her mind. Did she so want a child of her own—Justin's child—that she was deluding herself into thinking she was actually with child? She had heard of such a case before and had thought it the saddest thing imaginable.

She opened her eyes. And if she were expecting a child…she had no idea what she should do. Her mind had gone around and around with the possibilities until her head hurt. If only she could talk to Marguerite, but she knew what Marguerite would advise her to do—tell Justin.

But how could she? When she was not even certain? He was to marry Lady Clarissa; the current gossip claimed they were already secretly betrothed and as soon as Lady Georgina joined them, the betrothal would be made official. She would ruin more lives if she were to rashly claim she carried his child. And then, if she were wrong and there was no child…she shuddered to think of the consequences.

She looked up and saw Lady Georgina coming towards her. Her first impulse was to run but that would be far too obvious. In the last few days, Belle seemed to see Lady Georgina everywhere and had often found the Countess's sharp gaze fixed on her in a way that made her nervous. She forced a smile to her lips when Lady Georgina stopped in front of her.

'Good evening, Lady Milborne,' Lady Georgina said.

Her eyes travelled over Belle's face. 'I see you are not well again.'

Belle started. 'What do you mean? Of course I am well. Just rather hot.'

'Indeed.' She smiled, although it was not particularly pleasant. 'I will call on you tomorrow. I trust you will be home.'

'I…' Belle began but Lady Georgina interrupted.

'By the way, when my nephew returns to London, his betrothal to Lady Clarissa will be announced.'

Belle stared after her, her heart taking a sickening dive. She rose, wanting nothing more than to escape.

'Lady Milborne.'

Startled, she found Lord Salcombe next to her. He looked at her with a slight frown. 'Are you all right? You are quite pale.'

'Oh, yes,' she said brightly. Which was another odd thing. Since Justin had left Lord Salcombe had frequently spoken to her in a manner that could almost be deemed cordial.

'My aunt did not say anything to overset you, I trust.'

'She merely inquired after my health. I must look dreadful for everyone seems to think I am unwell. But it is nothing, just a slight cold I am still recovering from.' Perhaps if she made light of it then it would seem less remarkable.

'I hope that is all.'

'Yes, most certainly.' She smiled at him. 'You are kind to ask.'

'Not at all. My…' He stopped. 'Marguerite was looking for you. I will escort you to her.'

She went with him from the room. Marguerite was in the hall with Chloe. Marguerite had been as kind to Chloe as she was to Belle and it was easy to see that

Chloe admired her in return. However, Chloe's smile faded when she saw Salcombe. Her greeting was stilted before she turned to Belle. 'Lady Haversham has suggested we make up a party to Vauxhall before we leave London. Would that not be delightful?'

'It would, indeed,' Belle said.

'I trust I will be invited as well,' Lord Salcombe said. He looked at Chloe, his expression half-amused.

Chloe gave him a cool look. 'I suppose that will be up to Lady Haversham since it is her party.'

'Yes, although I recall you saying you cannot abide the place so I am not certain it is worth the trouble to ask you,' Marguerite said.

He smiled lazily. 'I could be persuaded to change my mind. Particularly if Lady Chloe is to be there.'

Belle stared at him and then at Chloe, who looked less flattered than angry. She had no idea why Chloe had taken him in such dislike, but then nothing made much sense any more.

She was glad when they finally left and Marguerite declared herself too fatigued to do anything but go home and go to bed. And then she was finally in her bedchamber and alone.

She climbed into bed and lay down on her pillow, but sleep refused to come. She could only think of the child she possibly carried. She felt caught in a trap where every possible move would only lead to more pain. How could she deprive Justin of his child and the child of his father in good conscience? That is, if Justin would even want to acknowledge the babe? Her every instinct told her he would, and, furthermore, he would never forgive her if she kept the knowledge from him. But he was already betrothed and how could she go to him?

But without a father, her child—their child—would

be a bastard. She could not bear to think of that, but she already knew she could not give the child to strangers to raise. She would find a way to care for the child herself. She would have to leave not only London, but her family and friends, before they suspected anything. By the time she fell asleep she was no closer to a solution than she had been before.

Lady Georgina called the next day. Belle and Marguerite were in the drawing room when she was shown in. She sat, a stiff, elegant old woman in a gown of puce silk, which suited her colouring to perfection. She refused refreshment and, after making a few sharp inquiries after Marguerite's children and the state of her health, announced she wished to speak to Belle in private.

After casting a hesitant look in Belle's direction, Marguerite rose and left the room.

Lady Georgina fixed Belle with her piercing gaze. 'You are breeding, are you not?'

Belle stared at her, her heart pounding. 'Why ever would you say such a thing?'

'Because it is true. There is no use denying it—after a half-dozen miscarriages and bearing three children, I know the signs well. Oh, I will grant that you have been very clever at concealing them. One might think Marguerite would suspect, but she only told me you had been ill with a cold and very tired. But I have been watching you since your return from Falconcliff.'

Belle felt angry and insulted that this woman would pry into her affairs in such a way. 'Before I left for Falconcliff you said I was barren. I have no idea why you would think anything else. I have merely been ill, that is all.'

'Perhaps it was your husband, then.' Lady Georgina's

voice was dismissive. 'You have not told Marguerite, which is good, for she would most certainly send word to Westmore, which would never do. He is to marry Lady Clarissa. He cannot afford the scandal of having his mistress bear a child which may or may not be his.'

'You have no right to insult me in such a way.'

Lady Georgina's brow rose. 'Don't I? Forgive me, but after the tales spread about you, I have no idea how many lovers you have had.'

Belle's hands clenched together and she rose. 'If this is what you have come to say to me, then I must leave you.'

'Sit down. No, that is not all.' When Belle remained standing, she raised her brow even more. 'I can see you intend to be stubborn. I wish to help you. You cannot, of course, remain in society while you are increasing as long as you remain unmarried. The best thing, of course, would be to find you a husband. I've no doubt Lord Ralston would be more than happy to oblige you.'

Belle kept her voice even. 'Would he? I did not think many men would be happy to marry a woman who is already increasing.'

'Lord Ralston could easily be persuaded to view it in the light of rescuing you from the arms of a wicked seducer. Of course, you still might miscarry and then he would be under no obligation to pass the child off as his own.'

Her monstrous callousness made Belle shake. She stared at Lady Georgina. 'But what if the child is Westmore's? He would be your great-nephew, your own blood? Do you not care about that at all?'

'My dear, for all I know, I have several bastard great-nephews or nieces whom I do not care to acknowledge. My own daughters have a number of illegitimate siblings whom I never felt the least obligation towards. Nor do my daughters. I will, however, be delighted to be a proper great-aunt towards Westmore's legitimate offspring. The product of the union between him and Lady Clarissa. And do you want to know why I would never consider you as a candidate for the next Duchess?'

'No.' But she could not move. It was almost as if she was mesmerised by the old woman.

'There was another young woman once. A widow with dark hair and a sweet beguiling face and eyes just like yours. I was betrothed. The match was arranged by our parents, but I knew he was the only man I could ever marry. But on the night of the ball when our betrothal was announced he met her. I knew from the moment she laid eyes on him that she wanted him. She pursued him shamelessly and he was foolish enough to fall in love with her. But I would not release him from our betrothal because I knew she would never make him happy.' Her mouth compressed in a bitter line and Belle felt a rush of pity for her.

Her pity vanished when Lady Georgina turned a look of pure hatred upon her. 'The young widow was your grandmother.'

Belle stilled. 'My grandmother would never do such a thing.'

'But she did. Just as you have used every wile to ensnare Westmore. But she did not succeed and neither will you.' She stood. 'If you do not marry your cousin, then you will go to Italy. You can stay there until after your confinement and then the babe can be placed with a suitable family.'

'No.'

Lady Georgina moved closer to her and smiled. 'But if you do not then I will spread it about that the child you carry is Lord Ralston's. You will be forced to marry him anyway. So, you have a choice: you can go to Italy or you can wed Ralston. You do not need to let me know now. I suggest you contemplate which course you would prefer and then you may let me know before this evening.'

She turned and walked away. Belle stood rooted to the spot. The trap was closing in on her and she feared she would not escape.

Chapter Twenty

She made up her mind within the hour. She would go to Italy. She could not possibly contemplate marriage to Arthur—the thought of having him near her or her child was repugnant.

She could run away, but where to? She suspected that Lady Georgina would make good on her threat to expose her. She finally sent a note to Lady Georgina and received a reply before the afternoon was over.

Lady Georgina was thorough, if anything. She read the note and then sought out Marguerite.

Marguerite was in her sitting room seated behind a small, elegant desk. She looked up from the pile of correspondence in front of her. 'You cannot know how much I loathe writing letters. I love to receive them but then I let them collect so I am forced to answer a great number at once. It is so tedious to write the same news over and over. If only there was a way to copy the letters and then I could add my signature and be done with it!' She glanced more sharply at Belle. 'What is it? You have been so subdued since Lady Georgina came to call, but I hated to interrogate you. Is something amiss?'

Belle took the chair next to the desk. 'She has asked

me to accompany a friend of hers to the continent. Her friend needs a companion and she thought I might like the chance to leave England for a while.' The lie was amazingly easy. 'I have decided to accept.'

Marguerite stared at her and then her eyes flashed with anger. 'Oh! How could she! She wishes only to get you out of the way so there will be no interference with her plans for Justin! I absolutely forbid you to even think of such a thing!'

'I have made up my mind. I rather like the notion of leaving England for a while. I think it would be the best thing for me to…to see new places.'

'But, Belle, you have not been very well since you have been in London and I cannot think that travelling would do you any good. I know you have not been happy and I cannot blame you at all, but at least you should be unhappy with friends, not among strangers!'

Tears pricked her eyes. 'Truly you have become a dear friend and I shall miss you so dreadfully, but I must do this.'

'But when will you leave?'

'In five days.'

'Five days? But that's not nearly enough time.' Now Marguerite had tears in her eyes. 'Oh, my dear, I will try my best to convince you to stay.'

Belle called on Maria the next day. She was not certain of her reception but her mother-in-law at first looked astonished and then almost uncertain. 'Please come in. I did not expect you. You must sit down.'

Belle stepped into the drawing room that had once been so familiar and realised, with a pang, that she might not see it again. 'I am sorry. I should have sent a note first, but I took the chance that you might be here.' She sat down on a striped chair. 'There is something I wished to tell you in person.'

'Of course.' Maria also sat down and looked at Belle. 'Is something wrong?' She looked almost apprehensive.

'Oh, no. I wished to tell you I am leaving England for some time.'

'Leaving England? But why?'

'There are so many reasons, but I think it best if I go away for a while. Lady Georgina has a…a friend who needs a companion to accompany her to Italy. I have agreed to go with her.'

'But you cannot! What will we do without you?' Maria's lip quivered. 'I have so often wished I had not said those words to you. It wasn't until you left London that I…I realised how important you are to us. I missed you terribly and Chloe…poor Chloe sank into such a melancholy state! I have been wrong about so many things!' She sniffed and wiped a tear away. 'I know Lucien was not always very nice. But he was such a sweet, charming boy and I…I always thought that perhaps he might be redeemed if only I…we loved him enough. You were so kind and lovely and I thought he might change when you married him but he did…did not. Chloe tried to tell me of some of the little cruelties he inflicted upon her and others and I…I would not listen.' By now the tears were flowing freely down her face.

Belle went to her and put her arms around her. Maria clung to her and sobbed and, after a while, drew away. Belle found a handkerchief and gave it to her and waited while Maria wiped her eyes. She sat back with a sigh. 'My love, can you forgive me?'

'Of course.' Belle caught her hand.

'You are too good.' She pressed Belle's hand for a

moment. 'But please say you will not go. You must come back to Dutton Cottage with us.'

'I cannot. Oh, I wish I could, but I think it best if I go away for a little while. There has been so much talk and scandal that it will be best for everyone if I leave.'

'But why? Is it because of Westmore?' She began to look distressed again. 'I do not understand what has happened. I thought he was in love with you—I do not know why he is suddenly to marry Lady Clarissa. If you wish to marry him you must—I…I, perhaps, was wrong about him. I have heard some of the rumours, you know. The rumours that said Lucien made it look as if Westmore cheated so that he might call him out. I did not want to believe them.' She looked at Belle with large, sorrowful eyes. 'I suspect that is true as well. Do you know why?'

'Yes,' Belle said gently. 'Lucien blamed Westmore's father for the death of his father. I believe he hoped that, by hurting his son, he would hurt the Duke as well.' Telling Maria that Lucien's intention had been to kill Justin would serve no useful purpose.

Maria was silent for a moment. 'I am sorry,' she finally said. 'I knew he blamed the Duke for Henry's death but I never thought he would…would do such a wicked thing. I should have told him the truth, that Henry had so many other debts that the one to Westmore hardly mattered.' Her face was unhappy. 'Please, you must not go.'

'I must, but I promise I will be back.' She forced a smile to her lips for fear if she didn't, she would end up in tears. 'I will miss you very much, Maria. You and Chloe. You have been my family ever since Grandmama died. I must speak to Chloe now. Is she home?'

'Yes.' Maria rose. 'I will send for her.'

* * *

Brandt glanced up from the calling card he held in his hand. 'Tell Mrs Pomeroy I will be with her shortly.' He glanced back down at the note and frowned. He finished tying the last fold of his cravat and then went to the small downstairs room where he usually met tradespersons, although not so commonly women of less respectable reputations.

His visitor rose at his entrance and held out her hand. 'Dear Brandt, it has been an age! You are still as handsome as ever, I see! And still not wed—I am certain there is more than one broken heart in your wake! But that is not why I am here.'

He took her soft, gloved hand and bowed over it before releasing it. 'Sit down and tell me why you are here. I will own that your reference to my cousin aroused more than idle curiosity on my part.'

She sat and the smile left her face. 'I had a visit nearly five days ago from a woman who wished to procure certain services. She told me that an acquaintance of hers has a daughter who is in an interesting condition and her family wished to send the girl off for a rather extended journey in the interests of her health. She has heard that there is a woman, a Mrs Foster, who will offer her services as chaperon for young girls in a similar state of health. For a fee, of course.'

Brandt leaned against his desk. 'I fail to see what this has to do with my cousin. He does not trifle with the affections of young girls.'

'You might be interested to know that the woman who called on me was your aunt, Lady Georgina.'

Brandt straightened. 'Who was the girl?'

'There is no girl but a young woman. Lady Milborne.'

For once, he lost his aplomb. 'Are you certain?'

'Quite certain. I was curious because of the rumours

concerning Westmore and Lady Milborne. I asked Mrs
Foster, who was quite willing to tell me once I offered
a suitable bribe. Your aunt made no attempt to disguise
Lady Milborne's name.'

Brandt stared at her. 'So you are saying Lady Milborne is expecting my cousin's child? She is supposed
to be barren, you know.'

Eliza raised her brow. 'My dear Brandt, what does
that signify? Perhaps she and Milborne were not suited
in that particular matter. It does happen, you know.'

'Hell,' Brandt murmured.

'Can you think of any other reason why Lady Georgina would want the services of a woman such as Henrietta Foster to act as chaperon for Lady Milborne?'

'My cousin is to announce his betrothal to Lady Clarissa Blackwood.'

'Is he? How inconvenient for Lady Milborne to be
increasing, which is precisely why your aunt wishes to
remove her. I suspect Lady Milborne is to be shortly
leaving England, is she not?'

'Yes. Why are you telling me this?'

'Because I want you to inform your cousin as soon as
possible. Preferably before Lady Milborne leaves England.' She smiled a little. 'Because if you do not, I will.
I doubt Westmore will be pleased if he discovers that
both you and your aunt hid Lady Milborne's pregnancy
from him.'

'He would most likely murder both of us.' Brandt
looked at her from under lowered brows. 'What I want
to know is why you have suddenly decided this is your
business. You were Milborne's doxy, why the devil
would you care about his widow?'

She stood. 'Because I have developed something of a
conscience in the past few years. I have told Westmore

that Lady Milborne knew nothing of Lucien's plot to kill her husband. She was innocent of any wrongdoing, just as Westmore was. I knew this and yet said nothing.' She looked at him. 'They are still in love—when I saw them at the Opera, I had no doubt. I rather think they deserve a happy ending together, don't you?'

'Yes,' he said. 'Which is why I am going to leave you if I hope to reach Blackwood's estate by dinner time.'

Justin glanced at the young woman at his side. They were strolling through the carefully manicured gardens behind Cheney Hall. As usual, Lady Clarissa was coolly reserved and said nothing more than she needed to answer his questions. She did not seem impressed with the flowers that were in bloom, or pleasant sunny weather or much of anything. Or with him, for that matter. He merely seemed to be another object in her landscape. He stopped and frowned. 'Do you know why I've been invited here?' he demanded.

She looked at him. 'I believe you are to offer me marriage.'

'Do you want me to?'

'No. I would rather you did not.'

'Have you given your parents any hint of how you feel?'

'No. They told me it was my duty to accept the best offer possible.'

He scowled at her. 'What is it you wish to do?'

'My duty, of course. If you offer for me, I will accept.'

He nearly gnashed his teeth. 'Then I will not offer for you. I do not think a marriage between us would bring happiness to you or me.'

'Do you think happiness is important in marriage,

your Grace?' For the first time she actually looked interested in something he said.

'Yes. So I suggest you think less about your duty and more about your own happiness before you consider marriage.' He suddenly felt as if he'd been released from prison. 'I will inform your parents that we decided marriage would not do.'

'My father will be angry.'

'I will see to it his anger is not directed at you.' He'd rather have Blackwood call him out than marry his daughter but he doubted it would come to that. Blackwood was no fool and he suspected the man knew matters between himself and Lady Clarissa were strained.

And then he planned to take his own advice. To hell with his duty; he was going to marry to please himself. He would have Belle if he had to abduct her and force her to the altar.

The interview with Blackwood was less difficult than he had anticipated. Shortly before dinner, Brandt arrived. He apologised for coming uninvited, but he needed to speak to Justin in private on a matter of no little urgency.

Justin heard him out, his mood growing more foul by the moment. He made his own apologies to Lord and Lady Blackwood and their daughter, and then he left for Dover.

Chapter Twenty-One

Belle looked across the table at her dinner companion. Certainly the prospect of leaving England did not diminish Mrs Foster's appetite. Or the less than palatable food this Dover inn served up. If her plump body was any indication, it was unlikely much did affect her pleasure in eating.

Mrs Foster glanced up and saw Belle watching her. 'Best to eat up, my dear. You will feel much better.' When Belle did not say anything, she gave a cackle, showing uneven, stained teeth. 'None of my girls believe me, but they discover they will do much better if they follow my advice.'

A feeling of pure revulsion shot through Belle. She looked around and suddenly had no idea why she was sitting in this dark, dank inn with this repugnant woman who appeared more and more sinister to her. From Mrs Foster's remarks she gathered this was not the first time the woman had accompanied a young woman 'in a spot of trouble', as Mrs Foster had put it, to some overseas destination. She was not a friend of Lady Georgina at all, but rather a companion hired to see she arrived in

Italy. And, she suspected, to make certain Belle did not bolt.

Belle put down her fork. 'I am not at all hungry. I wish to go to my room and rest.'

'You must wait for me to finish, my dear.'

Belle rose. 'I do not see why. I am tired now.'

Mrs Foster's eyes narrowed. 'The Countess wished me to keep an eye on you at all times. For your own good, my dear. It would not do for you to do anything that might endanger yourself or the babe.'

'I doubt if going to my room will endanger anything. But if you really must come with me, then you must leave your dinner because I am going now.'

Her pronouncement had the desired effect. Mrs Foster cast a longing glance at her plate of roast beef, peas and potatoes. 'Then go, but I will check on you as soon as I come up.'

That had been easier than she had thought. But perhaps Mrs Foster was used to dealing with very young frightened girls, a thought which was even more revolting.

She left the parlour, the smell of the hall making her more nauseated. She could hear coarse laughter from the taproom. She shivered and slowly climbed the stairs to the narrow hall above. With absolute certainty, she knew she had made a dreadful mistake. She could not possibly leave England. Not with this woman who watched her every move. She had no doubt it would be the same in Italy, perhaps worse. She knew too, with a sickening certainty, that Lady Georgina had no intention of allowing her to keep her child.

She had not been completely stupid, however. She had money, an amount sewn into the pockets she wore under her shift. She had more than enough to return to London, but she would not go to London, she would go first to Tunbridge Wells and then decide what she should do.

And if Lady Georgina chose to spread tales, then let her. But no one was going to take her child. Or control her in the way Lucien had.

She turned the key in her lock and stepped into the narrow room. She closed the door. And then nearly screamed.

Justin rose from the chair near the bed. 'Good evening, Belle.'

Her blood pounded in her head so hard she was forced to lean against the door for support. Her vision swam for a moment and then she felt strong arms around her. The next thing she knew she was on the bed. She forced her eyes open. Justin's dark face hovered over hers. His expression was grim. Relief and apprehension coursed through her in equal parts. 'Wh…what are you doing here?' she managed.

'First, I plan to take you to an inn that does not smell like a pig sty. Then I am sending for a surgeon.'

She struggled to sit up. 'I do not need a surgeon. I am rather tired from the journey.' She was completely confused.

'Perhaps, but you are also carrying my child. You will see a surgeon.'

'How did you know?' she whispered. Some part of her mind registered that he was already claiming the child as his.

'From Brandt, who was informed by Eliza Pomeroy.' His mouth was set. 'If it wasn't for the fact you're in the condition you are, I could strangle you for this. Why in hell did you not tell me the moment you suspected you might be increasing? Do you think I would ever allow any child of ours to be born a bastard and raised by strangers?'

The reference to Eliza Pomeroy and Lord Salcombe made no sense at all. She was beginning to think she was dreaming, but the cold fury in his face was all too real. 'I would never let my child be raised by strangers.'

'Then why did you agree to leave England under my aunt's sponsorship? Do you think she cares what happens to the babe? Or to you?'

She paled under his anger. 'I know she does not. But I was not planning to leave England. I…I realised that I could not.' Her words sounded weak and ineffective even to her own ears.

'So what, then? You thought to hide the truth from me? Allow me to marry, do my duty, as you said, while you raise my child? Perhaps you would marry yourself and pass my child off as another man's.'

Her own anger was starting to flare. 'The child is mine as well, your Grace. And how dare you throw such accusations at me? You have not even stopped to listen to what I might say. How could I tell you when you were about to contract a betrothal? And when I was hardly certain myself! I have always considered myself barren. Do you not recall that even a physician claimed I was? I thought my symptoms were due to ill health. Should I have come to you with only a suspicion?'

'Yes,' he shot back. 'And if you recall, the only reason we are not now betrothed or wed is because you refused me, which is about to change. You will do your duty now, madam, and marry me.'

He said it with such grimness that she nearly quailed. 'But there is Lady Clarissa—'

'Who has no more desire to marry me than I have to marry her. Do not argue with me, for I've no intention of letting you go. Nor will you be out of my sight until we are wed.'

She stared at him, her emotions and thoughts in turmoil. The rattle of the door startled them and Mrs Foster stepped into the room. Her eyes narrowed. 'So is this how you repay your benefactor? By meeting with a lover? You will leave, sir, at once!'

Justin whipped around. 'Who the hell are you?'

'Mrs Foster, companion to this lady. If you do not leave, I will be forced to take rather drastic measures.' She reached into the bag she carried and pulled out a small pistol and pointed it straight at Justin. Belle's blood ran cold.

'I doubt you'll get a farthing from my aunt if you shoot me,' he said coolly. 'You'll be more likely to hang.'

'Your aunt? And who do you think you are?' Her face was still belligerent, but a little less so although the pistol was still aimed at him.

'Westmore.'

'And how do I know that?'

He stepped forward. 'You will have to take my word. But I would not advise you to risk shooting a duke. The consequences will not be pleasant.' He now stood directly in front of the pistol. 'I am going to take Lady Milborne from this hell-hole. You may tell my aunt I have done so and that we will be married by special licence.'

She dropped the hand holding the pistol to her side. 'She'll not be pleased and I dare say she'll reduce my fee considerably. Won't do my reputation a bit of good either for I've not lost a girl yet.'

'You will be reimbursed suitably. You may apply to my secretary.' He took another step towards her and she backed out of the door. He shut it behind him and locked it. 'I am beginning to think Newgate would be too pleasant for my aunt.'

'She only wished to protect you.'

He stared at her. 'Protect me? She wishes to control me. And she does not care who or what is destroyed. Including you.' He moved to look down at her. 'I will pack your things.'

She rose from the side of the bed. 'I can do that. There is no need for you to do so.'

'Sit down. You are not well.' He had already found her valise and was lifting it to the chair.

'I am well. I am merely…' Her tongue tripped over the word.

'Carrying my child. Which is reason enough for you to sit.'

Her face heated. 'It is my child also. Not only yours. I will not have him treated as if he is a possession, nor will I be treated as if I am an invalid.'

He scowled. 'I intend to see no harm comes to you or the child. As my wife, you will do as I say.'

'Which is why I do not want to be a wife! Because I will become nothing again, only your possession to be ordered around as you please!' She regretted the words as soon as she spoke, but it was too late to pull them back. The words hung in the air between them.

He stared at her, his face unreadable. He finally spoke, his voice expressionless. 'You have no choice but to become a wife. It is your duty, as it is mine, to give the child a name and a home. I suggest you remember that when you find the bonds of matrimony too onerous.'

'Justin…' she began, but he had already turned away and she knew anything she said would only make matters worse.

She could only watch as he packed the few things she had laid out. He was amazingly efficient, although he fumbled over the folding of her nightrail. When he finally latched the valise he looked up. 'I will send the proprietor for your luggage. Can you walk or should I carry you?'

She bit back her sharp retort. 'I can walk,' she said quietly.

He took her arm, his familiar touch sending a spark of awareness through her. He did not release her even when he spoke to the innkeeper, and then he escorted her to the inn yard. The smell rose up and she instantly felt ill. She fought back the unfortunate sensation, although the interior of the carriage, clearly hired and strongly smelling of other occupants, was not much better. She closed her eyes and prayed she would not become sick.

Justin finally climbed in and seated himself across from her. 'Are you ill?' For the first time she heard a touch of concern in his voice.

She opened her eyes and resisted the urge to close them again when the carriage lurched forward. 'No more than usual. One of the unfortunate effects of this condition is that odours, carriages and a number of foods turn my stomach. I should warn you that, if you plan to take me anywhere in a carriage, I will most likely be sick a good part of the journey so it would be advisable for you to stay away from me.' The trip from London to Dover had been horrendous. Mrs Foster had handled each episode with skill but had shown little patience. Belle had felt too wretched to care.

'If Jackson can manage then I undoubtedly can. And you were planning to board a packet? I cannot decide if it would have been brave of you or foolish in the extreme.'

'I fear it would have been foolish,' she said in a small voice.

'I think you are right. Very foolish.'

She looked away, not able to meet his eyes. She had acted rashly, but at the time she could not think of what else to do. She had only thought of going away before anyone else discovered her secret. But someone else had known. Mrs Pomeroy? She could not have possibly heard correctly.

She wanted to ask him, but she felt too tired and ill to speak. She was grateful when the carriage stopped and she stepped down into the evening air. The inn itself appeared much cleaner and did not seem to reek quite as much. Still nauseated, she was forced to sit on the nearest bench while Justin spoke to the proprietor. Then they were shown up a narrow flight of stairs to a long hallway and finally to a room. She instantly sat down on the bed and decided she really did not care what arrangements he made. He finally shut the door and came to stand next to her. 'I have sent for a surgeon. I can help you undress and then you had best get into bed.'

Her head jerked up. 'I beg your pardon?'

He scowled. 'I am not planning to seduce you. However, I've no intention of allowing you to sleep in your stays and since there is no lady's maid at hand I will do the deed.'

'I can undress myself so there is no need for you to do so.' Her face must be on fire. 'And I am not wearing stays!'

'You are not well.' His brow rose a fraction. 'Besides, I have seen you on several occasions without your clothing so there is no reason for such modesty. You may leave your shift on, if you would like.' He sat down beside her. 'Turn around.'

She obeyed, knowing argument was futile and would only lead to more tension. But the feel of his fingers brushing the hair at the nape of her neck and then fumbling with the fastenings of her gown was akin to a slow exquisite torture and, despite her condition, she wanted nothing more than to press back against him and beg him to take her into his arms. Instead, she closed her eyes and sat as stiffly as possible and prayed her body would not betray her.

Her gown was finally gone. He stood. 'I will leave you so you may take care of any personal needs and then you should get into bed.' His voice was curt and he did not look at her as he gathered her discarded garments. She nodded and, after he had draped her clothing over a chair, he left her. By the time he returned she was in bed and under the covers. He was followed into the room by a short, balding man with a bag.

Mr Carver was soft-spoken and very thorough. Despite his kind manner, Belle was still embarrassed and it did not help that Justin stated he would remain in the room. He stood near the window, arms folded, and, although he seemed to be gazing off at a point across the room, she had no doubt he was aware of everything that transpired and of all her almost-whispered responses to the surgeon's questions. Mr Carver finally straightened and looked over at Justin.

As if on cue, Justin crossed to his side. 'How is she?'

'Your wife's symptoms are not uncommon for a woman in the first few months and sometimes the duration of a pregnancy. In fact, it is considered quite good for there to be some sickness as it indicates you will be unlikely to miscarry. She is healthy and I see no reason to worry excessively, but she should not overtax herself. I would encourage her to eat as normally as possible although she should not partake excessively of meat and eggs.' He glanced at Belle. 'I would predict that the child will be born in January.'

'In January?' For a moment she could have sworn Justin sounded bewildered, but he quickly recovered. 'Is there anything else?'

Mr Carver hesitated. 'The normal relations between a man and his wife are possible until the more advanced months. However, if any complications arise, abstinence is imperative.'

Belle wished she could bury herself under the covers but Justin looked no less confounded. 'Er, yes,' he said. He frowned. 'I wish to leave tomorrow for my estate. The trip will take nearly six hours. Will that harm my wife?'

His wife? He was already claiming her? Heat swept through her and she hardly heard the surgeon's answer or noticed when he took his leave.

Justin shut the door behind him. He stared at Belle for a moment and then crossed to her side. He looked down at her. 'So there will be a child in January,' he said softly.

'It appears so.' She dropped her eyes under his scrutiny and nervously plucked at the bedcovers.

'We will leave for Westmore House tomorrow. As soon as I procure the special licence we will be married. I presume you would like Lady Chloe and Lady Ralston present.'

She finally looked up at him. 'That would be very nice. Thank you.'

He ran a hand through his hair. 'You'd best sleep.'

'Where will you be?' She was starting to feel lost.

'Here.' A swift frown crossed his brow. 'But in the chair. Don't worry, I'm not so depraved I'd force my attentions on you. Either now or after we're married. But I've no intention of leaving you alone.'

'I will not run away, if that is what worries you,' she said, stung.

'That is not the reason.' He suddenly looked tired and she wondered how long he had been travelling. She realised she had not yet asked him about Mrs Pomeroy or Salcombe or how he had come to be here, but her mind was too tired to form the questions.

He leaned towards her and for a moment she thought he might kiss her, but then he drew back. 'Goodnight, Belle.'

'Justin, wait.' Her face heated. 'I…I think you should sleep in the bed as well. You cannot possibly be comfortable in the chair. I…I will not disturb you.'

His brow shot up. 'My dear, your mere presence next to me would be disturbing.'

'Oh.' His sarcasm stung. To her dismay, tears pricked her eyes. He undoubtedly detested her—she had nearly run away with his child and it was only because of Mrs Pomeroy and his cousin that he even knew. 'Of course. Goodnight, Justin.' She turned on her side and closed her eyes.

She could feel his gaze on her and then she heard his footsteps as he moved away from the bed. She fought back the tears and the urge to curl into a ball like a small, wounded child. Her body tensed every time he moved and she could almost imagine him as he removed his boots and stockings and then his coat. After a while he extinguished the light and then she heard the chair creak as he settled into it. And then she drifted into an exhausted sleep.

Justin eased himself from the chair in which he'd spent the night and slowly stood. His neck and back were both stiff but he had at least managed to prop his legs on Belle's travelling trunk. Surprisingly enough, after spending what felt like hours listening to her soft breathing, he'd finally fallen into a restless sleep.

The faint light showing through the cracks of the shutters told him it was past dawn. He wanted to leave early but he was loath to wake her. He walked softly to the bed and looked down at her. She lay on her side, one hand tucked under her cheek. Her dark hair was spread over the pillow and she looked vulnerable and lovely and completely desirable. It would be so easy to lie down next to her, gather her into his arms and kiss her awake as he had each morning at Falconcliff. He drew back—what the hell was he thinking of? She was carrying a child. He had never made love to a woman in that condition before, and despite Mr Carver's assurances, he had no idea whether it would harm her or not.

And she was not his wife. At least not yet.

His wife. He doubted if even then she would want him to touch her. She had made that clear—marriage to him filled her with fear. She still did not trust that he would not hurt her as Lucien had.

He'd run through a gamut of emotions in the past two days. Fury, fear, hope, disbelief, betrayal. He'd left directly from Cheney Hall and arrived at Dover. By the time he had combed the inns and finally discovered where she was staying his fear had turned to fury. At his aunt, most of all, but, until he laid eyes on Belle, he had not realised how angry he was with her as well.

His anger had dissipated, but that she had found it preferable to run away rather than come to him still wounded him. And that she would keep the knowledge from him that she carried his child touched something raw and primitive in his being.

She stirred at the sound of a coach horn. He had best wake her for he wanted to arrive at Westmore House as quickly as possible. He touched her cheek. 'Belle,' he said softly.

She murmured something and turned. 'Belle,' he said again.

Her eyes opened and she saw him. 'Justin?' She looked deliciously confused and he wanted nothing more than to kiss her.

'It is time to arise,' he said more curtly than he intended.

'Oh.' She blinked and sat up, the covers falling away to reveal her shift. She paled.

He frowned and sat down on the bed next to her. 'Are you all right?'

'Yes.' She swallowed. 'I usually do not feel very well when I first awake. Sometimes I feel better after I eat.'

'I will send for some food.' He started to rise.

She caught his arm. 'No, please do not. I can wait until we breakfast. I usually have only toast. I should be fine if I sit here for a little bit before I get out of bed.'

He gently removed her hand from his arm and stood. 'There is no reason why you cannot have toast now.' His brow rose at her expression. 'It is no use arguing with me because I've no intention of changing my mind. And when the toast arrives you will eat it if I must force it down you.'

She stared at him and, to his surprise, nodded. And

then she looked away. He had the most disconcerting notion she was fighting back tears. He restrained the impulse to go to her because he suspected she would only repudiate him. Instead, he left the room.

Chapter Twenty-Two

They reached Westmore House in the early evening. Belle had found if she curled up in the corner of the carriage and kept her eyes closed, the movement was not so bad. She actually fell asleep once and, when she awoke, discovered that Justin had covered her with a rug.

She wanted to thank him for the kindness but he had such a remote expression that the words would not come. So, she said nothing.

Westmore House was an imposing red-bricked building set at the top of a small rise and surrounded by a vast green lawn. The journey up the long, winding drive surrounded by neatly trimmed yews on either side seemed to last forever before the carriage finally halted in front of the entrance.

Justin helped her from the carriage and up the steps of the house. An elderly butler opened the door. 'Your Grace, we did not…' He cleared his throat. 'Welcome home, your Grace.' His gaze rested on Belle for a moment before returning to Justin.

'You may congratulate me. Lady Milborne has agreed to be my wife.'

Surprise crossed his rather austere face and then he smiled. 'Congratulations, your Grace.' He turned to Belle. 'May I offer you my felicitations as well, my lady?' His manner was a little more restrained.

It dawned on her that he saw her as the future Duchess. She fought back her sudden panic at the thought and managed a smile. 'Thank you.'

Other servants had appeared to welcome Justin home. As he had with his butler, he informed them Belle was to be his wife. Their expressions were a mixture of surprise and curiosity and by the time Belle was shown to her room by the housekeeper, Mrs Benton, she was exhausted from smiling. She was shown to a spacious bedchamber and, after Mrs Benton left, a maid came and helped her out of her dusty travelling clothes and into her nightrail, and then she was alone.

She sat on the edge of the bed. Everything seemed completely unreal. She was not on a packet crossing the channel, she was in Justin's house in Kent. Their child would not be born among strangers but among family.

The knock startled her and then Justin entered. Her heart slammed against her chest, and her eyes went to his face, but the cool expression on his face told her he was not here because he wished to be.

'May I speak to you for a moment?' he asked politely.

'Yes, of course.'

He moved to the side of the bed. 'I will leave for London to procure the licence tomorrow. We will marry the day after I return. I will also send word to your mother and sister-in-law that you are here and to Marguerite as well.'

'Thank you.' She pushed down the pit of despair that was growing in her. He was so impersonal that she knew he had not forgiven her.

'If you need anything you may apply to me or to my housekeeper.'

'You are very kind.'

He frowned a little. 'Not at all. This will be your home.'

Her home. Any words she might have said stuck in her throat and she could only nod. He still looked at her. 'I will also send for the local surgeon tomorrow.'

'Is that necessary? Nothing has changed and Mr Carver did not find anything out of the ordinary.'

'None the less, I would like Mr Thomas to see you. I would like his opinion as well.'

'Of course.'

'Is there anything you need?'

'No. I am very comfortable.'

'Then I will bid you goodnight. I will leave early so I possibly will not see you before I go.'

'Goodnight,' she whispered.

After he left the room, closing the door quietly behind him, she climbed beneath the covers. He was concerned about the babe and she was grateful. But, of course, he would be. She wondered if Lucien would have been equally solicitous and thought he might. He had wanted an heir so desperately that he would have done anything to ensure the child would be born healthy.

He would have cared about her health, but only because of the child. Rather like a prize mare. And when she proved to have no value, he did not hesitate to discard her.

She knew Justin was not so callous and he would never treat her cruelly, but she had no doubt that the child would always be his first concern. Which was, of course, how it should be.

But she could not quite quell the dart of envy that

pierced her. She felt instantly ashamed. For how could she possibly be envious of her own child?

Belle wandered to the window that faced the drive. The day was overcast, but at least there was no rain. Justin was to return today. The thought filled her with a sort of nervous anticipation. She had been seen by Mr Thomas, whose opinion on her condition did not differ much from Mr Carver's. She had rested and eaten and to her surprise found that her appetite had started to return and she did not feel quite so ill.

She turned when she heard footsteps. Her pulse quickened and she stilled. But instead of Justin, Chloe appeared. 'Belle!' Chloe ran towards her.

'Chloe! What are you doing here?'

'Westmore told us you were to be married and he said we might travel back with him, so we are here!'

'Maria as well?'

'I am here as well.' Maria appeared in the doorway, dressed in a grey travelling cape. She gave Belle a tremulous smile and Belle held out her arms.

Justin watched the reunion from the door of the drawing room. The happiness on Belle's face at seeing her family was evident. He only wished he was the recipient of the same welcome.

She looked up and met his eyes. The smile left her face to be replaced by uncertainty. He inclined his head and then turned away, not wanting her to guess how much he wanted her. He had no intention of being vulnerable to her again.

He found his butler at his elbow. 'Your Grace, Lord Salcombe has arrived.'

Brandt strode in, his boots and coat mud-spattered. 'Is our aunt here?' he demanded without preamble.

'No.' Justin frowned at his cousin's expression. 'Why?'

'She has left London. I feared she still might decide to…er…disrupt your nuptials.'

'How would she know?'

Brandt's brow rose. 'The news is hardly a secret. Lady Ralston apparently told her nephew of the good news and he is not exactly the soul of discretion.'

Justin cursed. He should have warned Lady Ralston to say nothing, but it had not occurred to him she would have time to send messages.

A sliver of apprehension darted down his spine. He fought it down. What could his aunt possibly do? Belle was under his roof and she had no power to stop his marriage to her now.

'You look lovely,' Marguerite said. 'See.'

Belle turned to the looking glass. There had been no time to think of wedding clothes so she wore the pale peach gown she had worn to the opera. Her hair had been caught up in a chignon that fell in ringlets to her shoulders. A feeling of unreality stole over her. In less than an hour she would stand with Justin and take vows that would bind her to him for the rest of their lives.

She fought the panic that threatened to swallow her. Marguerite's pleased expression changed to concern. 'Justin loves you, you must know that. Why else would he have stopped you from leaving England?'

Belle slowly looked at Marguerite. 'You have not guessed?' She bit her lip and knew she could not keep this from Marguerite. 'I…I am with child. His child. That is why he stopped me.'

Marguerite stared at her, her eyes round. 'Oh, my dear!' She pulled Belle to her. 'How could I not have known! The signs…you must think I was blind…oh, Belle, why did you not tell me?'

'I wanted to so very badly, but I did not know how it could be possible, and then I thought Justin was to marry Lady Clarissa—' She stopped. 'I still cannot believe it.'

'And you think Justin is only marrying you because of the child.'

'I cannot think why else. Oh, Marguerite, you cannot imagine how angry he was when he found me. I do not believe he can forgive me for running away.'

'You must tell him you love him.'

She was silent. How could she? If he hated her then it would only fill him with contempt. And she would be even more vulnerable.

'Tonight,' Marguerite said. She had a wicked smile on her face. 'You may seduce him as well. Men sometimes find an interesting condition, well, interesting.' She touched Belle's arm. 'Come, it is time to leave.'

Her heart was beating so fast she felt almost faint. Her stomach was starting to turn. 'In a moment. I think I will sit down.'

'Will you be all right? Shall I send for a footman to carry you down?'

'Oh, no. How odd that would look! I think if I rest for a little bit… Perhaps you could tell Chloe and Maria I will be down directly.'

'If that is what you want.' She gave her a dubious look and left the room.

She should have forced more than a piece of toast down herself but she had been so nervous she could hardly swallow that. The knock on the door startled her. She rose and opened it.

Lady Georgina stood on the other side. 'Good day, Lady Milborne. I have come to take you to your wedding.'

'I am to go with Giles and Marguerite.'

She smiled gently. 'I think not.' She pointed a small pistol directly at Belle.

Belle looked at the small dangerous weapon and for a moment had no idea what it meant. She looked back at Lady Georgina. 'What do you mean?'

'I mean that you will be married, but not to my nephew. I cannot allow that. Come with me, my dear. I am certain you would not want me to hurt you or your bastard child.'

'Giles and Marguerite are waiting for me below. I cannot walk past them with you.'

'But we are not going that way. We will take the back stairs which is how I came up unnoticed. Your bridegroom is waiting for you below.' She grasped Belle's arm in a grip that was surprisingly strong. 'Come, Lady Milborne. I do not want to waste time in idle conversation.'

She was still smiling but there was something in her eye that made Belle very afraid. Her sense of unreality only increased as she walked down the silent hall with Lady Georgina. All that she could think of was if she did not get away Justin would think she had betrayed him again. That she could not bear. Perhaps if she talked someone might hear them. 'Westmore is waiting below?' She tried to speak in an unnaturally loud tone.

Lady Georgina's grip tightened. 'Hush, you little fool. No, Lord Ralston. Do you think I would allow you to marry my nephew?'

'Lord Ralston?' Her voice rose whether she wished it or not. 'Arthur? I will not marry him!'

'Oh, but you will. He is waiting to rescue you from marriage to a man who will make you miserable. Very romantic, do you not think?'

By now they had reached the backstairs. She thought she heard a door close and then footsteps, but Lady Georgina had shoved her into the stairway and she could feel the cold pistol at her back. 'Go!' Lady Georgina said.

She started down the narrow steps, her heart pounding and her legs unsteady. By the time she reached the last step her stomach was churning in a way that was not promising.

There was a narrow passageway that led to the side drive. Lady Georgina pushed her through it and she saw the waiting carriage.

Lady Georgina grabbed her arm. 'Get in, my dear.' The pistol was still at her back. She had no choice. She stepped into the carriage.

'No!' But Lady Georgina had already shoved her in. Arthur sat in one corner, his face worried.

'Are you all right, Belle?' he asked.

'No. You must let me go! Please do not do this, Arthur.' To her horror, the carriage had started to move. 'I am to marry Justin.'

'Do not worry.' He cleared his throat. 'I will make certain you get to the church in time to marry Westmore.'

She stared at him. 'What did you say?'

'I intend to take you to your wedding.' He frowned at her expression. 'No matter what you think of me, I am not so base as to force a woman to marry me when it is clear she prefers someone else. Besides, I suspect you would become a widow again quite shortly afterwards.'

Had she gone mad? 'I do not understand. Why did you do this?'

'Lady Georgina was determined to stop your wedding. She approached me two days ago with a plan that entailed an abduction so you would be forced to marry me. I feared if I did not agree then she would find some other, perhaps more sinister, way to ensure the wedding was stopped. I wished to force her hand so that her perfidy would be exposed. I trust that, by now, she has been apprehended by the Duke's secretary.'

Her head was spinning with questions. But the carriage had stopped and she saw they were indeed in front of the small church. Her stomach had started to churn again. She had no idea whether it was from nerves or her condition. Arthur jumped down and held out his hand. She stepped down, just in time to see Justin emerge from the church. He took one look at Arthur, then stalked towards them with such a black look that Belle feared for Arthur's life.

She crossed to him. 'Justin, don't.'

The expression on his face was so icy she nearly quailed. 'It matters little to me whether you intend to wed Ralston or me, because I intend to put a bullet through him.'

She caught his arm. 'You must let me explain.'

He looked down at her hand and then at her face with cold deliberation. 'Very well, my dear Belle, explain.'

She heard another carriage arrive and a voice she thought might be Giles's, but her stomach had started to turn in an ominous way and she suddenly felt dizzy. 'Yes, but for now I do not feel at all the thing. I need to sit down. I did not have breakfast today.'

His face changed. 'Good God!'

She sat abruptly down on the grass and put her head between her hands, willing the nausea to go away. The last thing she wanted to do was lose the contents of her stomach in front of the others. She heard more voices around her and then someone knelt beside her. 'Are you all right?' Justin asked.

'Yes.' Although thoroughly humiliated. 'At least I did not cast up my accounts this time.

'I am sorry.' He handed her a handkerchief.

She took it and turned her head to peer at his face. The anger had been replaced by concern. 'You should be. You do bear some of the responsibility.'

A wry smile touched his mouth. 'Approximately one-half, I believe.' He held out his hand. 'Can you stand?'

'Yes.' She placed her hand in his and he helped her to her feet. By now the churchyard was filled with people who all seemed to be gaping at them. The spell was broken by the vicar who came down the steps of the church to their sides. His plump, pleasant face was creased with concern. He glanced down at their hands which were still linked. 'Are you certain you are well enough to stand for the ceremony, my lady?' he asked Belle.

'I think so.' If Justin still wanted her. She cast a quick look at his face, but his expression was difficult to read.

He did not take his gaze from her face. 'Is this what you want?'

'Yes, if you please. That is the only reason I am here.' She willed him to understand.

'I will save my questions for later.' His hand tightened around hers. 'Should we go in?'

She nodded, her mouth dry. He released her hand just as Marguerite appeared at her side with Chloe. They brushed as much of the grass and dirt from her gown as possible and straightened her bonnet which was completely askew. Chloe hugged her and presented her with a bouquet of flowers.

And then she turned to where Justin waited for her at the front of the church.

Chapter Twenty-Three

Belle sat down on her bed. The little maid had helped her into her nightrail and now she was alone in her bedchamber.

The day had passed in a haze. She could recall little of the ceremony that had joined her to Justin for the remainder of their lives. Not even the swift, cool, kiss he had brushed across her mouth had felt real. As soon as the ceremony had ended, Giles had appeared at his side and after listening to Giles's terse words, Justin had sent her home with Marguerite and Brandt while he and Giles went off with Arthur.

She had seen little of Justin the rest of the day. Marguerite had insisted she must rest and so had sent her straight to her bedchamber. From Marguerite and a horrified Maria, she learned that Justin, after listening to Arthur's story, had spent most of the day closeted together with Giles and Brandt. In the end, they had decided Lady Georgina was to be banished to a remote estate with a keeper.

Chloe came up a little later to report she had been quite stunned to see Justin and Arthur shaking hands in a most civil fashion. After delivering that piece of news, she looked rather lost and it wasn't until Belle assured her that she could come and stay with her very soon, that Chloe finally began to seem more cheerful.

Altogether Belle was certain it had been a most memorable day but, due to Justin's insistence that she stay in her room, she had missed most of it. He had even had a dinner tray sent up.

She scowled. He surely wasn't planning to keep her prisoner in her room during the rest of her pregnancy. Or avoid her. She had probably experienced almost every emotion possible today, but the most overwhelming one at the moment was anger, mixed in with frustration. He could have at least inquired after her health.

She rose from the bed and stalked to the door. She thrust it open and gasped. Justin stood on the other side. He looked equally startled to find her there.

He frowned. 'I would like to speak to you.'

'And I would like to speak to you.' She held the door open. 'Come in.'

He came into the room and she shut the door behind him. He turned and looked at her. 'Should you not be in bed?'

'No, I should not. I have been in bed or in that chair the entire day and I am quite tired of it. I am not ill, I am increasing!'

He stared at her. 'Which means you are to rest and do whatever Mr Thomas deems necessary to protect your health.'

'So that means I am to stay in my room until my confinement?'

'Of course not. Sit down.'

'I do not want to sit down.' His detached manner was infuriating her. 'Do you not care what I want at all? My only worth to you may be that I am carrying your child but that does not mean I intend to be treated like a...a brood mare!' She was undoubtedly making no sense.

He suddenly frowned. 'You think I care only about the child?'

'Yes! You have made that quite clear. You have done nothing but set surgeons on me at every turn. I suppose I cannot blame you but it...it still hurts.' There, she for all purposes admitted she cared for him.

He was stalking towards her and she found herself backed up against the dresser. He stopped in front of her. 'So, you think the only reason I married you is because of the child and that I am setting physicians on you because of the child?'

'Yes,' she whispered.

'Do you recall I asked you to marry me before? Even when I thought a child was impossible?'

'Yes, but I have betrayed you again.'

His eyes blazed into hers. 'You never betrayed me at all. Not at Greystone. Nor did you when you ran to Dover. Among the many things my aunt told me today was her threats to claim Ralston as the child's father. She lied as well when she said I was betrothed to Lady Clarissa. You did not have much of a choice.'

Her mouth was dry. She stared at him. He braced his hands on either side of her. 'I care about the child, but I still want you whether there is a child or not. Can you not tell? Every time I see you or I am near you I want to pull you into my arms and take you. Which is why I want to avoid you. I told you I've no intention of forcing myself on you.'

'Justin.' She stared into his dark face. He had not said he loved her, but at least he desired her. 'You would not be forcing yourself on me. I...I want you, too.'

The fire that blazed in his eyes at her shy admission

nearly consumed her. He groaned and pulled her against him, his mouth crushing hers in a kiss that seared her to her very being. She met his kiss with a passion that matched his until he finally lifted his head.

'I should not be doing this,' he whispered. 'The babe.'

'Mr Carver said there should be no problems with the normal relations between man and wife, do you not recall? Mr Thomas also said the same thing, although in a more indirect manner.' She pressed against him and cupped his face. 'I want to be with you tonight.'

He stiffened, the expression on his face that of a man about to be pole-axed. 'Belle. How can I resist you?' He almost groaned the words.

'Why do you want to?' She was filled with a heady sense of power. She took his hand. 'Come to bed with me.'

He followed her. She sat on the edge of the bed and tugged on his hand. Still looking bemused, he sat next to her. 'Now what?' he asked softly.

She draped her arms around his neck and slowly pushed him back on the bed. She half lay on him and looked down into his face. 'This, your Grace.' She lowered her head to his. He was still for a moment beneath her kiss and then his arms came around her and she was lost in him.

Justin slowly opened his eyes. The soft warmth of the womanly body next to him told him last night had not been a dream. He turned on his side and draped his arm over her, his hand protectively resting on the soft curve of her bare stomach. His loins hardened. Already, he could feel a hard roundness that had not been there before and the thought of the child inside filled him with a fierce, primitive protectiveness towards both mother and child.

He buried his head in her hair, and thought he could never get enough of her scent. Or of her. Even thinking of last night nearly sent him out of his mind with desire. Never had he thought his reserved, cool Belle could so thoroughly and satisfactorily seduce him.

He knew now, that no matter what else she felt, she at least desired him. Something he intended to take full advantage of. He would court his wife and make her fall as irrevocably in love with him as he was with her.

But first he had something he must do. He slowly removed his arms from her and slipped from the bed. He found his breeches and shirt and put them on and then quietly left the room.

Belle awoke. For once the all-too-familiar nausea was not present. Instead, her body felt deliciously warm and sensuous, her skin bare under the sheets. She moved and realised Justin was no longer with her although the bed-clothes still held his warmth. She was reluctant to open her eyes for fear it had all been a dream. He had made love to her with such exquisite tenderness that she had nearly wept.

She heard someone enter and she forced her eyes open. Her pulse quickened when she saw it was Justin. She sat up and then clutched the sheet to her chest. Her cheeks heated when she saw the flare of desire in his eyes.

So, at least he did not plan to avoid her. She would be as seductive as possible if it would keep him at her side. Perhaps she should drop the sheet. But there was something in his face that stopped her. 'What is it?' she asked, suddenly feeling apprehensive.

'I had something I wanted to discuss with you last night. Before you distracted me.'

'You certainly seemed very willing to be distracted!'

His lips curved in a rather wicked smile. 'I was. You may distract me any time you want.'

At least he wasn't planning to completely shut her out. He sobered. 'But I have something to give you. A wedding gift of sorts.'

She saw he held several papers in his hand. He held them out to her. She took them, her eyes on his face. 'It is a contract,' he said. 'A contract that stipulates the terms of our marriage. I know your marriage to Milborne was hell. He treated you in the vilest manner possible and I do not blame you for fearing the same thing will happen again. That you will be nothing more than a piece of property to be disposed of as I wish. So, I am giving you as much control of your destiny as possible. All property you bring to the marriage will be yours. You will have control of a sum that is your own. I will not question how you choose to spend it. You may choose to live where you want, although when our child is born I would, of course, wish to spend as much time as possible with him or her.' He moved towards her. 'Read it and if you agree with the terms then we will each sign it. There are two copies.'

She nodded, a dozen emotions tumbling over themselves. She quickly perused it and saw the terms were exactly as he said. The amount he proposed passing into her control nearly made her gasp. She finally looked up. 'When did you draw this up?'

He shrugged. 'While you were at Falconcliff. When I asked you to marry me then.'

'I see.' Tears were welling up in her eyes.

'So, do you agree with the terms?' Only the slight twitch in his jaw revealed his tension.

'No.'

His face shuttered. 'Why not?'

'Because I do not need a contract. I love you,' she blurted out.

He looked as if she had just hit him. His jaw dropped. 'You what?'

'I love you.' She had told him, just as Marguerite had said to do. And had seduced him as well, although not quite in that order.

He strode towards the bed. The next thing she knew he was sitting next to her and hovering over her with such a fierce look she nearly shrank back. 'I am sorry. I…I did not mean to tell you that.'

'You did not mean to tell me that because you do not love me, or because you did not want me to know?' he demanded.

'Because I did not want you to know,' she whispered.

'And why not?'

'Because I did not want to give you a disgust of me. I would imagine it would be uncomfortable to have someone love you when you do not love them in return.'

'And what makes you think I do not love you in return?'

She stared at him, hope starting to rise. 'Do you?'

He gave a strangled laugh. 'I have loved you since the moment I first saw you on Milborne's arm. And yesterday, when I discovered what my aunt had tried to do, I realised how deeply and thoroughly in love with you I am.'

'Then why did you not come to me yesterday?'

'Because, my love, I suffered from the same misapprehension as you. I did not think you would welcome a declaration of love from me when you obviously did not return my sentiment. However, last night gave me hope that I might persuade you otherwise.' His gaze fell to her lips and his eyes darkened for a moment. 'But there is the contract before we move on to other business.'

Her heart was pounding and it took all her willpower to keep from wrapping her arms around his neck and pulling him to her. 'Not unless we change the terms. I do not need such a large sum of money and I want it to stipulate I am to live wherever you live. Although I would prefer it would be at Falconcliff. And I would like it to say we are not to sleep apart.'

The smile that curved his mouth was wicked. He bent towards her and drew her into his arms. 'I would be more than happy to change the terms to your satisfaction.' And then he pulled her into his arms.

Modern Romance™
...seduction and
passion guaranteed

Tender Romance™
...love affairs that
last a lifetime

Sensual Romance™
...sassy, sexy and
seductive

Blaze
...sultry days and
steamy nights

Medical Romance™
...medical drama on
the pulse

Historical Romance™
...rich, vivid and
passionate

27 new titles every month.

*With all kinds of Romance for
every kind of mood...*

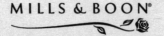

*Three brand-new,
sinfully scandalous short stories*

Regency BRIDES

Anne Gracie, Gayle Wilson, Nicola Cornick

Available from 20th September 2002

2 FREE

books and a surprise gift!

We would like to take this opportunity to thank you for reading this Mills & Boon® book by offering you the chance to take TWO more specially selected titles from the Historical Romance™ series absolutely FREE! We're also making this offer to introduce you to the benefits of the Reader Service™—

★ FREE home delivery
★ FREE gifts and competitions
★ FREE monthly Newsletter
★ Exclusive Reader Service discount
★ Books available before they're in the shops

Accepting these FREE books and gift places you under no obligation to buy, you may cancel at any time, even after receiving your free shipment. Simply complete your details below and return the entire page to the address below. *You don't even need a stamp!*

YES! Please send me 2 free Historical Romance books and a surprise gift. I understand that unless you hear from me, I will receive 4 superb new titles every month for just £3.49 each, postage and packing free. I am under no obligation to purchase any books and may cancel my subscription at any time. The free books and gift will be mine to keep in any case.

H2ZEA

Ms/Mrs/Miss/Mr ....Initials.....................................
                                                BLOCK CAPITALS PLEASE

Surname ....

Address ....

....

....Postcode..............................

Send this whole page to:
UK: FREEPOST CN81, Croydon, CR9 3WZ
EIRE: PO Box 4546, Kilcock, County Kildare (stamp required)